Last Will

Bryn Greenwood

Last Will

ISBN 978-0-9827734-7-5

Visit Bryn online:

www.bryngreenwood.com

STAIRWAY PRESS

A CURVA PELIGROSA BOOK
STAIRWAY PRESS
SEATTLE

Cover Design by Guy Corp, www.grafixCORP.com

www.stairwaypress.com
1500A East College Way #554
Mount Vernon, WA 98273

For my first readers…
with thanks to Sheila Walker,
in memory of Brianne May

CHAPTER ONE

WHILE YOU WERE OUT…

WHEN JOEL REACHED toward the van door, I said, “Don’t open it,” just the way my book on lucid dreaming told me to. The book said to contradict anything I didn’t like, but Joel ignored me.

“Well, hey, Bernie, what say we give you a ride home?” he said.

“Shut up and go away.” That didn’t work either. Amy stood next to Joel, her white-blond hair fluttering in the breeze. Joel’s fingers closed around the pitted chrome lever. Before I could protest, the door rolled open, and the back of the van gaped like the mouth of a hungry cave. *He* was in there.

“I’m not doing this, and if this doesn’t stop, I’m going to wake up,” I said. Then I did.

In that sense, the lucid dreaming worked. It kept away the nightmares, but it cost me sleep. Half an hour later, when my mother called, I had just fallen back asleep.

“Did I wake you?” she said.

“No,” I said, even though I knew my voice was gravelly with sleep.

“It’s not even ten o’clock.” She cleared her throat. “I’m afraid I’m calling with some bad news, Bernie.”

“Are you okay?”

She sounded fine, but in Boston it was nearly eleven, late for her.

"Yes, I suppose, but Virginia just called to tell me Pen is dead." When I didn't answer, she said, "Did you hear me? Your grandfather Pen has died."

I got out of bed, opened the closet and turned on the light. Looking for my suit, I fumbled through the clothes at the back. I saw already where the conversation was going: a trip to Oklahoma.

"Did she say what happened?" I asked.

"A heart attack. He was nearly ninety."

"I know. When's the funeral?"

"You'll need to make that decision, unless you're going to leave it all to Virginia, which I think is hardly appropriate. You really ought to decide."

"Okay," I said. There I was at the end of a long line of Raleighs; whatever decisions there were to be made for my grandfather, I would have to make them.

After I hung up with my mother, I felt myself drifting. The floor seemed less firm, and the bathroom tiles had already lost their tangibility. Afraid of drifting further, I brewed a pot of coffee and popped a few white crosses—enough speed and caffeine to keep me awake for two days, or give me a stroke. I spent the night cleaning house and making lists, until my eyes felt cooked in their sockets. By six I was on the phone buying my plane ticket, and at eight, I was standing at the Overland Park post office filling out the paperwork that would commit me to having my mail forwarded to my grandfather's house.

I went into work two hours late, and stood at the front counter watching Ellen, the second assistant librarian, check a customer out. The only sounds in the library were the creaking of book spines, the discreet bleep of the scanner, the reassuring thump of the book cover, the intimate whisper as she slid the books across the counter to the customer. Under the counter, the printer chattered briefly. Ellen tore the receipt off and slipped it into the top book. I let it wash over me, a little balance of pleasure to get me through the funeral, and whatever came after.

My boss, Beverly, was shuffling papers at her desk, and when I told her about my grandfather, she gave me a gentle smile of condolence. She never spoke when a look would have the same effect. It was the thing that made her a superior librarian.

"It's probably going to be a month at least, maybe longer," I said.

"Why so long?"

It wasn't a simple matter of an old man's house and car and checking account. I described the monumental nature of the task, the largeness of the estate, and when she still didn't understand, I told her that my grandfather was Pen Raleigh. Then I told her to read the front page of the Wall Street Journal. I saw the elements fall into place for her, like a Tetris game at work.

"I imagine a thing like that could take some time," she said. "It'll be fine, however long you need to be away." I read in her look the thing she would never say to me: they didn't really need me. Probably they never had.

I went back to my apartment to get my suitcase and told the apartment manager I would be gone a while, leaving my car parked. He offered to start it and drive it occasionally, then said, "Hey, you related to the Raleigh family in Oklahoma? The old guy just died and left a ton of money, my dad said." It was the most he'd ever said to me, including the day I'd rented the apartment. After twenty blissful years as a nobody, I was somebody again.

My grandfather's death didn't exactly leave me prostrate with grief, but at the funeral reception, I tried to be a dutiful grandson. Unfortunately, Meda Amos was a constant obstacle to my mournful sense of duty. I believe the polite word is *domestic*—she was one of my grandfather's domestics. She was always on some innocuous errand: bringing clean plates for the buffet or cleaning up a spill. At that moment, she opened the pantry door, crossed the dining room, and came into the formal parlor, where the dense Aubusson rug absorbed the sound of her footsteps. Conversation ground to an uncomfortable halt. Meda Amos began to gather up some of the dirty dishes, ignoring the stares of hushed admiration.

Clearly she was aware of the problem, because she'd done what she could to minimize it. She wore a featureless dress with an apron over it. Her hair was pulled back in a severe, black knot, and she wore no make-up, no jewelry, none of the artificial trappings women use to beautify themselves. Honestly, she'd been disfigured, and still we couldn't look away. That was the root of the problem: there wasn't any angle at which she was other than breathtaking and her allure wasn't diminished by the triptych of faded scars around her mouth. Two of them were more accurately the distinct halves of a single scar separated by her mouth, as though she'd had her lips tightly closed when the injury occurred. Her upper lip was sensually bowed, her lower lip a voluptuous invitation to a variety of obscene thoughts. I was grateful for the intervention of that scar; it slowed me down a little. The other scar was less dramatic, a secondary brush stroke above the left corner of her mouth.

When my mother cleared her throat, I wanted to protest. No one else was shamed out of looking at Meda Amos by my mother's disapproval. Taking the cue, Aunt Ginny said, "You can leave that until later, dear. We don't need anything else just now." Meda nodded almost imperceptibly and left. The spell broke. People went back to telling stories about my grandfather. I imagined my brother Robby remarking, "Ideally, the male of the species is the eye-catching one, because he has the numerical advantage of being able to reproduce with every female he can attract. For the female to hold that kind of magnetism—there's no benefit to the species."

My mother leaned toward me and murmured, "You know what Pen's will contains. He's left it all to you. You must consider that there are a number of very rapacious people waiting to take advantage of this situation. You need to visit Mr. Tveite. Establish your position with the board of directors." I hoped I would get a pass on the conversation if I kept silent, but she leaned closer, engulfing me in a cloud of *Chanel No. 5*, and said, "Are you listening to me?"

"Yes."

"Well, answer me then."

I was considering telling her that she hadn't asked a question, but Father Reginald stood up at that moment and made his excuses for leaving. The other guests must have felt the tide had turned, because they began to make their farewells, too, and I got up to see them out to their cars. When I came back into the parlor, I could tell my mother and aunt were annoyed with each other from the way they both smiled at me. Relieved. They reminded me of Nancy Reagan and Raisa Gorbachev, except that Aunt Ginny was much cuddlier than Raisa. To be fair, Nancy was cuddlier than my mother.

"Shall we have some dinner?" my mother said.

I went to help Aunt Ginny up from the sofa. As she took my arm, she smiled and said, "What a nice watch."

"It's the one Dad gave Grandpa Pen for his birthday."

"A very nice watch then, but it's a bit too big for you, sweetie. You need to have a link removed." Aunt Ginny took up the slack with her finger.

"You should have had it buried with him." My mother glared at me balefully.

"I—it never occurred to me." I felt like a cad. For the viewing, I'd given the funeral director my grandfather's wedding ring, his glasses and a tie tack. I assumed they'd be buried with him, but I hadn't thought to include the watch any more than I had thought to bury him with his wallet or his car keys. It wasn't too late. He hadn't been buried yet.

"Oh, Katherine, I don't think Pen will need it where he's going," Aunt Ginny said, causing my mother to turn on her.

"That is not the point." My mother swept out of the room, a thing at which she excelled, before we could respond. With the offending article on my wrist, I looked at Aunt Ginny, who'd suddenly become the arbiter of my relationship with my mother.

"Nonsense, Bernie. It's a nice memento."

After we finished dinner, Aunt Ginny and I went into the library, where my mother was reading a magazine. The room was just as I remembered it: too warm, too full of light glinting off polished wood. I could barely keep my eyes open, so I got up and went down the shelves of books on the north wall. I bypassed the interminable classics—Aeschylus, Byron, Dante, Descartes—most of their green leather spines unmarred by reading. I had learned at an early age that the unwieldiness of the books was intended as a stern warning against would-be readers. At one end of the top shelf was my father's secret stash of books. A testament to the cleaning regimen of my grandfather's housekeeper, the books were free of dust, but they hadn't been disturbed in years. I picked out *The Moonstone* and started reading. It's a book I find subtly pleasing, because no matter how many times I read it, or have read it (about four), I can never remember how the mystery is solved the next time I pick up the book.

"I can't see how Bernie will manage this, even with an army of lawyers and accountants," my mother said. She pretended I was deaf when I was reading, and I obliged.

"It was Pen's choice," Aunt Ginny said. "He always did what he wanted."

"I'm only worried that Bernie won't be able to handle it. So many decisions to make."

"He's a smart boy. Everything will be fine."

"Of course he's not stupid, Ginny, but I wonder if it won't be too much for him. Emotionally. He's not strong. Not like Robby." It was the point in my mother's disappointment when Robby once would have stood up and suggested he and I go for a drive. Aunt Ginny was simply embarrassed, folding and refolding her hands in the lap of her black dress.

"I'm sure he'll take care of it," she said.

"We'll see. When I told him what I expect Pen's will contains, he shrugged. And you saw that he's wearing Pen's watch."

"I don't see why that makes you so angry."

"The coroner brought Pen's personal items by and Bernie took the watch out of the bag and put it on. From his grandfather's body directly to his wrist. I think that's gruesome beyond words, apart from the fact that the watch had great sentimental value for Pen."

"Pooh," Aunt Ginny said. "The dead aren't sentimental."

"Bernham, do you hear me?"

"I hear you."

"Stop lurking and come sit down," my mother said in her dog-commanding voice.

The pages of *The Moonstone* had been polished smooth by my father's hands, and as I turned them, they gave off a whiff of his aftershave. I took the book over to where she was sitting and fanned it open in front of her.

"What is it I'm reading?" she asked.

"Nothing. Just breathe in."

She frowned and said nothing. The smell touched some part of her I couldn't.

The next morning my mother sat across from me at the breakfast table. She turned her magazine pages as if she were swatting at a fly. When I stood up to leave, she glanced at me as though she'd just noticed I was there and then went back to reading. She was leaving in the afternoon and considering the fact that we only saw each other for family funerals, the math was on her side. There were two more funerals that would require our mutual presence. Three, if I included hers, and she wouldn't be forced to speak to me at that one.

Because she'd insisted, I met with Mr. Tveite, the Chairman of the Board at Raleigh Industries. He was prepared, but for the wrong thing. In painstaking detail, his legal henchmen explained that although I was inheriting a controlling interest in company stock, it was structured in such a way that an intricate web of executive officers, managers, and board members stood between me and the actual management of the business. It was the one concessionary plan my grandfather put in place after Uncle Alan's death, when he must have realized I was his only heir. In terms which left no doubt as to the generally held belief in my inability to succeed at anything, the lawyers explained to me that there was no need for me to be involved in daily operation of Raleigh Industries.

They wanted me to serve on the board and they wanted my name on the company stationery. I was going to be a figurehead, trotted out at board and shareholder meetings and various community functions. I had such a reputation for incompetence that they suggested hiring an assistant to help me keep track of my little obligations. I don't know what response they expected from me, but they tiptoed so delicately around the central issue, that they must have been prepared for outrage. When they finished their presentation, I smiled and nodded in appreciation of their elaborate diplomacy. Leaning back into the leather chair that had been my grandfather's, I said the words they'd hoped for.

I said, "Okay. My brother was being groomed to take over this business, but I'm a librarian." Everyone in the room exhaled in unison and smiled at me. I felt like an ass for playing the simpleton, except I was relieved, too. What would I have done if my grandfather's dying wish had been for me to run the company? Killed myself and let the inheritance roulette wheel stop on someone else?

"You were wrong to worry," I told my mother when I came back from the meeting.

"What do you mean?"

"There's no need for me to 'establish my position' over at RI. I don't have one."

"That's outrageous. They can't push you out."

"They can't, but Pen did." I wanted to get the last word, to end the conversation. "Don't be upset. I'll still receive the dividends, the income. I just won't be making any decisions about the company. That's what Grandpa Pen wanted." She didn't say anything else, except to tell me she was ready to go to the airport.

With the big white house looming in my rearview mirror, and the line of trees that hugged the driveway reaching their bare limbs up to the winter sky, I felt my mother's relief. She was glad to be going, glad to be leaving behind all that good red dirt and that drafty old mansion. And me.

On the drive into Oklahoma City, she had nothing to say to me, and I found myself filling the quiet by describing the plot of *The Moonstone* as far as I could remember it, all the while hating myself for caving to her impenetrable silence. This was her idea of goodbye: "Oh, here we are. Take care of yourself."

She strode out onto the tarmac, her purse over one arm, and at the top of the stairs to my grandfather's jet, she gave me a little wave. Very Jackie. She had quite a repertoire of First Ladies.

"Good afternoon, Mr. Raleigh," Mrs. Bryant said when I got back to the house. She had been my grandfather's housekeeper for close to twenty years, and she had a way of moving that advertised her arthritis: stiff and careful. She calculated each movement before she made it. When she resigned, she would apologize and mention her health. She would not want me to feel that I was the reason she was leaving, but the truth was evident to us both: when a new tyrant takes the throne, the old tyrant's faithful retainer goes to the chopping block.

I wasn't even sufficiently tyrannical for her taste. She waited for me to tell her what to do, and when I didn't, she did what needed to be done. When she'd asked me about hiring extra help for the funeral, she was disappointed that I deputized her to do what she thought was best. Mrs. Bryant had a clear notion that there was a sacred order to the world. It started with God, the Pope, then descended through the ranks of the Church until it ultimately reached Mrs. Bryant, but in her mind her employer came ahead of her. I personally had always ranked the hierarchy of importance on usefulness, leaving me somewhere near the bottom. I wasn't sure where God fit in.

"What would you like for lunch, Mr. Raleigh?" she asked. "Mr. Raleigh usually preferred a roast beef sandwich on Tuesdays. Of course you can have whatever you'd like."

Feeling like an impostor, I agreed to prefer roast beef on Tuesdays also.

Over the next few days I learned to exist at the periphery of the cleaning that went on throughout the house. Mrs. Bryant had her two temporary helpers, Meda Amos and Mrs. Krause, and the three of us had an unspoken pact to pretend we couldn't see each other when we passed in the hallways.

At first, the only evidence of the phone calls was in the regularity with which Mrs. Bryant poked her head around a door and said, "The phone for you, Mr. Raleigh." Then I discovered that if I went up to my bedroom and shut the door, she wouldn't disturb me. It was the easiest solution to the phone calls, but after several days the evidence mounted: a pile of phone messages written on little pink pieces of paper that said, "While You Were Out..." They gathered in drifts across my grandfather's desk.

The messages were all the far-flung particulates of my grandfather's personal affairs. The people who called were assistants of attorneys, accountants, brokers, caretakers, consultants, and representatives from dozens of museums and collections. I didn't bother to count the calls from the news agencies, imagining the phrase "could not be reached for comment" printed after my name. I made haphazard attempts to return some calls, but I didn't have a particular system, and found that despite the best intentions, I couldn't develop one. Maybe they weren't the best intentions, but they were good intentions, arrayed one after another like so many paving stones. My failure was undeniable when the same names made third and fourth appearances, and the messages took on a tone of barely contained anxiety: questions needing answers.

I woke up each morning to discover the ceilings had been lowered while I was asleep. Every day the rooms in the house seemed smaller. I was a lobster put to boil on a low fire, feeling the water heating, but not realizing what the outcome of the hot bath would be.

By the time I realized what was happening, it was too late.

Or I never realized it at all.

It was that late.

I was a seafood metaphor.

I didn't know how many days went that way; I never did. I lost track, until I heard someone talking to me. I inhaled, smelling the dry, preserved familiarity of my bedroom, and over it, the scent of jasmine. A woman, not my mother.

It was the funeral stopper, Meda Amos. She stood next to the bed, looking down at me, and said, "Mr. Raleigh, your aunt is here to see you." When I sat up, she took a step backward, but I felt her looking at me—staring really—breaking the little agreement we'd had.

Creepy

Meda

I wasn't thrilled about working for Aunt Bryant again, but I was glad to get the money, even though it meant leaving Annadore with Gramma. The money for groceries had to come from somewhere. The work wasn't bad, because it wasn't like being a maid at a motel, which was the worst job I ever had. Mostly it was just keeping up with the way dirt sneaks in everywhere in a big, old house.

We didn't see much of Mr. Raleigh, which was fine with me, because I thought he was a little creepy. Not in a bad way, just kind of goofy and distracted. Aunt Bryant got nervous when we hadn't seen him in a couple days and the dinner tray we left out on the kitchen counter one night wasn't touched at all. Nancy knocked on his bedroom door, but he didn't answer, so Aunt Bryant said we ought to open the door and have a peek, just to be sure he was okay. I didn't feel like messing around, so I knocked louder and heard Mr. Raleigh mumble, "What? What is it?"

"Do you, um, do you want me to make up your room?" I said, like it was a motel.

"No, thank you."

I shrugged at Aunt Bryant, but she kept frowning.

When I asked what she was worried about, she said, "Now, I better not ever hear this come back to me, because I won't have you gossiping about the Raleigh family." She waited until Nancy and I nodded. "After his father and brother died, he took a whole bottle of pills that the doctor gave Mrs. Raleigh for her nerves. The evening after the funeral, his uncle went up to the room at the top of the stairs, just by chance, you know, because there must have been somebody using the downstairs washroom. Mr. Alan went up and found him. Came downstairs white as a ghost, shouting for us to call an ambulance. It gives me a chill remembering that. Mary Beth's Donald was a volunteer paramedic then. He says Mr. Raleigh was dead when they got here. They had to use the paddles on him."

"You don't think he would again?" Nancy said.

"Oh, I don't think so. He was just a boy then," Aunt Bryant said, but she looked upset.

The next day, Mr. Raleigh's aunt came to see him and asked me to let him know she was there. He didn't answer, even though I knocked really loudly, so I went into the room. He was sleeping, curled up on his side. His hair was matted to his head like he hadn't washed it in a while. When I said his name, he rolled over on his back and looked up at me. Then he sat up and looked around.

"Could I have some water, please?" he said. He was so hoarse I wondered how long it was since he drank anything. I filled the glass on his nightstand and when he finished that, I got him another glassful and he drank that, too. While he was drinking it, I looked at him sitting there in his underwear. Maybe I shouldn't have, but I couldn't help myself, because I'd never seen anyone like him. Without his clothes, he was bigger than I thought, but too thin. Just big, raw bones and not much meat on him. The way he was built, he looked like a giant ten-year old, all arms and legs. While I was watching him finish his water, his aunt came upstairs.

"That's fine, dear. Thank you," she said. That meant I was supposed to leave.

Weakness

Aunt Ginny

After I'd sent Miss Amos out, he said, "I'm sorry." He apologized because he'd been taught to think of it as his fault. His mother had never believed in his depression as a thing apart from his character; it was why she thought he was weak.

"You haven't been eating," I said.

"I'm sorry."

"Are you taking your medicine?"

"No."

"Oh, Bernie. What would your mother say?"

It nearly broke my heart to see him that way. He was even thinner than he'd been as a young man, when he was struggling to grow into his height. When you love another woman's child the way I love Bernie, you put your trust in God to keep you close, because no one else thinks of your bond as special. No one consults you when they're making decisions about his future. Yet, there he was, brought to me, for me to take care of. Whatever Katherine chose to believe about her sons, Bernie was as capable as Robby had been. He just hadn't seen the thing he was meant to do.

"Please, don't call my mother. Please," he said.

I was ashamed for scolding him, and for having thought of calling Katherine. Seeing the state he was in, I couldn't bring myself to do it. He didn't need her judgment or her doctors as much as he needed some kindness.

"No, I won't call her." I took off my glove, meaning to check him for fever, but when I tried to put my hand on his forehead he shied away. "I know she's a little hard on you, but you have to look at things as a whole. You know, when your grandfather was a little boy, no one thought he would amount to much. They used to call him Penny, because he misbehaved so much, and had a way of turning up at the wrong time, just like that old saying about bad pennies."

"That's apocryphal," he said.

"I beg pardon."

"It's not true, that story. People like the story so they keep telling it. Nobody ever called that man Penny."

"Yes, I know what apocryphal means," I said, a bit annoyed with his ten-dollar words. "I only wanted you to see that life isn't all set out for you. People change. And I think you should let an old woman tell her stories."

"I'm sorry."

"Do you still pray, Bernie? Would you like me to pray with you?"

He shook his head and wouldn't look at me.

I loved him so much and he was returned to me a stranger again. Secretly, I had always believed God sent Bernie as a blessing to Alan and me, to make bearable what might have crushed me under its weight. It seems shameful, considering how young he was, but there were many times I cried on his shoulder, especially after Joan died. He never used those stabbing words that adults offer: *She's gone on to a better place. You have to keep on living. There will be other chances. It must be God's will.* They appear to offer comfort, but behind them all are the suggestion that you ought to stiffen your spine and stop crying. I once thought Bernie would make a great minister, because when he was only five years old, he knelt down and prayed with his grandmother in her final hours. He had such healing in him, such compassion, and they saw to it that he became nothing inside. They made him into an observer.

"Well, why don't you take a shower and then we can go have some lunch?" I said, trying to be cheerful. I'd forgotten how angry I was at the Raleigh family, and I felt the sort of fury that isn't healthy for an old woman to feel. Once he was in the shower he must have felt better, because I heard him singing. That seemed more like the Bernie I knew, and just because he chose not to, it didn't mean I couldn't pray for him.

Changing the Guard

After Aunt Ginny left, I met up with Mrs. Bryant in the front hall and waited for her to say, "Good afternoon, Mr. Raleigh." Instead, she reached into her apron pocket, presented me with a handful of message slips, and said, "I need to speak with you, Mr. Raleigh." Five minutes later, she was sitting on the other side of my grandfather's desk, looking over the piles of phone messages at me.

"Mr. Raleigh and I had discussed me retiring. My health isn't what it used to be, what with the arthritis," she said. I accepted my defeat graciously.

After Mrs. Bryant's resignation, I called the office of the Chairman of Raleigh Industries, and his assistant said she would call the assistant of the VP of Human Resources, who would hire me an assistant, who perhaps would kill the rat that ate the grain that sat in the house that Jack built. Mr. Tveite was right. I needed help.

I hoped, too, that replacing Mrs. Bryant could be accomplished from a distance, but my grandfather had always managed his own household staff. The next day, Mrs. Bryant presented me with her replacements. She asked me into the kitchen and forced me to engage in a farce of an interview, as though my opinion could be of any value. I wasn't surprised that one of her prospective hires was her daughter, Mary Beth Trentam, who seemed embarrassed to shake my hand. Nepotism I had expected, but I was dismayed when she re-introduced the other applicant saying, "And you've met Mary Beth's niece, Meda Amos. She's been helping out temporarily."

We didn't shake hands.

Once we were seated at the kitchen table, Mrs. Bryant began by explaining, "Mary Beth's been working in retail, but she's really been looking for something more stable."

"And I've come in a few times as temp help for Mother over the years," Mrs. Trentam said. She was a younger version of her mother, well-built and just starting to go a little thick around the waist. Her hair wasn't grey yet, but it gave away her age all the same. It was styled with such exacting detail that she must have worn the same hairstyle for the last fifteen years. That or it was a wig.

In a tone of mournful confidence, Mrs. Bryant said, "Meda's been out of work for about two months now. On welfare. I used to have full-time help, but she quit this August and I never hired anyone to replace her. It's better to have two people steady. It's a big house."

I considered all of it unnecessary information. My personal policy toward most of humanity resembles the Army's policy regarding homosexuals. I won't ask; please, don't tell me.

"I'm sure you know best, Mrs. Bryant," I caught myself saying, for the third or fourth time in ten minutes. Meda sat to my right at the kitchen table, pretending to sip her coffee, although I could see the level in the cup hadn't gone down at all. Her serenity had a small chink in it.

If the lovely, shy creature tucked under God's arm in the Sistine Chapel ceiling fresco of Creation was intended to be Eve, she was nothing but a pale ghost of her Talmudic precursor. Meda was the darkly illuminated incarnation of Lillith, one of Adam's earlier wives, whom he repudiated for wanting to be on top during sex. As though she could read my mind, Meda glanced at me before I could look away. Her eyes were blacker than my coffee and just as liquid.

Based on my inability to look at her with anything like indifference, I knew it was a horrible idea to have her working in the house full time, but I agreed to it. I also agreed to the salaries Mrs. Bryant suggested. I would have agreed to almost anything to bring the interview to an end.

"You'll need to get the information to give the accountant for taxes," Mrs. Bryant said. "Or I could call the accountant." She was thinking of unanswered phone messages when she stressed the matter of paperwork. I couldn't be trusted.

Once they were gone for the day I wandered around the house, feeling like a time traveler. In my grandmother's sitting room, the same lace curtains hung against walls not papered, but hand-painted in complimentary stripes. The furniture was all upholstered in the same shades of blue. I half expected to find her at the piano, absently picking out a song with one or two fingers. I wasn't afraid of ghosts; as far as I knew, I was the only person who ever died in the house.

I sat down in the library, trying to decide what to do. Reading was a slippery slope that distorted time. I needed to replace my grandfather's TV. I needed to get cable or a satellite dish to give me a schedule. It was almost six o'clock and I couldn't go to bed before ten, because it was dangerous to allow the rules of time to be loosened by four whole hours. Those were the calculations that led me to do the thing my mother had discouraged. Like I was a rowdy kid, she warned me that I wasn't to be a "nuisance" to my Aunt Ginny, but the fear of my waiting bed won out. I drove into town.

After we exhausted our small talk, Aunt Ginny asked if it wouldn't be nice to look at some photo albums. I wanted to say no, but she had reached in with her bare hand and pulled me out of the boiling water. I settled in next to her with the albums across our laps and tried to linger over the oldest photos. My grandparents on their honeymoon in Paris. Aunt Ginny and Uncle Alan's wedding. My parents' wedding.

"Look," I said. "You're so beautiful." She still was beautiful. As we sat on the sofa, hip to hip, I took her hand into mine, admiring the slenderness of her fingers. Her skin had begun its decline into delicate crepe, making her hand an exquisite little creature in my own big, square hand with its ugly pinky stub. I couldn't resist the urge to stroke her hand after I captured it, and the cool distraction of her engagement ring only added to the pleasure. To drag out the happy memories, I tried to keep Aunt Ginny from turning the page, but she was having none of it. After a few moments of being petted, she slipped her hand out of mine and pushed past those photos rendered harmless by age.

On the next page was Aunt Ginny's oldest child. If he had lived he would have been ten years older than I was. He was almost lost in the lace of a christening gown. His eyes were glassy, and death was haunting him. The photos ended before he could appear in a picture of his second birthday.

Aunt Ginny's second child peered out of a bundle of blankets in the middle of July, going to his christening, and then a few months later to his funeral. There wasn't even a first birthday party. As we turned the pages, I recognized my brother by his glow of health. Robby was a non-descript baby, but he stood out in that procession of dying children. In later pictures, they went on being babies, while he moved toward adolescence.

I lost count, wasn't sure which cousin was which, until my own christening picture showed up as a milestone. I couldn't imagine how it had been for Aunt Ginny, to go through every pregnancy hoping that each one might be different. I don't remember the medical terminology, but the math was simple. Each baby had a fifty percent chance of inheriting that fatal gene. The odds don't seem bad, but statistically it's possible to throw a quarter up a million times and have it land tails up a million times. There were no points awarded for past efforts. Every time the scoreboard went back to zero.

Another photo showed a birthday cake with two brave

candles. The birthday girl slumped back behind her cake, her little face not plump, but swollen. In the chair next to her my brother devoured life in a fistful of cake.

The next cousin looked dead already in his christening gown.

One of the cousins didn't live long enough to be christened. The only photo of her was in a hospital bassinet, a plastic band ringing her frail wrist.

At last we came to the cousin I remembered most clearly: Joan, like a grey and wizened gnome, aged with the effort of living. We thought she would live, that she would start kindergarten in the fall, but she didn't. At the funeral her small face was peaceful and unrecognizable.

My cousins went on long past my ability to recall them. There were six of them altogether. Four basic elements recurred in the photos. Robby: sturdy and blond; me: taller, dark-haired; a succession of frail cousins: dying; my aunt: in a constant flux between the hopeful pastels of christenings and the determined black of funerals.

More bothersome than my cousins was the face of my Uncle Alan. Seeing pictures of him made me think of one of the last times I'd been to Aunt Ginny's house after I flunked out of McGill University. It would be a great story if after that failed venture into higher learning, I'd been stiff-necked and taken no beneficence from my grandfather, but that's not how it happened. Although I rarely saw the man, I was well aware my various career opportunities came to me through him. I didn't receive them directly from his hand, but through his dogged emissary, Uncle Alan.

They tried to make me a teacher, a production manager, even the assistant principal at a private school in Atlanta. They were all things dreamed up by my uncle and made possible by my grandfather's connections. I didn't have a degree in library science, but I worked at a library. I didn't have a degree in anything, because McGill wasn't the first college I failed out of. It was the last.

Uncle Alan gave up on having his own children sooner than my aunt did, and he staked his hopes on me. We were both younger sons. In Aunt Ginny's albums there were pictures of me on Uncle Alan's knee, standing in the car seat next to him, playing catch with him. Was I already failing there?

The visit I was thinking of, I listened to my uncle try to put a positive spin on my future. My grandfather, he said, was just as happy that I wasn't going to finish college. A waste of time and money. Then he asked what I really wanted to do, and I answered something I've long since forgotten, and then began the venture of me being an assistant librarian. A year later Uncle Alan died, so it was a good thing I managed to hang on as a librarian. In the five years since his funeral, I hadn't been to Aunt Ginny's house even once.

Aunt Ginny turned to the final pictures in the album and there I was graduating from high school, Uncle Alan's arm around me. At nineteen I towered over him in my mortarboard. Off to one side of the picture, my mother fished in her purse distractedly. I can't blame her for not looking much like a proud parent. I didn't even earn enough credits to graduate from high school; I have a piece of paper that cost my grandfather a donation toward a new football stadium.

As a courtesy, the corporate office sent out a girl named Celeste to be my assistant. She had a new blue suit and a blond bob, and every time I glanced at her she smiled brightly, either intending to become a VP of something or Mrs. Bernham Raleigh. Within half an hour she had created a calendar for me, and was returning phone calls, taking memos and typing up checks for household bills.

"I ordered checks for the household account with your name, but until then it's perfectly okay to use the ones with the late Mr. Raleigh's name," Celeste said when she passed me the checks to sign. Against my will I was influenced by the bold print that said 'Robison P. Raleigh, Sr.' in the upper left corner. For as long as I had been capable of expressing a preference I called myself Bernie, but I signed the checks 'Bernham S. Raleigh.' It was a case of medium writing, a spirit directing my hand.

By noon I felt hemmed in on all sides. In the study, Celeste was unflaggingly cheerful. Upstairs, Mrs. Trentam vacuumed in and out of the bedrooms. Mrs. Bryant put in her final days, inventorying the linen closets and china cupboards. Meda was a roving emissary of dusting; she was everywhere at once. I passed her in the hall and she said, "Mr. Raleigh."

"Bernie," I responded on autopilot. She acknowledged the correction with an uneasy closed-mouth smile, kept walking, and started up the stairs. Even her ankles were nice to look at.

Shamed back into my duty, I returned to the study and made phone calls to my lawyers and accountants about the money that was going to descend on me in the near future. My grandfather's money was reproducing itself while I was asleep. There was no way to keep up with it. While I lay in bed in the mornings, masturbating mindlessly, there were accountants, stockbrokers, and working stiffs putting in ten-hour days to make more money for the Raleigh family.

The first of many meetings that Celeste scheduled for me was with the executor of my grandfather's will. I might have thought it was my grandfather's way of apologizing to me, but it seemed more like a domino rally. I was the only one left standing. Most of the will was unchanged from when it had been written, except that after my father died, Uncle Alan's name replaced my father's. Over the years my grandfather had added some minor codicils to provide for my mother and Aunt Ginny, as well as a few employees, including Mrs. Bryant. Then, when Uncle Alan had his heart attack, someone applied the legal equivalent of Wite-Out® to the will and wrote in my name. At Uncle Alan's funeral, my grandfather must have already known what he was going to do.

"How's the book business?" he'd said to me in parting.

"Good. It's quiet," I said.

"Well, take care of yourself, son."

"You do the same, sir."

I shook his hand and then got in my rental car and drove to the airport. At the time, I assumed Pen had made other arrangements for the business that didn't involve me. I'd never given a thought to the money.

The will stipulated nothing for charities or schools. My grandfather believed in people "pulling themselves up by their bootstraps," and didn't think much of college degrees. His modest tithing had been a disappointment to the Church during his life, and in dying he chose not to continue it.

I got the impression that my grandfather's executor had wasted a lot of his own breath trying to convince Pen to leave some of it to someone or something more worthy than me. The Raleigh Industries company stock tipped the scale at over two billion. The rest of his stock portfolio and cash assets totaled another three billion. Then there was the house, plus an alarming array of real estate, the jet, seven cars, and the furnishings of the various properties: antiques, artwork, china, crystal and silver plate service for an army of 100. Lastly, I inherited my grandmother's jewelry, modestly appraised and insured at just under thirty-one million. That woman could wear diamonds.

When they showed me the numbers, I think I displayed stoic gravity in the face of the vacuum of emotion I experienced. I felt no elation or gratitude, which seemed to be what the lawyers expected. I realize I could as easily be dead. I realize there are much worse things than what happened to me, but the money didn't make it any better. It made it worse.

I left the meeting with my head full of insidious plans. I played with the idea of getting on a plane and going back to Kansas City for a few days, or forever. A visit, I speculated, would bolster the feeling that there were important things there for me to go back to, to reaffirm that I would be going back. In my heart, I knew it would have the opposite effect.

A feeling somewhere between panic and fatalism kept me driving around for hours after the meeting. It was my primordial feeling of a black hole sucking things inexorably into itself. The sensation would be bad enough if I felt trapped in the gravitation of it, but I never do. It's everything else slowly spinning inward, the whole of the world caught in the centripetal draw, while I watch from a distance. I taught myself it was better to stand aside and witness the destruction of the universe, but I wondered if I hadn't learned to fear the wrong thing.

A mile or so before the turn I should have taken to go to my grandfather's house—my house—there were two small white crosses planted by the side of the road. The names on them were Robison Raleigh, Jr. and Robison Raleigh III. I never understood the urge to create memorials of places where tragedies occurred. Misery landmarks itself, even when you want to forget. I resolved to have the crosses removed, even if I had to come out and take them down myself. I drifted briefly, the steering wheel becoming less real in my hands. I didn't turn toward the house and a little further on I drove by a familiar figure walking along the shoulder of the road. It bothered me that I knew Meda Amos so completely from a single glance, because I had no business filing away the shape of her back and her way of walking in my brain. It was perverse and useless.

I Couldn't Possibly

Meda

It was better than my other choices—at least I knew who he was—so I got in the car with Mr. Raleigh. My teeth were chattering so much I couldn't say anything. I waited for him to start driving, but he didn't.

"Your seatbelt," he said, and after I fastened it, he pulled back on the road.

He laid his arm across the back of the seat and his arm was so long his hand was almost right behind my head. It made me nervous, even though I knew there wasn't any reason to be. He reached over and turned the heater up a little higher, but didn't say anything else. After ten miles of that, the silence got to me.

"The car runs fine for a while and then it goes dead. It's an old car. I guess I shouldn't be surprised." He didn't answer, so I kept babbling until we got into the city limits. I told him where to turn. Right at the Presbyterian Church, then straight through to the T at the old train depot, and then a left.

"It's the third one on the left," I said, pointing because I couldn't think of how to describe which house he was supposed to stop at. My family called it the Blue Mushroom, and it was the ugliest house I'd ever seen.

"Is this your house?" he asked, surprised into saying something finally.

"No, it's my grandmother's house. Thanks for the ride." I started to get out of the car, but I still had the seatbelt on.

"Would you like to go to dinner?"

I couldn't believe I hadn't seen that one coming, so I tried to say what Aunt M. would have said to end the conversation: "I couldn't possibly. I need to get dinner for my grandmother and my daughter."

"They're invited, too. We can all go out to dinner," he said. "Please. I'd really enjoy some company." I felt silly for automatically thinking he meant something else. I didn't want to go, but I felt sorry for him.

"Well, okay, sure. It'll take us a minute to get ready. You want to come in?" He didn't pick up on the fact that I was just trying to be polite. Or he was that lonely.

Another Miss Amos

I knew I was taking advantage of Meda's compassion, but the seed of dread I was carrying around outweighed other considerations. Aunt Ginny was at her bridge group. I couldn't go home. Under the surface of Meda's kindness was a vein of anger; she scowled when I turned off the car. At first I thought her annoyance was because of the house, the fact that the house was more or less a shack. I'd have called it a lean-to, except that it wasn't leaning to anything. It was ancient, low to the ground and covered with faded blue corrugated siding that curled away from the house at the foundation. I thought maybe she was embarrassed for me to see the cracked plaster and sagging ceiling, or the wretched green, flocked-velvet lamp shade, or the coffee table with the warped veneer top or the sofa with its matted upholstery and cigarette burns. Possibly she didn't want me to see her grandmother sitting on that sofa with her feet—gone the way of all waitresses' and hairdressers' feet: corns and bunions and broken veins—propped on that coffee table.

Also, no one had mentioned Meda's daughter before, which invited questions about the fact that she was single again or still. Meda picked up the little girl, who looked about two, and escaped to some hinter region of the house, leaving me to introduce myself to her grandmother, who, like Meda, was also a Miss Amos. Not long after that introduction was effected, I discovered why Meda was uneasy about my presence. Miss Amos the Elder didn't waste time on small talk.

"You're the one who was abducted, aren't you?" she said.

I was momentarily stunned, because people don't usually ask about it. When I didn't answer she asked a second time, so I said, "Yes." She leaned closer to me, pointed at herself.

"I was abducted, too. Standing out in my garden one night—I can show you where it was—and they took me." At first I didn't suspect what was amiss with her story, only fearing that she would return to mine. "It was a real bright light, and then I woke up on this table and they were standing all around me. Is that how it was for you?"

"Don't tell him that. He doesn't want to hear your crazy

story," Meda said from the hallway. There was a patch on the shoulder of her coat. It was large enough that most people would have thrown the coat away, but she had patched it with a similar piece of fabric. Everything about Meda Amos made me want to help her, even her anger. I wanted to help her, but the complicated side of the equation was that I wanted her to need my help.

Once we were at dinner, Miss Amos returned to her story. "They looked like those mummies you see in National Geographic. Like they were all head and those big black eyes."

"Gramma! Mr. Raleigh doesn't want to hear this stuff." Meda muttered to me, "It's my mother and all those stupid newspapers she reads. Gramma can't remember what's real and what's not. She thinks half that stuff she reads happened to her. And Mom just encourages her. She's a UFO person. Believes in UFOs."

Meda and her grandmother bristled at each other.

"What's your little girl's name?" I asked.

"Annadore." I gave her what I hoped was a look of benign curiosity, but when she saw the look she said, "It's a long story," but didn't elaborate.

Meda was solidly real beside me, and I was half relieved, half disappointed that she seemed almost matronly with her practical shoes and her jacket on. As she leaned over to help Annadore with her food, she propped her bosom on the table. Terrifying, but in the lovely, rollicking way that a snake is terrifying. Fast, poisonous, slithering in the grass, but brilliantly designed. All sharp fangs, plated scales, and sinuous coiled muscle. Even if you're afraid of snakes, once you see their practical beauty, all the things you think you know fall away.

I caught myself looking at her, continuing my internal debate about why she was so riveting. It was not merely the juxtaposition of the scars to her beauty or the suggestion of perfection corrupted. I couldn't find a single feature in her face to improve upon, and that included addressing the issue of her scars. The problem was that the scars served as focusing mechanisms. They kept you looking when you wanted to be able to look away, and forced you to look at her face from new angles. In another woman you might have overlooked the subtle curvature of her upper lip that hinted at a smile, even when she wasn't smiling. You definitely would have missed the ethereal glow of the apple of her cheek. Since the Old Masters died, no one cares about that sort of thing.

Whatever it was about her, I didn't want to be parted from the sight. Meda didn't make the offer, but I accepted her grandmother's invitation to come in when I returned them home after the meal. Meda left the room briefly and her grandmother leaned close to me.

"I'm not crazy," Miss Amos said in a melancholy whisper. "She'll tell you I'm all loose in the head because of my stroke, but it happened. It happened and I didn't remember it at all until my stroke. Broke something open inside me so I could remember it. They were cruel little things, with the coldest eyes. No heart to them at all. You know. They say that it happened to you, too, when you were just a little boy. Someday you come when you like, when she isn't here to bother us. You and me, we'll talk. We'll talk. We'll talk." She said it like a mantra, drifting toward a trance or toward sleep, making me uneasy.

When Meda came back, she leaned over her grandmother and said, "Gramma, why don't you go to bed? It's late."

After the old woman shuffled down the hallway, Meda lifted Annadore out of her playpen and sat down in the chair across from me. After a few moments of quietly rocking her daughter, she said, "She hasn't been the same since her stroke. I think she realized she was going to die and that did something to her."

CHAPTER TWO

SMILING DOG

Meda

"DEATH MUST BE different for the elderly, though," Mr. Raleigh said. "As people get older, I imagine they start bracing themselves for it." He was waiting for me to answer, to disagree. He had some weird ideas about conversation. I couldn't help thinking about how he had died and been brought back. It made my skin crawl and he must have noticed. "What?"

"I was thinking about people who die young, about how they don't get any chance to get themselves ready." He was dead quiet and he sat back into the chair, staring off into space. I said, "Are you okay?"

"Oh…yeah. What were you saying?"

"I was going to say that people don't keep track of where they are in their lives, that's why they're not ready to die. It's not like you're looking out the window of a house, thinking, oh, it's spring, it's summer. We look out the window and think, looks like it's going to rain, I better take an umbrella. We're not thinking, I'm going to need my coat in three months when it gets cold." I said it in a big rush, wanting to get away from that other thing. I didn't want to think about it or see him thinking about it.

"Maybe we're not aware of the seasons of our lives at the

moment that they're occurring, but we can look back and see them. One morning you wake up and the season has changed. I wonder if my grandfather got up that morning and there were leaves falling from the trees."

"I think it's like being in a boat, sailing along, going some place, not realizing how close we're getting to the rocks until one day—we find out that's the only place we're going."

"Have you ever been sailing?"

"No," I said. Mr. Raleigh put his chin in his hand and we sat there not saying anything until he looked up at me and smiled. He reminded me of a dog my brother once had. The dog would smile if you petted him, but even when he smiled, he looked sad.

Subservience of the Flesh

I liked the sinister flash in Meda's eyes, when she talked about little sailboats colliding with sharp rocks. I was moved by her understanding of it, and pleased to find myself not thinking prurient thoughts about her. I don't discount the possibility that what I felt was due to the little girl she had balanced across her thighs. She spoke without a single gesture, both her hands trapped in the task of holding her daughter. That, I imagined, was the burden of motherhood: the actual subservience of the flesh. I was relieved when Meda stood up and carried her daughter down the dark hallway. A few minutes later she came back and said, "Well, goodnight, I guess. And thanks for dinner."

I was not completely unafraid, but was less afraid of going back to the house. I went upstairs and discovered that someone—Mrs. Trentam or Meda—had aired out my room, changed the sheets, opened the curtains, straightened everything, and taken away my laundry to be washed. The place was changed—the boiling lobster feeling dissipated.

The image of Meda resting her breasts on the table stayed with me, kept me awake thinking about the mystery of breasts. They have a very practical purpose in procreation: nurturing offspring. That practicality aside, however, breasts are an attractant, examples of the incredible marketing genius of biology. Imagine a toothbrush so alluring it made you want to brush your teeth. You couldn't stop thinking about brushing your teeth. It ate up whole hours of idle thought. That would be quite a toothbrush.

From what I had seen through her clothes, Meda's breasts were like that. They figured a great deal in my leisure thoughts, but it was her mouth I couldn't stop thinking about. Her mouth was such a form of torment to me that I forced myself to think about her ankles, or her hair or any other part of her, in order to avoid thinking about her mouth. The whole situation annoyed me; it was disgusting and vulgar to catalogue her physical charms for later perusal. Without a doubt, men regularly subjected her to that sort of mental delectation, but I tried to hold myself to a higher standard.

As much as I chastised myself, several mornings later I was in fact using her to animate my sexual diversions when she walked into my room. I had stayed up too late watching TV, then slept in without bothering to shut the bedroom door the night before. Maybe I was starting to feel at home. I struggled to whip the bed sheets up over me into some semblance of order, but it was futile. There was no point in hoping Meda didn't realize what she'd walked in on. Her face went pink, and she apologized softly: "I didn't realize you were in here. The door was open. I was just going to put clean sheets on the bed."

Her choice of words made her blush more and in the midst of an embarrassed giggle, she closed her eyes and opened her mouth in a lovely, wide smile, revealing that her right front tooth was missing and the bicuspid next to it was broken off at an angle. I'd only ever seen the tiniest smile from her—a curl of her lips—and sometimes she even put her hand over her mouth when she smiled. She was embarrassed about her teeth and I took her revealing smile to be an exchange: her secret for my secret, embarrassment for embarrassment. Saying, "I'll close the door," she backed out of the room and retreated down the hallway, still giggling.

In the aftermath of her laughter, I was utterly unable to finish what she had interrupted, so I showered, dressed, and entrusted myself to my eternally helpful assistant. Celeste was making phone calls, faxing paperwork, arranging meetings, all while maintaining a running commentary on a wide variety of friendly and bright topics.

"It must be so exciting for you to be home again," she said.

"It's nice," I said. It wasn't nice or exciting.

"I'm guessing you're a dog person. You are, right?"

"Hm." I'd never owned so much as a goldfish. I was a book person.

"I can always tell. I'm a cat person myself. I have a Maine Coon, a calico, and a Siamese mix," she said then quickly revised. "But I like dogs, too."

"That's nice."

"Mr. Tveite says this is the beginning of a new era for Raleigh Industries."

"I'm sure it is." Could she quote entire marketing brochures for RI?

"I think a small town would be a nice place to raise a family, but I really prefer living in the city, you know. Just more to do. I love going to concerts, don't you? I love live music."

"Mm-hm."

Our conversations didn't go exactly like that. Those were just highlights of a single day's conversation, but it was non-stop. She didn't have to stop talking to work, or vice versa. She could do both at once, seemingly with greater efficiency than she could do them separately. I didn't want to be a boor. I wanted to slap her. I ground my teeth until my jaw ached at the end of the day. It was like being trapped in a bad marriage and like many men before me, I took refuge in the garage. With a book hidden in my pocket, I stepped out of the room, as though I were merely stretching my legs, or going to the bathroom. I walked down the hall, past the kitchen, and once I was sure the coast was clear, I made a break for it. As are most people, I was taught to think of a car as a mode of transportation: a vehicle to convey me from one place to another, not a place itself. Sitting in the car, however, I began to think of things I could do to make it more comfortable. I needed a better light and something to drink. It might have seemed weird to an observer, except I was rich, so it was merely eccentric.

After a grueling day at my accountant's office, looking at indecipherably occult spreadsheets, I drove by Meda's house hopefully. I never would have done it, considering the embarrassment of her walking in on my act of self-pollution, except for that smile. Just as easily she could have been shocked or too appalled to speak, and I never would have stopped at her house. Instead she gave me that smile. Her old Datsun sat in the yard, but I got no response when I rang the doorbell. I knocked loudly and a woman I'd never seen before came to the door. Her hair was still dark, but her face was lined and rough, like she had lived hard. Her sunken cheeks hinted at missing teeth. She looked at me strangely when I introduced myself, but she let me in.

Miss Amos was sitting in her usual spot and Annadore was in her playpen, arranging plastic farm animals and chewing contemplatively on a cow. For several uncomfortable moments, we were all quiet, and then the woman put out her hand.

"So, you're Bernie Raleigh? I'm Muriel Amos. I'm Cathy's—Meda's mother."

"It's a pleasure to meet you."

"Meda's in the shower right now. She'll be out in a little bit." Muriel said it as though they'd been expecting me, so I sat down and waited.

"That's Bernie Raleigh," Meda's grandmother said to Muriel. "He was abducted."

"I know, Mom. I know that's Mr. Raleigh. You interested in

alien abduction?" Muriel took my uncertain shrug as an invitation to continue, leaning toward me over the coffee table. "You know a lot of people are starting to use hypnotism to find out they've been abducted. A lot of times the aliens will cause people to forget they were taken. They suppress the memories. I remember my own experiences, and my mother has been able to since she had her stroke."

"It's like that whole part of my brain got opened up, where I had the memories hidden, since I had my stroke." Miss Amos nodded to herself.

"I was just reading an article a friend of mine got off the Internet." Muriel indicated some papers on the coffee table. "About this woman who got hypnotized as part of a program to stop smoking. While the doctor was hypnotizing her, she had a flashback of being abducted. The doctor never believed in it before, but he says after that, he thought it had to be real, because he did a bunch more sessions with her and she remembered all kinds of things. It turned out she'd been abducted like fourteen times."

Down the hall, the sound of running water stopped.

"He's here," Muriel shouted.

At that same moment I added up the intricate web of alien abductions and multiple Miss Amoses. Parthenogenesis.

"I'll be out in a little bit," Meda called. "I'm almost ready."

While we waited, Muriel continued her story. "It was almost twenty years ago. We were living over off County Road 9, and I'd walked down to the grocery store. I was hurrying to get back, because I'd left Cathy—Meda—who was about five and her little brother alone. It was a spooky road to be on at night all alone back then, and I was thinking all kinds of things, when all of a sudden there was a big light shining down on me.

"It was too bright for car lights and it was coming from above me, too. I dropped the bag of groceries I was carrying and tried to run away, but it was like I was frozen, couldn't move, just like in a dream. And then I felt this really strong pull on me that made all the hair on me stand up on end. My arms and legs were dangling, and I could feel this pulling right in the center of my chest, that's where the light had latched onto me, right in my chest. That's how they took me up into their ship."

"Wow," I said, trying to maintain a look of polite interest.

"That was the first time they took me, but they've taken me a lot of other times since then."

We all straightened up when we heard a door close down the hallway, and then Meda came around the corner, dressed to go out. She had on a slithery black skirt that swirled around her calves and a dark green turtleneck that left my speculations about breasts in the dust. I came up out of my chair in a purely reflexive gesture of good manners; I don't know what I would have fallen back on without them.

"That's not—you know what Jeff looks like. This is Mr. Raleigh." Meda looked at her family with undisguised suspicion. Belatedly, she turned to me and said, "Hi."

"Hi. I was on my way back from the city and thought I would stop and see if you—all of you—would like to go to dinner with me."

"I can't. I—" The other three Amoses in the room looked at me expectantly, but without giving me any hints about what they expected. Then someone knocked on the door, and Meda never finished the statement. "There's Jeff."

She gave a sigh that spoke so eloquently of the discomforts of her situation that I regretted increasing them.

"I'm sorry. I should have called," I said.

Her date knocked again, and for a ludicrous moment I wondered if I should answer the door; I was closest. Finally, Meda stepped past me, her sweater-clad breast making contact with my arm, and reached for the door.

A Million Bucks

Meda

I opened the door just a crack and said, “Hey, Jeff, let me get my coat.” Jeff can’t take a hint to save his life, so he came right in. His head dropped back so he could look up at Mr. Raleigh. It was about the only way to look at Mr. Raleigh, but Jeff got all prickly about his height. He was even shorter than me, only 5’8”.

“Hi, I’m Jeff Hall.” He stuck out his hand, and I knew he was going to give Mr. Raleigh a tough guy handshake. I don’t think it worked, because Mr. Raleigh went on being polite.

“Bernham Raleigh. I was just leaving, Mr. Hall. It was so lovely to meet you, Miss Amos,” he said to Mom. “And a pleasure to see you again, Miss Amos,” he said to Gramma. Then he turned to me and said, “I hope you have a nice evening, Miss Amos, Mr. Hall.” It was all I could do not to laugh. Was he kidding?

“Nice to meet you, too, Mr. Raleigh. I hope we see you again some time,” Mom said.

“Is that your boss?” Jeff asked after he was gone. “I didn’t know you worked for Lurch. Christ.”

“I’m ready to go.” I managed to get Jeff out of the house before Mom could start in.

“You look like a million bucks,” Jeff said in the car. That was the kind of compliment he always gave me. I hated it, because who wants to be told how much money they look like? Really, no girl wants to be told that, or anyway, I don’t.

“Thanks,” I said.

“You better watch out. I’m guessing your big geek boss is going to put the moves on you.”

“I don’t think so.”

“Oh, please, he’s a guy, he’s thinking the same thing every guy is thinking. And he’s rich, so he thinks he can buy whatever he wants.”

"He's not that rich."

"Aw, that's sweet, baby," Jeff said. He didn't understand what I meant.

Debunked

I believed Meda's mother. I don't mean that I accept the notion that aliens came to our planet and took Muriel into their space ship. Although I don't dismiss that idea as impossible, it seems like the least likely of several possibilities. I believe something happened to her, something that made her feel taken away from herself, something that returned her not quite as she had been.

I was nine, nearly ten. They were waiting for me as I walked home from school. I was taking a shortcut through the city park, and someone called my name. Amy waved at me. She was a blonde girl who had worked for my parents as a maid for a while. I had a little crush on her. I remember that she asked me about Robby. When I told her he was sick at home, she looked upset. I followed her gaze to a battered van parked up the hill, where the path widened into a little lane that eventually emptied onto a side street. There was a man leaning against the van watching us. Amy's boyfriend, Joel.

"Hey, come over," Amy called to Joel. "This is Bernie."

"Where's his brother?"

"He's home sick today." There was an uneasy silence between Amy and Joel.

"Well, hey, Bernie, what say we give you a ride home?" he said.

"You sure?" Amy asked.

"What's that supposed to mean? Come on, Bernie." Now I understand the silent conversation that was taking place, but at the time I noticed nothing. I can't remember if I'd been admonished against taking rides from strangers, but even if I had, Amy hardly qualified as a stranger.

In the back seat of the van there was a second man. When I sat down next to him, he said, "This isn't him."

"I know," Amy said.

"Damn it." He punched me in the face, harder than Robby ever had, hard enough that the world started to fall away from me. I never even saw the man, because I must have blinked as I turned toward him, and all I felt was the impact of his fist. Then the man I never saw pressed a rag that smelled like a hospital over my mouth and nose. I suppose it was ether.

Mrs. Duncan, the housekeeper before Mrs. Bryant, answered the first ransom call. Thinking it was a prank, she disconnected. Until then, my family thought I was missing, and all kinds of people, neighbors and employees, turned out to look for me. When the kidnappers—I hate that word, so stupidly melodramatic—when they called the second time, they were allowed to speak with my grandfather. His response was vitriolic rage, as evidenced by the newspaper quotes at the time. Within two hours of the second phone call there was a full-blown FBI task force operating out of the formal parlor. The newspapers ran pictures of cops and agents, crowded around recording devices and maps in my grandmother's parlor. It was weird to see that, and a little embarrassing, like a copycat Lindbergh scenario.

My grandfather was defiant. He refused to pay the money demanded, or any amount negotiated by the task force. Initially he even refused to allow them to play out the decoy payment scenario the FBI developed. It wasn't the money; it was a matter of principle for him. I was twenty-one before I knew that, before I knew he had refused to pay.

The next day Celeste went to the corporate office for what she said was "training," and what I suspected was a debriefing. Mr. Tveite wanted to know what I was up to. In her absence, I walked down the hall to the kitchen, hoping for some different lunch conversation. As I opened the door, I heard Meda say, "It's the only day they could fit Mom in. The Saturday appointments fill up fast."

"It's just that Thursday is so inconvenient, Cathy," Mrs. Trentam said. "I already have to take Samantha to school that day, and then I'd have to stop for you and then for Muriel. And then the drive into the city at that time of day."

"I know it's not convenient, but that's what they had, and she needs to go. She's been putting it off and she needs to go. Couldn't I borrow your car and then you wouldn't have to take the time?" Mrs. Trentam was silent. Meda sighed and, with honest submission and no anger, said, "If you can't, you can't. I'll figure out something else."

"It'll be less of a headache if I just take you. You'd have to be back by two, because that's when I have to leave to pick Samantha up from school and I can't be late picking her up. And Mr. Raleigh isn't going to be happy about us taking the whole day off." I hated hearing myself referred to as some distant authoritarian, and although it was an admission I'd been eavesdropping, I interrupted them.

"I have to go in for a meeting on Thursday. I could drop you off before and pick you up again afterwards."

Mrs. Trentam cringed when I said it, and answered for her niece: "Oh no, we couldn't possibly. That would be so inconvenient for you."

"I don't want to put you to any trouble," Meda said. "You know how doctor's offices are. You might be stuck waiting to come back."

When I insisted, she didn't waste her breath on any more protests.

When we picked her up on Thursday morning, Muriel had the aura of those Mexican women who speak with the Holy Virgin. She came to the door of her trailer in ragged sweat pants, slippers and a man's work shirt. She looked like she hadn't been awake long, but she lit up when she saw me and said, "Well, good morning, Mr.

Raleigh." At her mother's enthusiastic greeting, Meda gave me a defeated, almost reproachful look and led me up the steps.

"Bernie, it's just Bernie," I said.

Meda's shoulder blades tightened together. It occurred to me there was a limit to the degree of acceptance I could obtain through kindness.

The trailer had the cave-like quality that is native to mobile homes: paneled walls, brown carpeting, and windows covered in dark curtains. It was decidedly lived in.

"It's so nice of you to help us out like this," Muriel said to me. Then she opened a can of beer. Meda had been digging through a pile of clothes on the sofa, but at the familiar pop and hiss, she turned with a beat-up sheepskin jacket in her hand and snapped at her mother.

"Why'd you go and open that? You can't take a beer. You want him to get a ticket for driving with an open container?"

There was a storm of sadness and aggravation in her face, and as wrong as it was, it gave me an erection watching her wrangle with her mother. Meda snatched the beer away and forced Muriel's arms into the jacket, the same way she had put on Annadore's coat ten minutes earlier. Not with brutality, just an abruptness born of frustration.

We rode in silence until Muriel said, "Hey, Bernie, maybe if we have time we could go down past Tinker. There's this field east of there, and if you're there in the early morning you can see the ships."

"We're not stopping, and they're fighter jets from the airbase," Meda said.

"That's what they want you to think."

"We're not stopping." Meda stared straight ahead, picking at the seam of her jeans.

"Such a nice car." Muriel sank back into her seat with a sigh of pleasure. "Leather seats. That's quality."

For the rest of the drive, she limited herself to such mundane conversation topics, for which I was grateful, and eventually Meda thawed out a little. To Meda's embarrassment, Muriel took out her wallet to show me family pictures. She passed forward a picture of a thin girl who looked like a shadow of Meda, a brunette with brown eyes, whereas Meda's were true black. "That's my other girl, Loren, Meda's little sister." She passed me a small photo of Meda from many years before, and I saw then that the scars had imparted calmness to her face. In the picture she was in the third grade and her face was a riot of feeling: some disagreement with a classmate, or a fight with her mother over the shabby, too-small dress she was wearing. The expression on her face was feral. She hated. Something. Someone. It was the only picture of Meda that her mother carried in the plastic folds of her wallet.

Mr. Tveite, the Chairman of the Board of Raleigh Industries, spent almost two hours walking me through his ideas for my little presentation at the annual shareholder meeting. He thought I was an imbecile; I reciprocated by thinking he was an ass. Once we'd finished our meeting proper, the Chairman started to talk about going to lunch. The look of breathless opportunism on Celeste's face confirmed to me that the meal should be avoided at all costs. Then the Chairman began talking about his New Year's party, which he really hoped I'd come to. As I was trying to figure out how to escape, his secretary rang on the intercom and said, "Lionel Petrie has arrived, sir."

"Great! Send him in." Mr. Tveite flashed me a big grin. "This is the best part. Bernham, meet Lionel Petrie. Lionel, here he is, in the flesh."

Lionel Petrie looked at me with the same excited fervor of a birdwatcher seeing a rare specimen. He was not quite five and a half feet tall, and was swathed all over in dark hair, from the top of his head down to the collar of his shirt. As he shook my hand, his mouth opened in the midst of the fur and said, "Good to meet you. Good to meet you. Did you tell him already?"

"No, I was waiting until you got here. Lionel is going to turn his camera on Raleigh Industries, Bernham."

The name seemed familiar, because he had directed a car commercial a few years before that had famously pulled the manufacturer's sales out of the doldrums. I'm sure he'd done other things, but that was what I knew him from. I decided to pretend a polite interest.

"We're doing a new advertising campaign then?" I said.

"We're not just doing an ad campaign. You're doing an ad campaign. Lionel and our marketing people have come up with a great idea. We want to make a commercial featuring you." Mr. Tveite smiled when he said it, and for the briefest moment I tried to think of what he was waiting for me to say. Then a wave of horror rose up and obliterated my natural tendency toward compliance.

"I don't think so," I said. I picked up my briefcase, but Celeste balked at her cue. She sat at the conference table, her tablet full of notes before her, looking attentively at Mr. Tveite. There were her loyalties.

"Oh, come on, Bernham. Don't decide so quickly. Let's talk about it over lunch. I've got a table at the Coach House and—"

"No. I didn't agree to that. I didn't agree to do any commercial. I've got to go now. Celeste, I'll see you tomorrow morning." I made it to the reception area before Lionel Petrie came puffing up behind me.

"I'll call you, so we can chat about it," he said.

"Nice to meet you, Mr. Petrie." I didn't pause, and at least he didn't follow me into the elevator.

My heart had finally stopped pounding by the time I reached the hospital. In the waiting room, Muriel greeted me like her best friend. Meda gave me her usual smile that conveyed discomfort, but still contained an erotic allurement. I could only guess at what it was like going through life with a face that carried that suggestion no matter your mood, and it made me even more ashamed of my masturbatory pursuits. We made small talk for half an hour, with Meda apologizing every five minutes. Eventually a nurse came to tell them they could go in and see the doctor, and Meda began the process of gathering up Annadore's things.

"It's okay," I found myself saying. "I can watch her while you two are in with the doctor." Meda looked at me in surprise. If it had been possible, I would have looked at myself in surprise.

"Okay." Meda stopped her gathering efforts and got up to follow Muriel and the nurse. After they were gone, Annadore looked at me for a moment, and then went back to the coloring book she was scribbling in on the floor. I sat for a while and thought of all the things that could go wrong. What if she started crying or needed to go to the bathroom? She didn't. She continued coloring in her book, while I flipped through a *National Geographic*. When she got tired of coloring, she gave me a copy of *Stellaluna* and held her arms up to me. I didn't know what else to do, so I set her on my lap and read to her. Twenty minutes later, Meda and her mother came out. Muriel was oddly quiet and Meda seemed more brooding than usual. I didn't ask. Annadore showed off her various coloring activities and Meda smiled at her, complimented them. She even smiled at me.

"Thank you for watching her," she said, granting me a reprieve from her earlier annoyance.

About Money

Meda

"The blood test is essentially good news, because there's no increase in antigen production. The little cancer tag cells we talked about last time, we're not seeing those. The largest of the cysts, however, are worrying." The doctor used his really calm, don't-scare-the-rednecks voice. He treated us like idiots because we were poor.

"So, it's basically the same as it was," Mom said.

“I expect we’re going to see the same thing when we take a closer look at the biopsied tissue, but the blood work looks about the same.”

“That’s good, right? That it’s not any worse?”

“It’s not any better, however. We really need to do a better imaging test, and honestly, the best next step would be lumpectomy to remove the largest of the cysts.” Mom looked scared, even though she kept acting like it wasn’t a big deal. “Now, Mrs. Amos, again, I just want to caution you not to look at this too negatively. This is not like a mastectomy. We would make several small incisions to reach the cysts that we consider a concern.”

I hated the next question I had to ask next, because it was about money.

It turned out the answer was that Mom was out of luck. It pissed me off royally that the doctor could be that dense, to be talking to us about what kind of treatment we ought to do, when he had to know we couldn’t afford it. Or maybe that was why he was so careful to let us know that Mom’s problem wasn’t really serious, yet. Anyway, it was mostly a wasted day. It was good to know Mom wasn’t any worse, but she also wasn’t getting any better from us waiting to see what was going to happen.

When we were done with the doctor, Mom said, “Gosh, I’m hungry. I hate skipping breakfast.” Her idea of breakfast was the beer she almost drank.

“Let’s get some lunch, then,” Mr. Raleigh said.

He was so easy about everything that I said okay. We went to a Chinese place, because that’s what Mom wanted.

My fortune was: “All things beautiful will come to you.” Right.

Mr. Raleigh’s fortune said, “You have an iron will, which helps you succeed in everything.” He thought it was very funny.

“That’s not a real fortune.” Mom had this idea that fortune cookies ought to tell your future.

“You really don’t have to do that, Mr. Raleigh,” I said, when he reached for the check. I thought I'd made him mad, because he frowned at me.

"Just Bernie, okay? I hate it when people call me 'Mr. Raleigh.'" He paid the waiter before I could say anything else and then he asked if we wanted to go to a movie. I tried to say no, because he'd already spent so much time waiting on us, but he said, "Honestly, I don't have anything else to do. I'd like to see a movie."

Thinking about going into his room and seeing him asleep, I wondered what he did in the evenings after we all went home.

He was a nice guy, but I didn't know what it was about, his being so eager to help me out, and then paying for lunch and a movie. I figured it was about sex, because it's almost always about sex. During the movie, I thought about how I felt about that. Even though he definitely wasn't my type, he wasn't bad. He was too tall and he wasn't handsome, but he had a nice face, with those sad dog eyes and his crooked nose. I liked that he was so polite, and it didn't hurt that he had money. Except he was a disaster waiting to happen, being who he was, being my boss, being so sad.

Proposition

We ended up seeing a children's movie about some toys that come to life, the safest choice considering Annadore. She and Muriel at least had fun giggling and chattering. Next to me in the dark, Meda was tense, and I didn't attribute it to me. Maybe Muriel's visit with the doctor had been bad news. I had my own tension, and I wasn't sure how I'd ended up sitting next to Meda. I'd intended to avoid it at all costs, but I wound up in the aisle seat with Meda next to me, and Annadore in between her mother and grandmother. Meda's hair smelled like jasmine, and despite her tension and mine, the afternoon was pleasant.

We dropped Muriel back at her trailer, and then at Miss Amos' house, Meda asked me if I wanted to come in and have dinner.

"It'll just be our Chinese leftovers." She said it so casually I didn't feel guilty saying yes. The defense she had mounted against me before was relaxed. Once we'd had dinner and Annadore had been put to bed, Meda tried to explain to me about her mother: "It bothers her going to the doctor. If I didn't make her go, she wouldn't. She's really difficult about it."

"She's so hard-headed," Miss Amos said from her corner of the sofa. "She shouldn't be surprised that he left her. When she would get an idea in her head that was it. And mean, was she mean. Used to beat us with her shoe."

"No, Gramma, no, we're here. It's Meda. It's Cathy." She whispered to me, "She's talking about her mother." When I asked if Muriel had been sick long, Meda thought about the question for a long time. "It's hard to know, because she doesn't always see things the way other people do. So you don't know is it real or is it what she thinks?"

"You mean she's a hypochondriac?"

"No, it's that she thinks her cysts are caused by alien experiments. So it's hard to tell how long she's been sick, because she's been telling me that the aliens were making her sick since I was a little kid." Meda blushed and shrugged.

"She mentioned that, but she didn't say what kind of aliens. Were they Grays? Or Reptilians?" It was a whim asking her, but I liked hearing that hushed tone of skepticism that was mitigated by concern for her mother.

"I had no idea normal people knew about this." Meda laughed, her hand creeping up to cover her mouth.

"I watch a lot of late night TV," I confessed. Because I have often been unable to turn off that link to the rest of the world, I've learned a lot about the fringes of humanity. "The Discovery Channel. They have several different shows about aliens. I like the ones where they have experts on to debunk the myths about aliens."

"Those shows always get Mom worked up."

"I particularly enjoy their absolute contempt for anyone who suggests it might be real. They always call it the 'alien abduction phenomenon.' And they're so superior when they talk about 'the power of suggestion and subconscious knowledge assimilation.'" Meda looked amused, either by my monologue or by what a jackass I was. I shut up.

"The abductees are just as bad. Mom and her alien friends go on for hours. And if anyone's ever stupid enough to disagree with them, they have this whole thing about how you're 'blind to the truth' and how you're 'buying the government's lies.' They're not mean about it, because they feel so sorry for you."

"I like the shows with the religious experts, too. That's funny. I mean, God's an all-knowing, all-powerful alien overlord. If people can believe in that, how can they cast aspersions on people who believe they've been abducted by aliens? You talked to Jesus Christ. You got taken up into a big space craft."

"But really, doesn't it seem awfully far-fetched to you?" Meda said. "That aliens would keep coming down here and keep doing experiments on us? Which is what Mom always says they're doing."

"I think it's interesting that we assume aliens wouldn't do that, the body cavity probing and whatnot. Look at the Nazis. Germany had advanced technology compared to a lot of other countries, but Nazi scientists conducted terrible experiments on people. And our culture still does it, on monkeys and rabbits and all sorts of animals."

"I know, a couple years ago somebody gave me a brochure with all this gruesome stuff in it about animal testing. I had to quit smoking. I needed to anyway, because of Annadore, but I couldn't take it, knowing the tobacco companies were doing stuff like that to puppies," Meda said.

It surprised me. I hadn't pictured her as a smoker or an anti-vivisectionist.

"If the aliens keep probing us, maybe they haven't gotten the information they want," Meda said. "But you didn't answer my question. What do you really think about it?"

I weighed all the possible answers as quickly as I could and decided on something that was very close to the truth.

"I think alien abductees are suffering from the social equivalent of religious persecution," I said. "They believe. It's a matter of faith. The archaeological evidence for Christian mythology is no more solid than the evidence for alien abduction. It fails to establish the existence of God. All it can do is establish that humans believed in God all those years ago."

"Like quoting a Spiderman comic book to prove that Spiderman really exists." When I stopped laughing, Meda said, "I can't take credit for that. My brother always used to say that whenever Mom quoted her alien experts at him. But why do people believe? In aliens or God?"

"I think it's about what these people are missing in their lives that they fill with this belief. With religion and with alien abductees, I think it's an admission of powerlessness. Like a twelve step program," I said. Meda scowled. "That's just my opinion."

"Admit that you're powerless, that only your higher power is in control," she said with contempt. "My mother's been a recovering alcoholic almost as many years as she's been an alcoholic."

"Can I ask whether you believe?"

"Mostly I think it's group craziness," Meda said, and not one word more, before she stood up and walked down the hallway. After she was gone, I realized I hadn't specified which belief system I was asking about.

I almost called out to her, but didn't want to wake Annadore. I put on my coat and fished the keys out of my pocket, waiting for Meda to pop her head back out to say good-bye. Several minutes passed, and I was about to let myself out, when she came finally back. She had changed clothes and wore a soft white blouse and a long dark skirt that cast a shadow over her bare feet. She crossed her arms just below her breasts, so that I couldn't avoid looking at them.

"Do you want to stay? The night?" she said.

I was mortified by the question, not so much an invitation as a gesture of acquiescence. She stood there, all solid practicality, waiting for me to say something, maybe waiting for me to follow her into the bedroom. Her physical mysteries were peeled away, leaving her spiritual mysteries intact, glowing openly on the surface. In a flash, I understood. There was a limit to how much help she would accept, unless I was her boyfriend. Sex was more expedient. She would be more comfortable, because it would be an arrangement she understood better than my attempts at friendship. I don't know what I said or did to make my exit, but I knew I'd had a close call.

Lying in bed an hour later, I tried to remember the course of my precipitous flight, tried to remember what had been said. I thought of a hundred different, if not better, ways I could have handled it. I worried that she was offended, and I worried because among the hundred other scenarios I thought of was one in which I said yes.

He's Gay

Meda

He looked so uncomfortable I thought, *Oh, he's gay*. A lot of things about him made more sense when I thought about that. On the other hand, if he was gay a lot of other things didn't make any sense. Enough guys have stared at my breasts, I guess I know what that look means, and he was definitely looking at them like that. I wouldn't have asked him, except I thought that would put an end to it and I could stop wondering what he wanted.

"No, but thank you," he said, when he got over being shocked. "So did you—are you—when's your car going to be fixed?"

"Soon." Just as soon as $300 fell out of the sky into my lap.

"Well, if you need anything, I mean any help or anything, let me know. I'd be glad to." He sounded like the clerk at the hardware store.

"Thanks." I hoped he'd go soon, but he stood there jingling his car keys, not looking at me.

"Thanks, for this. I enjoyed talking to you," he said and actually blushed. So maybe he was just shy. I kept thinking, too, about what a little boy he looked like: so skinny and that ugly scar on his chest. Maybe he hadn't been with many women, or any women. I guess a guy could get to be his age and still be a virgin.

"I enjoyed it, too." I wanted to be nice, to make up for being so stupid. Who knew a person could have a halfway normal conversation about aliens?

CHAPTER THREE

MONUMENTAL INJUSTICE

DAILY, I WAS held prisoner by Celeste, who made me review donation solicitations from museums. Celeste lived for that sort of thing, going over the fine print and consulting the inventory list. It was her pleasure in the thing that made me feel I was her prisoner. The donations in question were my belongings, my responsibility, and Celeste worked for me; I should have been able to dictate the agenda. I had to admit to myself, however, that she took my job more seriously than I did.

Celeste took most things more seriously than I did. A few days later I looked at my calendar and saw: "10:30 Mr. Cantrell/Holy Mount." Mr. Cantrell had been hired to oversee the construction of my grandfather's monument and he occasionally called to update me on the work being done. He'd suggested that I go out and see how things were "shaping up." I wasn't susceptible to the suggestion, but Celeste apparently was.

Not trusting anyone else to do right by him, my grandfather had made the arrangements three years before. Construction had been underway for almost eight months, and if my grandfather had waited, it might have been done in time for him. Instead, he was at an "interim" location. I didn't know exactly what that meant, but I imagined him somewhere like the passenger waiting room of an

Amtrak station, tapping his foot impatiently. He'd be checking his watch every few minutes, except I was wearing it.

Going to the cemetery would have been bad enough, but Celeste made the assumption that she would accompany me and I couldn't uninvite her. I tried, and she wouldn't let me. As we were leaving, however, we passed Meda in the hall and I saw a new opportunity. She refused.

"I have work to do."

"No, come with us, it'll be fun," I said, trying for jocularity instead of outright begging. "You need a break, some fresh air."

"At a cemetery."

"Oh, come on." I dared to give her a chummy pat on the shoulder, drawing her toward us. Whether she heard my desperate plea or decided that a break from work would be nice, she got her sadly patched coat and came with us. In the car, Meda gave a cry of happiness and held up a blue, stuffed dog she found in the backseat.

"Annadore will be happy to get him back. I was worried the aliens had taken him." She laughed while Celeste rolled her eyes at me. I concentrated on driving.

As soon as we pulled through the main gates of the cemetery we saw my grandfather's monument. There was no way to avoid seeing it. It was a monstrosity, a word which at any rate shares the same etymological root with the word *monument*. For more than seventy years my family had owned an elegant, but fairly discreet mausoleum on a small hill that overlooked the older part of the cemetery to the south. The new structure was fifty yards away from the original mausoleum, and even unfinished it dwarfed its humble predecessor. It dwarfed the rest of the cemetery. The foreman led us around, detailing some of the finer points of the structure. Not surprisingly, they were of an esoteric nature, as that which makes a mausoleum a standout among mausoleums involves a lot of specialized features. We surveyed the marble, the granite, the engraving, the statuary, all the subtle glories of that strange little mansion, and tried to make complimentary remarks.

"It's so impressive," Celeste said.

Meda mumbled some nicety like, "It seems very cozy," and then clamped a hand over her mouth, casting me a look of muffled horror. As casually as she could muster, she said, "So, what's a thing like this go for?" I had asked the question myself when I first spoke to Mr. Cantrell and I knew by the tone of his voice he felt it was inappropriate. Maybe he'd been an undertaker in his early career, because I could imagine him saying, "How can you put a price on commemorating the loved one?" The look on Celeste's face was a mixture of things. Maybe she felt the question shouldn't have been asked, but she was curious.

I was so embarrassed to be faced with the question myself that I lied. I told them about half of what the actual cost was, but my lie made both of them open their eyes a little wider. Celeste recovered quickly, but Meda stood there shaking her head in amazement. Despite the dimensions of the new mausoleum, the point of it all was reasserted by the natural draw I felt to visit the older mausoleum where so much of my family was actually at rest. They were stacked three deep in chronological order: my grandmother on top of her mother-in-law who was on top of her youngest daughter. On the other side of the aisle were my father and my brother, one Robison Penry Raleigh on top of another. On top of them was my Uncle Alan, hidden behind a blank face of marble that said Starkalan Sevier Raleigh. In the plots around the mausoleum were some miscellaneous Seviers and Raleighs, and even one lingering Penry. We'd left the Bernhams in the old country.

Perhaps after the immediate family was moved to the new place, some of the more distant relatives could move into the old mausoleum. Like buying a coach ticket and getting bumped to first class. I made a mental note to ask Mr. Cantrell about it. When I walked around to the north side of the old mausoleum, I saw the six small headstones huddled together. Meda followed me and, in a gentle voice, said, "Babies. That's sad."

"My cousins." I steered us back toward the car. "We've been

walking around here for half an hour and I still haven't seen any Amoses."

She laughed and looked away. When she slowed, I lagged with her, letting Celeste get ahead of us.

"People like us don't get buried in this cemetery," Meda said. "You have to go up north of town to see where my family is buried. It only costs two hundred dollars to bury somebody there. And you don't have to have one of those concrete vaults. This guy named Varney who lives on German Road builds coffins. Roger—my mom's boyfriend at the time—and I drove up there and got a coffin when my brother drowned."

It was the sort of thing you expect would bond you to another person, that we both had lost a brother, but we were so far apart standing there in the shadow of my grandfather's stupid mausoleum. She felt it, too, and to reaffirm it to myself, I drove out to the other cemetery. I also reaffirmed what it meant to be in charge; neither of the women asked me where we were going.

I'd driven by the cemetery before, and even from the road it looked raw and bleak, like a place of mourning instead of a golf course. Celeste's usual chatter died out when she saw it. There were few trees, and while some of the graves had shrubs or flowers planted on or near them, there was no attempt at formal landscaping. Instead there were rows of headstones, running in irregular formation up the face of the hill. Meda headed out with certainty toward an area where the graves were gathered inside crumbling stone boundaries. Beyond that were headstones older and more worn than the oldest ones at Holy Mount.

"There I am." Meda pointed to a small white stone that was barely legible. I squatted down and by angling my head against the glare I could just make out the ghost of old letters. "She was my grandmother's great-grandmother." There was a Star of David carved into the stone and below that the words *Meda Amos Aged 26 yrs. Let her rest*. The next grave over had a marker that read: *Ann Adore, Friend*.

There was a stone that read *MaeLee Chinese gal* and one that said *Buffalo Nell O'Hara, She was a good one.* A more elaborate, expensive one said *Tamaura, Beloved Concubine of J. Tidwell.* Most of the others were barely marked, some with wooden planks that must have once had names on them. Other graves were mere depressions in the soil. Meda led me a little further to a stone that said *Zipporah Amos 1858-1897 With Her God.*

"That's Meda's younger sister," she said.

The Other Meda Amos

Meda

Celeste hated me because somebody, probably her mother, told her that all girls are competition, and I guess she thought we were competing for Bernie. That was the way she looked at me. Standing in the middle of all those headstones with Bernie kneeling in front of Meda Amos' marker, I could tell she was thinking bad things about me. I was a slut, trailer trash.

"Why do they all have such weird names? Here's one named Shuck Lou Anne," she said.

"They're prostitutes, aren't they? From when this was a boom town," Bernie said.

"Yeah, except those are people who can't afford to be buried in the other cemetery." I pointed over at the new part of the cemetery, because I wanted to be fair to them.

"Prostitutes," Celeste said. "How funny. And you're named after her?"

"I'm related to her." That was what she wanted to hear.

"Your great-great-great-grandmother, right? Do you know what year she died?" Bernie said.

"I think a lot sooner than her sister, but I'm not sure."

"You have a very interesting family tree."

I guess I did, if that was his idea of interesting.

Let Her Rest

Celeste rubbed her hands and blew into them until we got the hint. I tossed her the keys and she grumpily started toward the car. We wandered back across the field, Celeste in the lead, and Meda pointing out graves to me. There was her great-aunt Leah. There were two of her grandmother's babies, which I supposed she remembered from the recitation of family lore, because the little indentations were unmarked. She stopped abruptly in front of a marker that was made of hand poured concrete with metal letters stuck into it. It said: *David Amos 1976-1993 Miss You*. Her brother.

"Do you ever think about what you'll have put on your headstone?" she said.

"I hope I won't end up like my Uncle Alan with a slab of stone that says Bernham Sevier Raleigh."

"I meant besides your name. I like the ones that have little things written on them. Like the one that says, 'Too good for this world,' or 'Beloved Concubine' or, I don't know. I don't like the boring ones, like your family's. I like the ones where you can tell that somebody else wrote it about the person."

"'Let her rest'?" I said.

"No. I always thought that was sad. Like she'd never got to rest while she was alive. Or scary, like they were afraid she wouldn't rest when she was dead. I want something nice on mine."

"If there was a verbal equivalent of a shrug, that's what they'd put on my headstone." I shrugged at her. She obliged me by giggling. "Or, 'He was okay.' Did you write what's on your brother's headstone?"

"Yeah. I didn't have a lot of room for what I wanted to put," she said, embarrassed.

"I like it. You read it and you know someone was thinking of him. It's like a message."

"That was what I wanted. I don't know if I believe he's looking down and can see it, but I wanted to send a message just in case."

Celeste was waiting for us in the car and we were getting closer despite our wanderings. It seemed in poor taste to ask what I wanted to ask in a cemetery, but I wasn't sure I'd get a better opportunity. "Would you go out with me on a date?" I specified the date part, because I didn't want to confuse the situation.

Meda laughed out loud as soon as the question was in the air. Then she swallowed the laugh with a hiccup.

"I don't think that would be a good idea."

"Why not?" I said.

"The last time I dated my boss I got fired. And I really need this job. And my aunt would kill me."

"I'm a little confused." I debated with myself how to phrase what I wanted to say. "I got the impression that—maybe I misunderstood. If the date you had the other night, if that's something serious, I'm sorry, but I got the impression that you would be willing to go out with me." I didn't want to blurt out what I really meant: *tell me if I've misunderstood that we can have sex, but we can't go out on a date*. I was prepared to let it go rather than say what I was thinking.

She frowned. "Look, this is a lose-lose situation for me. If we go out and it doesn't work, maybe later you'll fire me, but if I won't go out with you, maybe you'll fire me anyway."

"I'm not going to fire you. That just seems mean, and I don't have a mean bone in my body," I said, my mother's somehow derogatory words coming out of my mouth. When had she said that? "Honestly, it didn't occur to me that you would see it that way. I'm sorry. I apologize."

We were only ten feet from the car, so I walked over and opened the door for her.

"I think I must have such a boring family," Celeste said, as soon as we were in the car. "There's nothing interesting in our family tree. Both my parents are teachers. And my grandfather was a bricklayer. Nobody ever did anything very important or very bad either. No scandals or anything."

I wasn't sure if she was waiting for us to pitch in, but since I knew her to be capable of holding a conversation without second party input, she was on her own. Meda sat quietly and I tried to figure out how to undo my stupidity. At the house, as I prepared to follow Celeste back to the office, Meda stopped me.

"I'm just being silly," she said, once we were alone. She didn't look at me, but kept her gaze on the little blue dog as she made it walk up my arm. "I guess it would be okay for us to go on a date. Since you don't have a mean bone in you."

"Not a one." I was conflicted. I was getting what I thought I wanted, but I felt belittled by the terms under which I was getting it. I had admitted I didn't have a spine. The vertebrae are the meanest bones in the body.

We went on the default first date: dinner. I thought my mind was playing tricks on me, when Tilda came to the table to take our order. She'd grown substantially in girth since the last time I saw her, but everything else about her was just the same as the day she stood stoically in her good navy dress at my brother's funeral. I would like to say that she had a beautiful smile or an inner glow, but she was the girl my brother had loved, grown into womanhood. Her face had settled into the predictably jowly weight of her thirties, and sunk into the ruddiness of her face, her eyes were still small, her nose still snubbed and upturned. With no sign of recognition, she took our orders and prepared to leave.

"Tilda," I said. I wasn't sure what I wanted from her, but it was like looking at a museum display of my childhood.

"Yes, hon?"

"Do you remember me?"

"Bernie, of course I remember you. I'm surprised you remember me. How are you?"

"I'm okay. How are you?" I couldn't think why it was so important for me to talk to her, but we filled up several minutes with small talk. Meda watched me with a squint of curiosity that made my skin crawl. At the moment I thought I ought to introduce the two of them, Tilda sprang her condolences on me, and before I recovered from that, she left to put in our order.

"My brother's fiancée, when she was in high school," I said to Meda. Some explanation seemed required.

"So, what do you do? I mean, what did you do before now, before you had to start being Bernham Sevier Raleigh? What kind of job did you have?" Meda asked the question, almost as though it were the only sort of conversation that could be made on an official date. It was odd, considering the other conversations we'd had. Her discomfort made me wonder if I'd imagined her asking me to spend the night with her.

"I'm a librarian. Actually, I'm an assistant librarian. All of the pleasure, none of the responsibility."

"A librarian," she said slowly. "And now you're just you."

"I'm planning on being a librarian again when I get all this mess straightened out."

"Really? You're just going to go back to being a librarian?"

"I plan to. This isn't what I'd intended to do with my life." I gestured uselessly, not sure how to describe the contours of what I was doing. She watched me, puzzled, but didn't offer any assistance. "What about you?"

"You know what I do. I suppose I'll keep doing it," she said.

Of course, it was the wrong question. By the time our dinner came, the restaurant was so busy there was no need to worry about what to say to Tilda. She put the food on the table, smiled at us and moved on. Meda began to eat, but the conversation died from there. I'd been on enough bad dates to recognize what had just happened. After dinner, I assumed I would just take her home, but as we crossed the parking lot, she turned to me and said, "Can you dance?"

Little Bernie Raleigh

Meda

He laughed so hard I expected a totally different answer, but he said, "It depends on what kind of dancing you mean."

"Can you two-step?"

"Absolutely. That's one I know. And I can waltz. I think I know the fox-trot, but I may have that confused with something else."

There's no way to know which guys will dance and which ones won't until you get them on the floor, but I figured I'd give him a chance. It was just a bar with a small dance floor, but I always liked it, because it wasn't full of show offs. You could go and dance and have a place to sit down and drink a beer.

"Sorry I'm so tall," he said when we finished the first dance and found a table. I thought it was sad, him going through life apologizing for something he couldn't help. He wasn't a bad dance partner, but he was too tall. While he went to get us a beer, this girl Carrie, that I used to work with at the motel, came over and sat down at the table with me.

"Holy crap," she said. "Is that little Bernie Raleigh? You're dating Bernie Raleigh? I don't know why I ought to be surprised, I mean, it's not like you don't get whoever you want, but he's so rich. I mean, like millions and millions."

I knew that's what everybody was going to think. Oh, look, there's Meda trying to snag a millionaire.

"It's not really a date. He just wanted some company. He doesn't know a lot of people here."

"Well, great, you can introduce us and then he'll know me," Carrie said hopefully. When Bernie came back with our drinks I introduced him to Carrie, and then she just sat there staring at him.

"So." He looked at me, wanting help.

"You don't remember me do you?" Carrie said.

"I'm sorry."

"I used to always sit behind you in grade school. Walker, Carrie Walker, you know so I was always behind you in the alphabet." After a while she got the hint and left, but people kept bothering us all night.

"I forget sometimes that you have a past here," I said. It was strange to think about all the people who knew who he was.

"Sometimes I forget that I do, too."

"You didn't go to high school in town, did you?"

"No, fourth grade was my last year here. I went to a private school after that."

Never Nice Enough

"Did you like school?" Meda asked.

"No one was ever as nice as I wanted them to be." I hoped it sounded sufficiently neutral.

"Are they ever? Is it a lot different from when you lived here? Is it true how they say you can't go home?"

"Oh, you can go home, but why would you want to?" I said. She rewarded me with a beautiful giggle that seemed to be part of her date mode. It made people turn and look at her.

"What was going to a private school like?"

I tried to tell her, but there was so little to tell. I went to a very exclusive school in Maryland, the kind of place where the students wear ties and blazers, and have to learn the fox trot for the annual dance with the girls' school. If there are even two kids out of two hundred who remember me from school, I would be amazed. Maybe there was bonding and friendship. Maybe there were late night parties and boyish pranks and secret societies. I just don't know, because I wasn't there. I was the invisible student. I went to class, went to the dining hall, went to the library. I didn't talk to anyone and the only people who noticed me were the staff members, who were obsessed with my curfew. There were a lot of sons of wealthy and famous families at the school, but the security paranoia focused on me. Pretty silly. I didn't have any statistics on it, but I think the odds were against me being kidnapped. Again, I mean.

When I asked about her school experience, Meda said, "I think what you said is true. No one was ever nice enough. But I bet they were nicer to you than they were to me."

"Were they really mean to you?"

"You've met my mom and she's always been that crazy. What do you think? The worst thing is how people say things to you that aren't very important to them, but that ruin the way you think about the world. It even screws up the nice things people say to you, because you remember the bad things, even while people are saying the good things. So I get dressed up for this date, and you tell me how 'lovely' I look, but what I remember is Aunt Bryant telling me I looked like a tramp when I was dressed up for a date. And that was years ago."

Meda took a deep breath and seemed embarrassed to have said so much on such a personal topic, so I asked her to dance again.

"You do look lovely," I said while we were dancing. The compliment was inadequate.

"In a trampy kind of way." She laughed darkly. "My sister does it, too, that poisoning thing. She likes to remind me of how fat I am. Stop. Not fishing for a compliment there. I am a little heavy since I had Annadore. Loren says it to make herself feel better, but when she does it, I don't think about why she's saying it. It poisons the way I think about myself. I bet girls like your brother's fiancée have this about their whole lives. I wonder if the rest of their life is poisoned by the first time they found out they weren't pretty, even if they find someone who thinks they're pretty. I mean, your brother must have thought she was pretty."

"Why do you think your sister does that to you?"

"I don't blame Loren, because she's been poisoned, too. Aunt M. had made a dress for me and dressed me all up for this stupid thing. My mom and Aunt Rachel were telling me how beautiful I looked, and Loren—she was only five or six—said, 'What about me?' Mom said, 'Oh, sure, baby, you're pretty, too.' But she was just dismissing Loren, and little kids aren't stupid. Loren knew what she meant. That's why she hates me."

It was why I always hesitated to judge my mother. The very idea of her had been poisoned for me.

We didn't actually manage to have the entire conversation at once, because when we weren't dancing, a dozen different people stopped at our table, ostensibly to say hello to Meda, but they always expected to be introduced to me. After an hour of that, Meda and I were both ready to go.

As I was driving her home, Meda said, "Can we stop somewhere? I need to get milk." We stopped at a convenience store on the highway and while we were waiting for the cashier to quit talking to her boyfriend on the phone, a man and a woman came in.

"Hey, Meda. Haven't seen you in a while," the man said. The woman with him gave Meda a look of pure hatred.

"Travis. Connie," Meda said flatly and turned back to the cashier.

"Well, how are you? How have you been?"

"I'm fine." To the cashier: "Could I pay now?"

Without putting the phone down, the girl rang Meda up.

"Where have you been keeping yourself?" Travis said.

Connie glared at him harder.

Without waiting for a bag, Meda picked up the carton of milk and headed toward the door.

"It was good to see you," Travis said, mostly to my back by then, as I followed Meda outside.

Only as I pulled up in front of her house did Meda grudgingly say, "I used to date him. Before he got married."

"Didn't end well?" I didn't think I had any ex-girlfriends to whom I wouldn't have made at least some effort to be polite, but then I'd never had a girlfriend with whom I had anything I would describe as chemistry, which Meda and Travis had.

"He wouldn't even help me get money for an abortion, and now he acts like Annadore doesn't exist." Meda didn't say anything else, and I tried to fill in the blanks for the two dozen other questions I wanted to ask.

The Whole Stupid Story (Condensed)

Meda

I didn't want to have tell him the whole stupid story about me and Travis, so when Bernie looked at me like he was waiting for me to explain, I said, "His family didn't like me and that goes a long way toward screwing up a relationship. His mother hated me." I didn't mention what a jerk Travis had been and how he'd broken up with me, it seemed like a hundred times, and come crawling back.

"My mother hasn't ever been interested in whom I was dating," Bernie said. *Whom.* I went to put the milk in the refrigerator and checked on Annadore and Gramma. They were both sleeping. When I came back, Bernie was sitting on the sofa with his coat off. He looked too comfortable for me to let that ride.

"Does that mean you think your mother wouldn't approve of me?" I said.

He laughed. "I don't have a clue what my mother would think of you. Like I said, though, she's never been interested in my girlfriends."

"She'd get interested real fast if you were going to marry one of them." Travis' mother didn't hate me until after I got pregnant and he decided he wanted to get married.

"I doubt it," Bernie said.

"You don't know your mother very well, if you think that."

"That's true, I don't. So, does he ever see Annadore?"

"He may have seen her from a distance, but he's never met her." The worst part wasn't that he broke my heart, but that he didn't have any interest in her.

"Aren't you glad, though, that he didn't help you get an abortion?" Bernie said. "You wouldn't have Annadore, then."

"No, I wouldn't." I was ready for him to get pissed off, because people get so crazy about abortion. He frowned, but I couldn't tell if he was upset or if he was just thinking. I didn't want to have to tiptoe around with him, so I said, "Would it matter? If I hadn't had her, would it matter?"

"I think it would."

"I'm not saying I don't love her. I'm not saying she doesn't matter. But would it matter if she hadn't been born? I wouldn't know, would I? I know what those religious nuts say, 'How would you feel if your mother had had an abortion?' And no offense, I know you're Catholic, but I guess I wouldn't feel any way about it. I wouldn't be here to mind."

"I'm not all that Catholic. And I suppose you're right. You can't know what you'd do if the situation were different. Anyway, I'm glad you had Annadore."

"So am I." Most guys I dated weren't even a little interested in her. Jeff pretty much pretended she didn't exist.

"I confess I'm surprised that Travis picked, um, Connie, over you, regardless of his mother," Bernie said.

"Why? Because his wife's not very good-looking? That's what everybody says, 'he picked her over you?'"

"Well, because you seem like a kind and interesting person to me, and that you're the mother of his child. Okay, and yes, that you're astronomically more beautiful than his wife."

"You know, that's just—it's the kind of thing that's a bigger problem than it is a help."

He laughed, because nobody ever thinks about what it's like to go through life being 'astronomically' better looking than other people. It's an idea, not something real. It's not like being astronomically richer than everyone else. Also guys always end up being bothered by my scars. A guy asks me out and we date and he thinks I'm still pretty even though I have them, but then they start to bother him and that's when the relationship is over. He can't stand to look at me anymore. If I dated a guy long enough that always happened.

After a while Bernie stood up and said he ought to go, since it was late. I guess that was to keep me from making another stupid invitation to spend the night.

"Would you like to go out again next week? Saturday night, maybe?" he said, like he thought I was going to say no.

"I can't on Saturday night, but if you want, we could do something Saturday afternoon. Like a movie or something."

He leaned down from way up high and gave me a little peck on the cheek.

Poker Face

There was no excuse for it, but at the end of our date, I kissed Meda on the cheek and fled. Days later I imagined I could still feel the softness of her cheek against my lips. When I went to dinner with my aunt I was strangely aware of kissing her the same way I had kissed Meda and with the same restraint of feeling. I was a coward.

When I asked Aunt Ginny if she remembered Tilda, she said, "Oh, of course. She's such a nice girl. She married one of the Bierchen boys, you know, who own the German restaurant." Then she went on about the Bierchen family for ten minutes.

"I saw her when Meda and I went out to dinner and it made me think about Robby. About what an odd couple they were."

"I think they have two children, Tilda and her husband. I can't remember which one he is, Karl or Rex," Aunt Ginny said, as though I hadn't interrupted.

"Doesn't it seem strange that Robby was engaged to her? Not that I don't like Tilda, but I hadn't really thought about how odd it was that he went after a lot of girls who were kind of chubby and homely."

"You said you went to dinner with—what was her name?"

"Meda Amos, you met her. She and her aunt took over for Mrs. Bryant at the house." I wasn't sure what was the best way to describe our relationship.

"Oh, my, the pretty one with all that black hair? But so sad, about what happened to her. Was it a date that you went to dinner with her?"

"I guess so." Waiting for her reaction made me nervous.

"Oh, Bernie, dear. I don't suppose you stood a chance at resisting her."

It was done nicely, but there was a barb in it, for me and for men in general. Aunt Ginny shifted the conversation several more times and I began to realize my aunt was purposefully avoiding the topic. It confused me. I wasn't sure what I wanted from her, but she seemed intent on denying me.

I think I just wanted to talk about Robby, to hear my own memories of him confirmed. He was such a stranger to everyone; I was closest to him and barely knew him. Not that he couldn't talk. He could keep a conversation going on anything. The pride and joy of the high school debate team, he could discourse on any topic from any perspective, never once being held up by his personal convictions, whatever they were. If he had lived, he might have been the president. Not just of Raleigh Industries, but of the country.

It was not just seeing Tilda that made me think about Robby, but what Meda had said about them. I agreed with her that the little things people say poison you, but she was wrong about Robby and Tilda. Robby never thought Tilda was pretty. He loved her because she wasn't.

His idea was that a shy ugly girl, especially a fat one, will never try to get inside your head. She is so grateful to be on a date with you that she will never have any expectations of where that date is going to go. If you never call her again, she'll consider herself lucky to have had the one date. That kind of girl is going to be happy to sit next to you in the movie and hold your hand and talk about trivial things. An ugly girl isn't going to ask, "What are you thinking?" After a lifetime of being the butt of cruel jokes, she doesn't want to know what you're thinking.

Tilda was the perfect girl for Robby: chubby, heading to fat on good German food, middle-aged homeliness already settling into her sixteen-year old face. She had two older sisters who offered proof that she wasn't going to bloom into a swan someday. Her hair was in a frazzled page-boy and she always wore heavy wool sweaters that looked hand-knit. When people spoke to her, she looked down shyly at her enormous, sweater-encased bosom. She had no confidence in the reasons Robby wanted to date her, that was clear from the awkward way she spoke to my parents, like an uninvited guest.

After he proposed to her, he later confessed to me, she shook her head. So he kissed her and kissed her and kissed her until she stopped shaking her head. According to Robby, that was how they got engaged. He put the ring on her finger, and she didn't take it off, but she never agreed to marry him. She didn't know why he'd chosen her, and if Robby was right, she didn't want to know. I wondered if her sisters ever spoke to her about him, warned her against getting her heart broken.

He did break her heart, through no fault of his own. About three months after Robby and Tilda got engaged, he and my father were coming back from the city, heading home for dinner. The roads were icy and the car slid across the center lane and under a cattle truck. My father was three days dying from his injuries, but Robby was dead before anyone could get down the road from the house.

Almost everything I knew about Robby I knew from the letters he sent me while I was away at school. Mostly he filled his letters with trivial things, but he also wrote to me about my mother's frustration with my lack of progress in therapy. His letters like negative images of my mother's, he wrote, "You're right not to tell them anything. They don't have any business trying to get inside your head. Neither does she."

I vacillate between two notions about Robby. Sometimes I imagine his distance as a profound shallowness. He never revealed his inner self, because there was no inner Robby. At other times I imagine there must have been something incredibly deep, perhaps dark, within Robby that he held it all so close to himself. I suppose it doesn't matter. The point behind a poker face is to keep others from guessing which kind of hand you're holding. Robby loved to drive around in the car at night, looking at lights in the windows of houses from a distance. Or I've misremembered and I was the one who loved that.

When I made a final attempt at the conversation I wanted to have, Aunt Ginny said, "Robby was afraid of women, that's why he liked shy, homely girls like Tilda."

For the first time it occurred to me that my aunt hadn't liked Robby very much.

An Aunt's Love

Aunt Ginny

It upset me that Robby was still so important to Bernie after all those years. I'd never thought Robby was particularly good for Bernie. I thought he was a bully. Of course Bernie had been taught to think of Robby as larger than life, because everyone in the Raleigh family was so enamored of him, the first son. Robby was the sort of boy everyone liked right away. He was very handsome and charming, but aloof, and people are often attracted by that perception of distance. You could spend a day with him and come away impressed with his intelligence, with his looks, but not really feel that you knew him. Least of all would you know what he thought about you, and it caused a lot of confusion with the girls he dated. They came away from a single date with him, already in love, and probably he'd never call again.

Bernie was his opposite, very open and affectionate. It was good that he had so much to give, because his mother wasn't very generous with her affection. Katherine was always pursuing Robby and most of her maternal efforts went toward wooing him. It's difficult to describe, because it might seem a little odd to someone who didn't know them well. Oh, it was odd, but not unnatural. Robby wasn't particularly given to confidences and Katherine wanted to live that old cliché: a boy's best friend is his mother. All the time I could see how Katherine was taking Bernie's love, but was too busy giving to his brother to spare much for him. I don't think she saw the ways in which Robby was like her.

Victim Blaming

Meda

"It wasn't a date, so before you start in," I said, as soon as I got to work on Monday. As sure as anything, I knew Aunt M. had already heard about it.

"What does that mean?"

"It wasn't a date. We just went out to eat and we went to have a beer afterwards."

"Well, the last I heard, dinner and dancing were a date. Damn it, Cathy, why do you always have to do this?"

"Do what? I don't do anything." I knew what she was going to say, and looking at her getting ready to say it, I wished I hadn't taken the job.

"You know what I mean. You don't learn. It's just like what happened with Jim Weaver. At least it took you two months to lose that job."

"What did I do? I didn't do anything. You really think I did something to get that disgusting Jim Weaver to make a pass at me?"

"And what about when you worked at Davenport's?"

"No, no, this isn't about Davenport's. You tell me what I did to make Jim Weaver act that way. You tell me what I did to make that creep come on to me."

"Whatever you do that causes problems everywhere you work," she said.

Like it was some one thing. I was just about ready to tell her what Jim Weaver had done, because there was no way I was taking the blame for that slimeball putting his paw down my blouse and pinching my nipple. I was guilty of slapping him, but everything that happened before that was his fault. I didn't get a chance to tell Aunt M. any of that, though, because Celeste walked into the kitchen like she owned the place.

"I'd like some hot tea, please," she said.

"Of course," Aunt M. said. "We'll bring it right out for you."

"Thank you." Celeste went back out, practicing her sexy secretary walk. I wondered if she walked around like that in Bernie's office, waiting for him to look at her butt when she bent over to pick up something she'd dropped on purpose. While we waited to be sure Celeste was gone, Aunt M. filled the tea kettle and put it on the stove. I got down the tea tray and the tea pot and all the accessories, waiting for her to say something. I didn't even know if Celeste ever used the stuff, but I filled the creamer and the sugar bowl, and put lemon slices on a side plate, just like Aunt Bryant had taught me.

"I'm not blaming you," Aunt M. said finally. "I'm just saying, you need to nip this in the bud. You cannot date Mr. Raleigh."

"I know that, but what am I supposed to do? You want to go in there and tell him I can't go out with him? Because that would be a huge favor to me."

"You know I can't do that."

"Why the hell not? You say whatever you want to me." I reached up to get a second cup and saucer down—in case Bernie wanted tea—but I wasn't paying attention. I tilted the saucer too much and the cup slid off onto the tiled countertop. It blew apart into tiny pieces. For about fifteen seconds Aunt M. was quiet. Then she started bellowing at me.

"Meda Catherine Amos. You did that on purpose. Do you have any idea how valuable that china is? That's Limoges. That cup cost more than you'll make today."

I hadn't done it on purpose, but it was useless to say anything. She knew it was an accident.

"I ought to fire you. I ought to," she said, but it was a lie. She couldn't fire me, for the same reason she wasn't going to tell Bernie that our next date was off. I was so mad that my hands were shaking when I carried the tea tray into the office. Bernie got up when I came in, and I thought he looked embarrassed while he cleared papers off a corner of the coffee table. It was a good sign. When my boss asked me out and then got embarrassed because I was doing my work, it meant he was getting ready to fire me or lose interest. I hoped he was as nice a guy as he said he was.

Little Miss Pageantry

For our second date, Meda suggested a movie in the city, and I appreciated her reasons. At least if we left town, we were substantially less likely to run into a dozen people who knew us. We left Annadore with Mrs. Trentam, who gave me a look I couldn't quite identify, but she looked at Meda with undisguised disapproval. She suspected some unnamed impropriety.

We saw yet another American remake of a French romantic comedy, and half an hour into the movie, Meda leaned over to me and said, "You know, a lot of people like to hold hands at the movies."

"Really?" I said like a jackass.

"How is this a date?"

I reached for her hand and she let me have it rather grudgingly, considering she'd practically demanded that I hold it. Once her feathers were smoothed, she made the obligatory comparison of our hand size. Her hand was not quite small enough to fit entirely in my palm. I am a human cartoon, laughably out of proportion to the rest of the world. She chuckled and then laced her fingers into mine. She didn't remark at all on the two joints missing from my left pinky, although that was the reason I had hesitated to hold her hand.

When we returned from our date, Mrs. Trentam was altering a small yellow dress that was four inches deep in lace and ruffles. Half-buried in the dress, Annadore stood unsteadily on a coffee table, her owl-eyed beauty dissipated into baby doll cuteness. It reminded me of a girl I dated in college who later married an acquaintance of mine. I was insufficiently marriage-minded for Caroline's taste, but Les was willing. At the ceremony, Caroline trawled up the church aisle like some connubial barge. I imagine there are few things more terrifying to a man than seeing the love of his life decked out in a bead and lace bedizened, rustling showboat of a wedding dress. Thirty yards of gleaming white satin, a 12-foot long train in tow, like a giant New Year's parade float. I suspect it's the same horror one feels on spying the loved one in a casket, rosy-cheeked, pressed, primped, and primed for the family viewing.

I was about to make a snide comment to Meda, when a growl escaped from her throat. Dogs usually make the same sound to warn you away, but contrary to that warning, and driven by an instinct I barely recognized, I put my arm around her. She pulled away from me, and went to Annadore.

"Come on, Baby Girl Amos, it's time for us to go. We're going home."

"Almost done," Mrs. Trentam said around a mouthful of pins.

"No, done." Meda began unfastening the dress, nearly tearing it in the process. "She's not going to that pageant. I already told you that."

"Don't be stupid, Meda. Look at her. She's cute as a button. Couldn't you just eat her up?" Mrs. Trentham pinched Annadore's cheek.

"She's not going to be in any of those fucking pageants."

Back in her play clothes and strapped into her car seat, Annadore was her owlish self again. She squawked fitfully, troubled by her mother's upset. Meda couldn't even speak. Riding in the passenger seat, she white-knuckled her hands together as we drove away from the scene of the crime. It was an instructive experience for me; there are more ways to destroy a child's soul than shutting him up in a dark closet.

Miss Amos and I lingered in the brittle half-life of Meda's anger, drinking coffee in the kitchen, pretending we couldn't hear Meda sobbing in her bedroom. Her grandmother talked about the experiments the aliens conducted on her, discoursing in great detail on nasal probes and the migraines they caused.

"Did they do experiments on you, too?" she said. It wasn't morbid curiosity. She was as concerned as the facilitator of a victim support group.

I sipped my coffee to give myself time to think. "If they did, if you could label it an experiment, then I would say it's on-going. Data is still being gathered."

Miss Amos nodded knowingly.

It wasn't a room, just a walk-in closet. Even If I hadn't been bound hand and foot, I wouldn't have been able to stretch out full length. I was blindfolded, but not gagged, because of my broken nose. It was days before I could breathe through my nose again, and once I could, I wished my sense of smell was still gone. The carpet smelled artificial like teddy bear fur. There was a nylon sleeping bag that smelled of dust and mothballs. Overpowering those scents was the odor of cork. They had covered the walls and interior of the door with heavy corkboard, rudimentary soundproofing.

I lay there one hour after another, and when I couldn't stand the smells anymore, I breathed through my mouth. Then the pounding in my head receded and I felt the coolness of the cuffs on my wrists and the chain that drew them down to my ankles. The light that crept under the blindfold was itself a dilution of the light that managed to sneak through an infinitesimal crack under the door. During the day it was yellowish. At night it had the blue glow of TV.

I suppose they knew I wouldn't fight Amy and that's why they made her feed me and take me to the bathroom. Or maybe it was for the humiliation of having to perform bodily functions in front of her. It was a pendulum that swung between us, because every time she touched me she cried and whispered reassurances in a low, fearful voice. Twice I was brought out of the closet and made to talk into a tape recorder. They wanted me to sound tearful and afraid, but everything was blunted for me, because of the sedative they were giving me. Whereas the violence of the unseen man didn't work, the sound of Amy crying did. Her fear was real in a way mine wasn't.

The second time, after the recording was made, the unseen man said, "I swear, if they want their proof, I'll cut his little fucking prick off and mail it to them."

Joel laughed. The remark was meant to scare me, except I didn't know what *prick* meant. They used a pair of bolt cutters on my pinky. I probably screamed or cried when they did it, but all I remember is the sound Amy made. Like a horse with a broken leg, right before someone shoots it. High, terrified, hopeless.

They didn't kill me, I suppose, because they believed they were going to get the money out of my grandfather. That was the only reason for the corkboard, the sleeping bag, for me being alive. If they hadn't believed, I would have been as dead as Bobby Franks.

CHAPTER FOUR

GIVING THANKS & THE BENEFIT OF THE DOUBT

WORKING UNDER THE misconception that it was a private call, Celeste stepped out of the study while I spoke with my mother. She and I exchanged our usual pleasantries, updating each other about the weather and our extant relatives, a club that grew smaller all the time.

Toward the end of the call, my mother said, "I do wish you'd come visit for the holidays." It sounded like some insincerity out of a Victorian novel. I tried briefly to pursue the idea, and couldn't get any particulars out of her. It was a gesture, not an invitation, and when I extended my own invitation for her to come and have Thanksgiving or Christmas with me, she began a list of reasons that made the suggestion impractical. The reason she didn't mention was the only one I believed: Boston was a safe place for her. After my father and brother died, she moved back to Boston, to be near her own family, to be among familiar places. I think she wanted to go home and to return to the person she had been. I envied her.

In keeping with tradition, she took a deep breath and said, "What else?" That was the signal that the conversation was over.

I mean always to be fair to her, but I'm aware of the futility of my affection for her. I'm not irrational. I don't believe she blames me for being kidnapped, but it ruined things for her. It upset her world and made everything less perfect, including her. What came after, my other failures, her other disappointments, they only added insult to the original injury. In my efforts to be fair to her, I've done my best to avoid any interpretation of her words or actions. I try not to infer motive from the fact that I can't remember her visiting me in the hospital. I don't look for meaning in the calm way she declined to hold my hand at the funeral service for my father and brother. I was seventeen and, when I reached for her hand, she very politely extricated herself. I don't pretend to know what she was feeling. As for the gauntlet of therapists and psychiatrists she made me run, I believe she wanted to help me, but the thing she wanted didn't exist. She wanted meaning out of a world of chaos.

I wonder about the different ways the phrase "benefit of the doubt" can be used: the benefit of doubting what?

After I hung up with my mother I called and made plans with Aunt Ginny. When she said dinner was at two o'clock, I knew she meant it literally. It wasn't a gesture.

Wanting to be nice, I sent everyone home for the whole week of Thanksgiving, but there was danger lurking in solitude. I didn't see Meda the rest of the week, through my own stupidity. I hadn't made any plans to see her, I didn't even know her phone number, and it seemed rude to drop in during a holiday week. The first two nights I was fine, but by Monday I was afraid to go to sleep at night. It wasn't so much the sleep I feared as the bed, my lobster pot. Instead of sleeping, I found myself watching Bette Davis movies at midnight on public television and infomercials at two a.m.

Lured into the routine, one night I found myself strangely transfixed by an infomercial for a product called Progenis. I noticed, after staring at the screen for some time, that if the letters r-o-g were removed, the name of the product became Penis. Subliminal marketing. Perhaps it was meant to pass by the average person, to slip into the subconscious mind of the flaccid TV viewer. In the commercial a man distanced himself from a woman who was interested in him. Not because he didn't return the sentiment, but because he was ashamed of what they labeled his "erectile deficiency."

I wondered what Meda thought about my refusal to sleep with her, whether she ascribed my reluctance to some sort of "problem." My main difficulty in the sexual arena had been a consistent and wholly humiliating history of being unable to ejaculate. Nothing easy to explain like impotence or premature ejaculation. I was the worst kind of failure. I couldn't even fail within socially acceptable parameters.

It's one of the loneliest feelings in the world, being in the intimate embrace of some girl, and thinking that at some point I'm simply going to have to cut my losses. In most cases, she's there in good faith and I'm there in the best faith I can muster, wanting to be sure she's enjoying it. I've always been keenly interested in the pursuit of other people's pleasure. All the same, it's a lonely moment, when I make the decision that it's time to stop trying.

As bad as it was not sleeping at night, I was more afraid of sleeping during the day. It was a slippery slope. On Wednesday I got lucky. I lay down in the afternoon and took a nap on the sofa. It was one of those late-afternoon naps that steal the entire day, lasting until the next morning. I got up, showered, shaved, and read a little. There was nothing scary about being alone then, because I knew Aunt Ginny was expecting me. I went a little early and found her house filled with the serenity of a library on a rainy day. The meal was surprisingly casual for a woman I had always seen as my mother's equal in the pursuit of elegance. Of course, we ate off a staggering assortment of china and crystal, but the food had been prepared beforehand, and we reheated it in the microwave. I found myself on the verge of tears when Aunt Ginny squeezed my hand over the pumpkin pie.

"This is the nicest Thanksgiving I've had in years," she said. "I'm so glad you're here this year. I've missed seeing you."

I worked my jaw, trying to dissipate the nagging catch in my throat so I could say, "I'm glad to be here."

I imagined the grim scene of Aunt Ginny and my grandfather in the dining room up at the house. I dismissed it as unlikely, substituting the image of my grandfather in his study, ignoring the holiday, my aunt at the senior activity center, eating an institutional turkey and dressing, trying to steer clear of old men on the prowl for a widow. I was ashamed of myself, because I didn't know what she'd been doing for the intervening years between funerals. To atone, I suggested we look at the photo albums.

I was so happy to have everyone back after the holiday—Meda most of all—but even Celeste briefly. I lingered in the kitchen chatting until Mrs. Trentam began working on her to-do list for the week, making it clear that it was time for me to leave them alone.

Celeste and I went into the study and polished off the rest of the paperwork for some paintings I was donating. Representatives from the Smithsonian were coming out later in the week to look at them, and Celeste wanted to be sure that everything was squared away beforehand. Then we started on the various documents my lawyers had sent about creating a charitable foundation, the only solution I could think of to the money that was piling up. My grandfather had gone on stockpiling and reinvesting. I couldn't see myself doing the same.

The horror of horrors was lurking in the mail that had accumulated over the week: a letter from the corporate office telling me that my grandfather was going to be posthumously inducted into some sort of Business Hall of Fame. The Board of Directors at RI wanted me to accept the award. It involved sitting through a presentation about my grandfather's "entrepreneurial spirit," the blurb about the event said, and then getting up on the dais and saying a few words. Celeste in her usual freakish way seemed to bask in the reflected glory and made several excited remarks about the award and the ceremony. "I saw the pictures from when Mr. Tveite went last year. It was gorgeous. RI bought two tables and one of the executive assistants got to go to fill space."

I wondered if that was hope in her voice, all the while asking myself how fabulous something could be if people had to be invited to "fill space." There had to be more than enough VP's and upper managers and their spouses to fill two tables; whither had those cowards slithered when the time came to attend the event?

After lunch, I did my disappearing act on Celeste and wandered around the house, in search of Meda. I found her in a bedroom, where she was struggling to turn a mattress. She looked embarrassed when I helped her, but nothing worse than that. I asked her if she'd like to go out again on Friday, and she said flippantly, "I am so gonna sue you for sexual harassment." It killed the words in my mouth, and when she saw that, she started apologizing. "It was a joke, I don't really think that. I believe you when you say you wouldn't do anything bad to me. I don't think you're harassing me."

"No, if you don't want to go out with me anymore, all you have to do is say so. It's fine. I won't take it the wrong way."

"Not 'not anymore,' but I already have a date on Friday."

"What about Saturday?"

"Sure," she said and started making the bed. I was dismissed.

I didn't know how I felt about Meda's date. There was competition for her attention. Once I acknowledged there was competition, I realized I was willing to compete. She had planted the seed when she asked me to spend the night. It never would have occurred to me except for that. She needed a friend. I was trying to be her friend. I spent a good hour, pacing around the house, attempting to organize my way of thinking on the topic. To begin with, I tried to address the strange hopefulness I had felt when I went into her house, thinking that she might be pleased to see me. She'd gone on two dates with me. She went on dates with a short guy named Jeff, but she'd asked me to stay the night. That was the rat that ate the grain that lay in the house that Jack built.

Later in the afternoon, the phone rang. After answering it, Celeste put the line on hold and said, "It's Lionel Petrie."

"Tell him I'm not here."

She looked at me reproachfully, not upset at being asked to lie, but at my failure to appreciate how wonderful it was to have Lionel Petrie call me. I glared at her.

"Oh, Mr. Petrie, I'm so sorry. He's not here right now. Can I take a message?" She didn't even try to make it sound like the truth. After she hung up, she walked over to my desk and put a pink phone slip on the blotter. While I was out, Lionel Petrie called. I needed to return his call. The box for that line had been checked a bit more thoroughly than was necessary.

Borrowing the Cadillac

Meda

When I told Celeste I needed to talk to Bernie, she gave me a prissy frown. I think it rubbed her the wrong way that I used his first name. She didn't have a choice, though. I didn't whisper or anything, and he had to have heard me ask for him, so she let me in.

"Could you give us a minute?" Bernie said.

Celeste looked even more miffed, but she went into the library while he and I talked.

"I'm really sorry. I know I haven't been a very good employee lately, but Gramma called and said Annadore's sick, so I need to take her to the doctor this afternoon." I felt like I was in school again, standing in the principal's office. That's what I didn't like, not being sure how to feel about where he and I stood with each other. He was nice, but he was my boss.

"It's okay. You don't need to apologize. Do you need a ride?" As soon as he said it, I felt stupid for being uncomfortable.

"It's just Dr. Hendershot at County Hospital, the doctor I take her to. My car's okay. Thanks for being so understanding."

"If Annadore's sick, I'd hate to think of her out in the cold if you had car trouble again. Why don't you take the Fleetwood, and I'll take another car to my meeting." He took the keys out of his pocket and tried to hand them to me.

"That's so nice of you to offer, but I couldn't."

"Would you rather drive the Bentley? Or a Rolls Royce? Those are your other options." He opened his desk drawer and took out two other sets of car keys. He was teasing me, but I got the feeling that if I said yes, he really would loan them to me. I guess that's what being rich is for, being able to loan someone a Rolls Royce, but it made me feel like he was so nice that I was never going to be nice enough back to him.

"No, I guess I would rather take the Cadillac," I said, because I figured it was about the only graceful way out of it. "Thank you. That's really nice."

"Do you need some money for the doctor's visit?"

I turned around and walked out, because I didn't want to think about what something like that would mean.

Being Meda

I tried to give Meda money. She was taking Annadore to the doctor and she looked worried and tired; it was a simple mistake. I wanted to help her, and I guessed that money was tight. I was annoyed that Mrs. Bryant hadn't asked for a better salary for Meda, knowing she had her family to take care of, and I was annoyed at myself.

After I made the offer, Meda wouldn't even look at me. The one mistake was forgivable, but what I did next wasn't. I got out the phone book and dialed the number for the County Hospital, not knowing what I was going to say until the receptionist answered the phone. Then I realized it was quite simple. I told the receptionist who I was and asked her to send me the bill for Annadore Amos' visit.

When it was time to go to the attorney's office to meet with the museum representatives, Celeste gasped when she saw that we were going to take the Rolls. "Where's the Cadillac?" she asked. Wanting to tell her it was none of her business, I explained that I had loaned it to Meda. Celeste remarked that I was "very generous," but it was tinged with disapproval. The meeting was brief, and when I dropped Celeste back at the house, I worried about tensions that might be created by Meda's situation. Were Mrs. Trentam and Celeste doing their jobs, perhaps angry that Meda got special treatment? I didn't know how those things went. I didn't want to know.

Meda's grandmother had told me to come by some time to talk, about aliens she meant. I went anyway, intending to pump her for information, and with a little prompting, she offered to show me some family photos. I couldn't help but contrast the bound volumes of my family's photos with the mousy smelling shoebox Miss Amos retrieved from her bedroom. She spooled through story after story of her dead relatives, until I wanted to pluck the box out of her withered hands, dump the pictures out on the coffee table and paw through them like a dog. Almost when I couldn't take any more, Miss Amos pulled out a school photo of Meda. She looked ten or eleven, and I was astounded by the subtle changes brought about by the years since the photo in Muriel's wallet: the thinning of her face, the way the hate in her eyes had blossomed into something more pragmatic. Her eighth grade picture, however, defied all my expectations. Meda's gaze was distant and devoid of hostility. I had viewed the procession of photos like a ripening process, but there it was interrupted. Her lips formed a shy smile.

Returning the box to its storage place, I found a real treasure. Amid a clutter of pharmaceutical products on Miss Amos' nightstand was a framed photo of a young man in a World War Two-era naval uniform. Tucked into the lower corner of the frame was a newer photo. The familiar shape of Meda's face caught my eye. She wore a deep blue formal dress and a rhinestone tiara. In the crook of her left arm she held an avalanche of roses. Her hair was tamed into convoluted waves and curls, her eyelids drooped sensually under the weight of mascara, and her lips gleamed red with an invitation to debauchery. The feral eight-year-old Meda looked out of a woman's face. Someone had cropped the photo at Meda's right elbow, leaving a slivered vestige of her escort: the edge of a shoulder, a wedge of head and hair, perhaps topped by another cheap crown. From behind me, Miss Amos said, "Billy Gertisson. I loved him, but he died at Midway."

"What's this picture of Meda?"

"Oh, that. That's when she won the Winter Homecoming Queen. I cut that wicked boy right out." It was a story I could have gotten from anyone in town, if I'd asked. My aunt would have told me, and it was only a matter of time until somebody told me. I hoped the inevitability of it made it less of a betrayal that I heard it from her grandmother.

"Her ninth birthday she wanted to have a sleepover party, but no one came. The other little girls in her class didn't want to go. Or their mothers wouldn't let them go. Their mothers didn't trust Muriel to stay sober and take care of the girls." Miss Amos interjected this in the middle of the larger story, perhaps to illustrate the odds that had been against Meda winning a popularity contest.

In the mutilated picture, the failed party was behind her. She was the first sophomore girl ever to win the Winter Homecoming Queen, a title usually accorded to the prettiest senior. It all came out in a gush from her grandmother: a tangled web of pride and sorrow, the sort of story that doesn't bear dramatizing. Her escort, the boy clipped out of the photo, had some particular ideas from his father about the sexual availability of the Amos women. When Meda didn't want to play along, her date and his two friends beat her up and raped her.

And they lived happily ever after. That's the part of the story Miss Amos didn't have to tell me. I figured it out myself. Meda had no father, an uncle who was a wandering spirit, and her brother had been a little boy. I thought of Robby, who despite his charm and reserve had a certain brutality to him, an eagerness to punish wrongdoing with violence. Miss Amos' silence told me that nothing had happened to the boys who did it. She looked up into my face with eyes as black as Meda's, full of a lifetime of disappointment. I had to look away.

By the time Meda came home, Miss Amos and I were recovered, sitting on the sofa talking about aliens. Meda gave me a funny look, and I gazed at her in amazement, knowing all the people she was carrying around inside of her. The Ghost of Winter Homecoming Queen Past.

"Ear infection," she said, laying a fussy Annadore on the ottoman and sitting on the sofa between her grandmother and me. "He gave her some drops, and uh, some Amoxicillin." She fished the bottles out of her coat pocket.

"How much?" Miss Amos said.

"Nothing. The receptionist said it was taken care of." She sounded angry.

"So sue me for trying to help." I was startled to hear something so flippant come out of my mouth. Meda was not impressed. Instinctively, I leaned closer to her, enjoying the aura of cold around her, and the smell of warm skin sneaking up out of her coat collar.

"You don't know what it's like, having people think, you know, because you were paying."

"It's part of your benefits," I said.

"That's not true. And you know that's not what people think."

"You," I started, but stopped, wanting to find a diplomatic way to say it. "You wouldn't do it the easy way. That's why I called."

"I don't like taking your money."

"Why?"

"You don't know what it's like being me!" The outburst startled Annadore into tears. Meda reached out and stroked her hair until she settled down again.

"You don't know what it's like being me," I said quietly.

Meda took off her coat, picked up Annadore, and carried her down the hall. A little later, I heard Meda in the kitchen and then she poked her head into the living room.

"Come eat," she said.

The kitchen was like a movie set, everything in it straight out of the Forties, including the refrigerator and stove. The wallpaper and cabinets had once been white, but were yellowed with age. Fifty years of foot traffic had worn a ring in the linoleum around the table. Only Meda looked out of place, in the wrong costume for the movie: a black thermal undershirt and a pair of men's corduroy jeans, both of them unnervingly tight.

Meda seemed embarrassed when she put the meal on the table, and there was nothing to alleviate that except to eat it. I liked soup and grilled cheese sandwiches fine.

When the railroad crossing bells began to clang outside, I was the only one who flinched. I nearly choked on a bite of grilled cheese, but Miss Amos went on grumbling into her soup. Meda went on cutting the crust off Annadore's sandwich, and Annadore went on dabbling in her glass of milk, making a mess. I half-expected the train to come through the room next door, but I focused on getting my sandwich down the right way.

After Annadore's bedtime, we sat on the sofa, watching TV. I was acutely aware of the pressure of Meda's arm against mine. I thought of putting my arm around her, but reminded myself of all the reasons I wasn't going to succumb to the temptation. We sat for almost an hour, her grandmother next to us, Mutual of Omaha *Wild Kingdom* flickering across our faces.

Meda jumped up when someone knocked on the door. I had a sinking feeling I had again intruded on her personal life, but when she opened the door it was her sister Loren. I'd seen photos of Loren, but in her current incarnation, she was making every effort to be Meda's opposite. Where Meda curved, Loren was rail thin. Loren's hair was as blonde as Meda's was black. So blonde it had to be bleached. While Meda was fair, Loren was tanned, again I assumed artificially.

"Did you know there's a Cadillac and, I think, a Rolls Royce in the front yard?" Loren said.

Meda shifted to look at me and Loren followed her gaze.

"This is Bernie. This is my sister, Loren."

I stood up to shake her hand, but she ignored the gesture.

"So now you're borrowing his car. Did you get to drive the Rolls Royce?"

"No," Meda said. "Which sweater did you want?"

"The sexy red one with the V-neck. The one that makes your boobs look big."

"My boobs *are* big. I don't have a sweater that can do that for you." Meda gave me a smile that carried more warning than amusement, and I had to bite the inside of my mouth to keep from laughing. I was sorry I hadn't seen that sweater in action.

"You're such a bitch." Loren flopped onto the chair opposite me. "Her boobs wouldn't be so big if she weren't so fucking fat."

"Watch your mouth, Muriel," Miss Amos said.

"I'm Loren, not Muriel," she snapped. When Meda went down the hall, toward her bedroom, Loren turned back to me. "So, Bernie. Meda says you won't sleep with her. Never happened to her before. Maybe you like blondes better. Thin blondes?"

I hoped some catastrophic incident would occur and end the conversation. I envisioned a train derailing into the house. I wasn't surprised that Meda told her sister things of that nature, but I didn't like being asked to comment on them.

"Well, her boobs *are* big," I said, pretending to have an internal debate about the sisters' respective charms. Loren narrowed her eyes at me.

Meda came back with a red sweater and threw it in Loren's lap.

"Gramma says you're an abductee, too," Loren said to me.

"No, Gramma's confused," Meda said.

"Mom said so, too."

"Shut up, Loren. He was kidnapped, you moron, like for ransom. Not by aliens. Now that you have what you came for, maybe you could leave."

"Why? Are you going to try to get laid again?" Loren said

Meda answered with a malevolent smile and grabbed Loren's arm.

"My boobs *are* big," Loren mimicked in a whiny little girl's voice, as Meda walked her to the door and pushed her out.

With Loren gone, Meda considered me with a look of annoyance. It was late.

"Look, for whatever reason, I know you won't stay, so I'm not sure I should keep asking. Except I don't want you to think that the invitation's closed just because I don't keep asking." She rested her hands on her hips and glanced at her grandmother, who did not seem to be listening.

"It's okay. I like you asking," I managed to say, surprising myself.

"You want to come and help put up Christmas lights Sunday?" she said.

Being Bernie

Meda

Bernie didn't even need a ladder to put lights on the edge of the roof in front. We were almost done when Gramma came out to tell me I had a phone call, which I knew meant it was a guy. If it was Loren or Mom or Aunt M., she would have said so. It was Jeff.

"I wanted to come over for a little while tonight," he said.

"I don't think tonight would be good. Besides, I'll see you Friday, right?"

"Just for an hour or so. I want to see you, give you your Christmas present." He had this cocky voice he used when he was trying to get people to do what they didn't want to do. He thought I was too stupid to notice he was using it on me.

"I don't want you to give me anything, and tonight's not a good night." I wouldn't even do Christmas except for Annadore. I hated to think about what he was giving me for Christmas, but I guessed it involved him trying to talk me into letting him spend the night. I'd slept with him once, almost three months before, and he wouldn't let me forget it. I don't know what it was. I would have let Bernie stay if he wanted, whether we had sex or not, but the idea of Jeff coming and staying the night depressed me. They say you always want what you don't have, so maybe that was it.

"Come on, Meda. Don't be so hard on me."

"Please, don't come over. I have someone over."

"Your boss, right?" He must have driven by and seen Bernie's car.

"Bernie's helping me hang Christmas lights."

"So it's Bernie, now, not Mr. Raleigh. Bernie is helping you put up your Christmas lights. How nice." Jeff went on like that for a while, so that I kind of tuned him out, started wondering what Bernie was up to. I tuned back in to hear Jeff say, "I guess bowling doesn't hold a lot of appeal when you've got that kind of money dangling in front of you."

"God, if you don't want to go out with me, just say it, okay. Stop with the 'poor, poor Jeff, mean old Meda has another guy at her house' routine. I wasn't aware we were seeing each other exclusively."

"I guess we're not," he said and hung up.

When I came out of the bedroom, Bernie was sitting at the kitchen table, working on a string of lights, going through it one bulb at a time to find the one that wasn't working.

"Who was that?" He didn't know the code. He didn't understand that I wasn't going to say, "my mom."

"Jeff Hall. You met him," I said, curious to see his reaction. He nodded and kept working on the lights.

"What does Jeff do, for a living, I mean?"

"He's the gym teacher at the high school," I said. Bernie made a face.

"He's taking you out next weekend?"

"I don't think so. He called to dump me or to get me to dump him. Same thing."

"I'm sorry."

"He says he can't compete with you." I wanted to see if I could get any kind of reaction out of him. What I got was a half smile, and then he went on to the next light bulb. "Says you're too rich, too tall, too good-looking."

"You're just teasing me."

"That wasn't really what he said, but that's what he meant."

"Well, I'm not an electrician, but there's something else wrong with this string of lights," Bernie said when he reached the end of the cord. He was looking at it like he was an electrician, like he was going to try to fix it, so I took it away from him and put it in the kitchen trash.

Fair to Middling

"So, what are you doing for Christmas?" I asked, when Meda sat down across the table from me and started to sort through a box of tree ornaments. The oven door was open, heat radiating out of it. I was sweating sitting in front of it.

"Well, Annadore and I are going to Aunt M.'s for the day and then probably everybody will get together here for the evening. Christmas Eve we're going to hear my cousin Stephanie sing with her church choir. She gets to solo. What about you?"

"Nothing special," I said carefully. I didn't want to spring the trap too soon.

"You're not doing anything with your aunt?"

"She'll spend the week with her sister in Ohio, like she does every year." As much as I was operating on ulterior motives with

Meda, I was also facing the prospect of several days of utter aloneness, watching awful Christmas specials on TV, or not watching TV, knowing there were awful Christmas specials playing while I wasn't watching.

"What about your mother? Aren't you going to see her for Christmas?"

"She prefers not to." Meda gave me a quizzical look, so I added, "She wouldn't enjoy it."

"Spending time with her son?"

"Well, I'm not the son she wanted." As soon as the words were out of my mouth, I regretted them. I didn't want Meda's pity. I wanted her to like me. I glanced up, but couldn't read her facial expression.

"What does that mean?" she said.

"Have you ever read a children's book called *The Devil's Storybook?*" She shook her head. "In the book, there's a story about a perfect little girl who never lost her temper, no matter what evil schemes the Devil devised to upset her. She was perfect until she had a 'fair-to-middling child.' Then she lost her temper every day. Her happiness was destroyed by a less than perfect child."

"Are you saying you're Satan's revenge on your mother?"

"No. All she sees is that I'm not as smart or as capable as my brother was."

"Too bad for her, she got an average kid."

"Fair-to-middling," I corrected. "Every time she sees me or talks to me, it reminds her of what happened. In her mind, she had a perfect life, until that. It started all the other bad things that happened to her."

"You mean, you getting kidnapped? You're not serious."

Meda wasn't going to let me move on without an explanation, so I waded in as far as I was willing.

"The kidnapping, a little, but more that I'm alive and Robby is dead. It's me as much as it is her. I get tired of being reminded that I'm damaged goods, that I'm a disappointment. It's the reason your mother is anxious when she's with you. She's always aware that she failed you."

"I don't want to talk about that," she said without irony.

In the end, I had to ask to be invited and albeit grudgingly, the invitation was extended.

"Well, sure, if you really want. You can have Christmas with us," she said. When I started asking her about what Annadore wanted for Christmas and what other kids would be at Mrs. Trentam's, she frowned at me unhappily. "You don't need to get anyone presents. That's not necessary."

"You sound like Mrs. Trentam when you say that."

"I do not! Oh. I can't believe you said that." She was absolutely silent for a good thirty seconds, thinking. "I'm always worried I'm going to turn into my mother. I never knew I was turning into Aunt M. Look, it's just that you don't need to bring presents to be welcome for Christmas." She was all generosity once I'd wrested the invitation from her.

"I know, but I want to bring presents. That's what's fun about Christmas, especially for kids."

"Oh, Bernie," she said.

I could see she didn't like the idea, so I let it go.

When I got up to leave later, she smiled at me in her inscrutable and completely desirable way. "The invitation's still open," she said. It took more work to get invited to Christmas than it took to get invited to bed.

I turned our Saturday date into a shopping date, and although Meda started out as something of a killjoy, she eventually warmed to it enough to suggest things she thought her little cousins would like. She said outright that she wanted "absolutely nothing" from me for Christmas, but she weakened enough to tell me what Annadore wanted and needed. Thoughtfully, she pointed out something I could get for my aunt—a cashmere sweater shawl—and she even suggested a gift for Celeste. Once her blood sugar was low from a day of shopping I asked her about going to the Hall of Fame dinner and the Chairman's New Year's party. Celeste had dutifully returned the RSVP card weeks ago, and on it she advised my hosts I would be bringing a guest.

Meda recognized she was being sucked into my devious plans, but she was in a good mood. Also she had a plan for revenge that involved a western clothing store. "My date dumped me because of you, so you're taking me somewhere that has an actual dance floor, and you can't go dressed like that." She looked me over and shook her head.

"I doubt they have anything to fit me."

"Guys named Slim and Tex shop here. They've got something to fit you." She laughed long and loud at her joke, and I was only slightly less enamored of her for it.

Broken Furnace

Meda

We snuck in through the back door, so Gramma wouldn't ask us what we were up to, and also because I didn't want to get Annadore all worked up about presents. I took Bernie into my bedroom and it cracked me up how he acted when he realized he was alone in my bedroom with me. He kind of pulled into himself.

"So, what does your family usually do on Christmas?" he said.

"Well, we don't do caroling or you know, that sort of thing." I imagined he had those storybook Christmases when he was a kid. The whole sugarplums dancing in his head business. "Anyway, it's not the Amos family Christmas, which I won't invite you to, because of Gramma's weirdness. It's Aunt M.'s thing, so usually it's just sports on TV and lunch and opening presents. Not very religious, which always makes Aunt Bryant mad."

When I brushed past Bernie to get to the bed, he tried to get out of my way, but my room was just big enough for the bed, the dresser, and a path around them.

I reached past him to get the wrapping paper and, mostly for fun, to see what he would do, I pressed up against to him to reach it. I liked that he seemed so skittish, so I put my arm around his waist and stood up on my tiptoes. He leaned down like he was going to kiss me, except we both breathed out these little white puffs of air from the cold, and he pulled back and gave me a funny look.

"Why is it so cold in here?" Whatever he'd been about to do he wasn't going to, so I let him go. He came back to tell me that the heater was set for 72 degrees, but it was only 43 degrees.

"Yeah, I know. There's something wrong with the heater. There always is."

"Maybe you'd like a new furnace for Christmas," he said.

Not Enough Wrapping Paper

"No, I don't have enough wrapping paper for that," Meda said.

"I'm serious. You and Annadore shouldn't be living like this." I wished I'd phrased it better, because I could see that made her defensive. "How much do you need? How much would help you get a new furnace?"

"I can't take something like that from you," she said. I asked why not and got an unpleasant answer: "I'm not a hooker."

"If I were sleeping with you, you might have a point, but as the situation stands, that's not fair or accurate."

"I'm sorry. It's not that, you're right, but I can't. I'm not a charity case."

I sat down on the edge of the bed, which dipped arthritically under me, and looked up at her for a change. "Meda, let's consider a hypothetical situation. If you had $20 million, and somebody you knew, somebody you liked, needed help, needed a new furnace, or whatever, wouldn't you want to help them? Wouldn't you be frustrated if they wouldn't let you?"

"Yes, of course." She rubbed at her temples in confusion. "Do you really have that much money?"

"I have a lot more than that. I could write you a check for $20 million today and I'd never miss it. Would that be enough?"

She finally laughed and looked less ill.

"So you can tell me, between friends, do you need help? Will you let me help you?" I said.

"The thing is…my mom does, more than I do. More than we need a new furnace. You know, she's got these cysts. They need to operate, but I don't know where the money is going to come from. She doesn't qualify for any kind of medical help or anything." Meda's voice got shaky. I had to look away from her.

While she was wrapping presents, we worked out an agreement. I would pay for her mother's operation, and it would be okay for me to buy her grandmother a new furnace. Helping her mother was the first and most practical sort of distribution from what would eventually be the Raleigh Foundation. The idea had formed like nacre in an oyster. The thing to do with the money was the exact opposite of anything he would have done. He never would have thought it was important to help poor women get medical care. It really put a song in my heart and a smile on my face.

Big Deal

Meda

When we went into Aunt M.'s house, she looked at Bernie like she'd never seen him before. Then she stared at the presents he was piling around the tree.

"Merry Christmas, Mrs. Trentam," Bernie said in his little boy voice.

"Well, Merry Christmas, Mr. Raleigh. I wasn't expecting you. Not that you're not welcome. Of course, we're happy to have you."

While Aunt M. glared at me, Bernie introduced himself to Uncle Donald and my cousin Doug and my cousin Terry's husband, Chris. Aunt M. was upset, but Aunt Bryant acted like I'd committed some kind of unforgivable sin. She came out of the kitchen and said, "Merry Christmas, Mr. Raleigh."

I think Bernie would have hugged her. After all, he'd known her since he was a kid, but she wasn't having anything to do with that. Terry acted dippy like she didn't know if she should shake Bernie's hand or curtsey. I sent Annadore to play with Terry and Chris' kids, and then as bad as I felt doing it to him, I went into the kitchen and left Bernie out there with Uncle Donald, Doug, Chris, and Aunt Bryant's Aunt Georgina, who was about a thousand years old. Bernie was just going to have to deal with them on his own. He asked to be invited.

As soon as I went in the kitchen, Aunt M. jumped on me.

"When you said you were bringing someone, I thought you meant Coach Hall. For God's sake, you should have told me you were bringing *him*."

"That's the least you could have done," Aunt Bryant said.

"Oh, Meda," Terry said.

"What were you thinking?" Aunt Bryant said.

"You should have told me," Aunt M. said.

"Why? What would you have done different for him that you didn't do thinking Jeff was coming?"

"I would have dusted the ceiling fans and the tops of the cabinets," Aunt M. said. I guess because Bernie was tall.

Aunt M. always made me feel like I was a little kid again, and how I'd never been clear on what all the rules were when we lived with her. She had rules about how you were supposed to close the doors. She had furniture that no one was allowed to sit on. She had three different sets of towels that only got used for particular occasions, and all these different sets of dishes that were only for such and such company. That was on the list of what she would have done different, too, because she made Terry and me get the best china out and wash it so we could use it. I couldn't wait to tell Bernie that he was the only guest worthy of the best china since some priest from Italy came and had dinner at Aunt M.'s house like fifteen years before. Then she made us put a different tablecloth on the table. When I came back from doing that, they were still harping on what a terrible person I was.

"That little witch actually shrugged and smiled at me. Brings him into my house without a word of warning," Aunt M. said.

"That's how she's always gotten out of things," Aunt Bryant said.

"It was just the sort of look she gave me when she was little and did something she wasn't supposed to do. Just like that, like that will make it all better." Aunt M. glared at me. "Don't think you're charming your way out of this."

"I'm sorry, but what was I supposed to do? Make him spend Christmas alone?"

Like the ditz she is, Terry said, "Well, if he's her boyfriend she ought to be able to invite him."

"God forbid," Aunt Bryant said. "Her boyfriend."

They decided not to say anything else about Bernie or me, but I got the job of peeling all the potatoes for lunch, which was Aunt Bryant's way of punishing me. The funniest thing that happened all day was when we were going into lunch, Bernie hit his head on the doorway arch. Aunt M. started flipping out and apologizing. He just rubbed his head and said, "My own fault. Happens all the time."

Who's your team?

I spent the several pre-dinner hours watching football on TV with Meda's uncle and male cousins. The advantage of that form of socialization was that I wasn't required to say much of anything about a sport I knew nothing about. I was in the embarrassing position of knowing the rules to such sports as water polo and lacrosse, and I could hold my own on the topic of baseball, but I didn't know a safety from a first and ten. Mostly, I sat and listened to them talk about the game.

At one point, Mrs. Trentam's husband Donald turned to me and said, "So, who's your team, Bernie?"

"I live in Kansas City, so I try to root for them." For all I knew, they were watching college football.

"Ah, God, the Chiefs," his son said. "I never saw a team try so hard to lose." That was the sum total of that conversation.

A little later, Donald turned to me and said, "Want a beer, Bernie?"

For the most part, as long as the women were out of the room, the men behaved like normal people toward me. The rest of the time, the Trentam/Bryant family solved the discomfort of my presence by not talking to me. They weren't rude, but almost every conversation I attempted to be part of died a terrible death if Mrs. Trentam or Mrs. Bryant were in the room. I spoke and everyone looked at me and nodded. Then they started talking about something else. They weren't the warmest people either, so that I wondered why Meda came to Christmas with them. I guessed it was because they were the closest thing she had to normal relatives, and she seemed intent on Annadore playing with her cousins.

Shortly after the meal, the massacre of the gifts began. Mrs. Trentam, I think, would have enjoyed it if her mother hadn't so clearly disapproved of the "shenanigans." The kids at least didn't let that bother them.

I gave Meda her gifts on a wave of nonchalance. Gifts were being handed around to everyone, so I simply gave the packages to one of Meda's cousins and asked him to pass them to her. I didn't dare glance up at her and busied myself with helping one of the younger cousins put together a racetrack. The new coat was simple enough, but as for the other gift, I was worried it might upset her. Gifts of jewelry have always seemed fraught with meaning, and I worried that she would infer the wrong things from the necklace I bought her. It was two strands of pearls with an elaborate gold and opal clasp, not quite a choker, but meant to be worn close to her bare neck. I hoped it was a discreet gesture of admiration, and of necessity I didn't get to see her expression when she opened it.

After the kids had been dispersed to play with their new prizes, while the women were cleaning up after dinner, Mrs. Trentam handed me an album full of Terry's and Meda's pageant photos. I had a feeling I was risking Meda's wrath if she caught me looking at them, but I couldn't resist. I turned over the pages slowly, trying to fit Meda into a mental file folder labeled "Beauty Pageant Contestant." The photos started when she was four or five. She was a little like Annadore, but less owlish, more elfin, a changeling. Later photos showed her prepubescent glory nearly camouflaged in an effort to make her seem suitable in a pink satin dress. Through the ruffles I glimpsed the misguided reason for her aunt's efforts. She had seen how beautiful Meda was, but she hadn't realized it was obscene to paraphrase that mystery into mere pageant-winning prettiness.

Meda would never have made it to a Miss America pageant, or even to the Miss Oklahoma pageant. She was not blonde enough, perky enough. Her beauty didn't bloom up with a smile and sparkle. It was more like a blow to the head, insufficient to knock you out, but enough to make your eyes ache in their sockets half an hour later. At my height, it's a sensation I've experienced a few times, but with less pleasant consequences. Passing through on some cleaning mission, Mrs. Trentam paused to remark on the photos I was looking at.

"She always hated those pageants, as queer as she was. What little girl wouldn't want to dress up like a princess and look beautiful? Not her, though. The way she'd scream and cry and carry on sometimes, you'd have thought she was being murdered. And you can see what she looked like. You can see."

"And the trouble you went to," Mrs. Bryant's aunt prompted.

"The trouble I went to, sewing all those dresses, taking her to those contests. She never did appreciate what I was trying to do for her. Not until she got chosen Winter Homecoming Queen. She was pretty excited about the other kids voting her to be Queen. That Ray Brueggeman ought to be whipped." Mrs. Trentam closed her mouth tightly and went on with her errand.

When I came to the last pictures in the book, Meda at fourteen or fifteen, I was ashamed that her underage lips and breasts aroused me so much. Chris leaned over to see them and said, "God help me. Don't tell Terry I said this, but her cousin makes my mouth water." I was the only one who seemed bothered by the remark. Terry's own brother and stepfather chuckled.

"You're a lucky man, Bernie, if you can keep her," Donald said.

"I bet that won't be a problem for him," Chris said, I suppose referring to my money.

"She could have been a movie star with looks like hers," Mrs. Bryant's aunt said.

She was thinking of a different place and time. Meda might have been a silent film star, but today she is too unlike anyone else. American culture takes refuge from true beauty by idolizing women who are all alike in their prettiness. My theory was validated by the other photo albums Mrs. Trentam produced, when I asked about her own pageant days. She had been, as I'd suspected, a very pretty woman. Blond, shapely, with even teeth and a cute little nose. In her photos of the Miss America pageant, Mrs. Trentam's bathing suit was charmingly old-fashioned, and she filled it out nicely, with her Miss Oklahoma sash across her chest.

"Damn, now she's pretty, isn't she?" Donald said proudly.

CHAPTER FIVE

SLEEPING OVER

BY THE TIME we left Mrs. Trentam's, it was late. At Meda's, there were cars in the yard and all the lights were on. The mysterious Amos family Christmas. Meda put her hand on my leg and said, "Let's not stop. Can we just stay at your house?" I hesitated, and she said, "Never mind. You can just drop us off."

It was a classic moment of failure for me. She needed something from me, and I had no clue what it was. I turned the car around. She was silent for the rest of the ride, and once we got to my house, she saved her words for small remarks to Annadore, who was excited by the change of scenery. The brief spurt of energy gave way quickly and Meda put her to bed in the room across the hall from mine. I'd picked that room because it had two beds, but after Meda got Annadore put to sleep, she came into my room and said, "Can I sleep with you?"

"Oh, Meda, I don't think so."

"We don't have to do anything, I didn't mean it like that. I just don't want to sleep by myself." The idea made me feel sick to my stomach, but I gestured what I hoped was a wry invitation to the bed. While I was in the bathroom, Meda took over my bed, appropriating all the pillows. When I came out, she asked, "Is that just for me or do you brush your teeth that long every night?"

I looked at her lying in my bed, and considered what to do. From the pile of discarded garments on the chair I saw that she had stripped down to her panties and her sweater. Her bra was folded on top of her slacks, one cup into the other. I tried to pretend that it was any other night and stripped down to my shorts, counting on a level of politeness I didn't get. She watched me undress. She gave up one of the pillows to me and waited for me to lie down, before turning out the lamp. Once I had finished my vague attempt to get comfortable, she scooted over and snuggled her bare legs against mine. Pulling my right arm around her shoulders, she curled up to me, and the unrestrained weight of her breasts rested against my side. She put her hand on my chest and touched the scar that was almost directly under her cheek. I hoped that if she wanted to know, she would ask someone else about it. When she slid her hand under the covers, I misunderstood what she intended, until she touched the matched pairs of scars on my legs.

The scars are a textbook study in the phenomenon of wound shoring. When you shore a target against another object of similar density, like one body part against another, the secondary target, the shoring object, takes the brunt of the injury. The bullet goes through the primary target and passes most of the kinetic energy to the secondary target. The exit wound of a shored target is usually small and neat like the entrance wound, while the exit wound of the shoring object tends be quite ugly.

Meda touched each scar once, only once, and each in its proper order: entrance, exit, entrance, exit. She wasn't going to ask me, because she'd already asked someone. She put her hand back on my chest without a word. I was grateful that the thing could be done so easily. We knew each other's secrets, but didn't have the burden of talking about them.

Even so I lay there with my stomach full of acid. When Meda hadn't moved for a while, I reached down and touched her cheek, felt her breath against my fingers. She stirred and asked if I was okay. I tried to be okay, but eventually I slid away from her and stood up. She sat up and looked at me in the near dark.

"What's the matter?"

"I just can't."

"You can't what, even sleep with me, just sleep?" she said.

"It's not you, it's just I can't sleep with someone else in the room." The same lie I'd told my second girlfriend. I preferred the way it sounded to the way the truth sounded.

"You can't at all?" She laughed.

"I know it's abnormal, but I really can't sleep with you. I'm sorry. I'll go sleep in another room."

"It's okay, I'll sleep with Annadore," she said and crawled out of the bed. As she crossed the room in the dim light, her pale legs seemed disembodied below her black hair and dark turtleneck.

Baby Girl Amos

Meda

Bernie knocking on the door woke me up in the morning. He was standing in the doorway in his blue jeans, but he looked more naked in his skin than most people do.

"Hey, are you awake?" he said.

"Kind of. You can come in."

He came over and sat down on the foot of the bed, but didn't look at me.

"I didn't get to say thank you for the necklace and the coat," I said. "You really didn't have to. You've done so much already. I feel bad that I can't get you anything as nice as what you've done for me."

"I know you said you didn't want anything, but I'm glad you liked it anyway."

"If we promise there won't be any sleeping, would you like to get in bed with us?" I said. He looked like he couldn't quite make up his mind, so I lifted up the edge of the covers for him, and he crawled into bed. It was silly, because he was too tall for the bed and it was too small for all of us. That was half the fun, being packed together like that. "We used to play sardines when we were little, Loren and David and I, we'd all get in one twin bed together to get warm." He relaxed a little then and put his arm around me, so that we were like three spoons in a drawer: iced tea, soup, baby.

Lying there pressed up against him, I could tell he had a hard-on. I looked at him over my shoulder, because I was curious what he was thinking. I couldn't tell, so I slid his hand up my belly to my breast and said, "Are you happy to see me?"

"I always am." He laughed and he wasn't even embarrassed. He didn't do anything else, but he didn't move his hand.

After about ten minutes of being cuddled together with us, Annadore started to get wiggly. "Santa Claus come?" she wanted to know.

"No, Baby Girl Amos, you know there's no Santa. We don't play that game at our house. I guess her cousins gave her the idea."

"Santa come. More pressies."

"You'll get more presents for your birthday," Bernie told her and then looked at me. "Why do you call her Baby Girl Amos?"

"I didn't name her for a couple of weeks, so when she first came home from the hospital, that was her name. You know those plastic hospital bracelets? That's what they put on them. Baby Girl Amos, Baby Boy Raleigh."

"I was never Baby Boy Raleigh. Bernham isn't really my name, just a name they give boys in my family." He sounded kind of surprised at himself.

Annadore started crawling on top of us, jabbing us with her sharp little knees and elbows. "I know what you want, good girl," I told her. "You want scrambled eggs, don't you?"

I was sorry to have to get up, we'd gotten so warm and cozy, but Annadore was hungry so we went downstairs and I made breakfast.

"Why did it take so long to name her?" Bernie wasn't eating, just moving his food around on his plate.

"Because I'm stupid? Maybe they'll put that on my headstone: 'She was stupid.'"

"You're not stupid," Bernie said. Bless him.

"Well, Travis and I broke up the last time about a month before she was born, but I thought we'd get back together. I thought once he saw her he'd get a backbone or figure out a way to make things work or something. He didn't, which is okay with me now. She's better off not knowing him."

After we had breakfast, Bernie took a shower. I went into his bedroom to get the rest of my stuff and heard him singing. He had a nice voice, so Annadore and I lay down on his bed and listened to him sing. I was brainless, lying there and feeling sort of sappy about him. I was so stupid that I was relieved thinking about how he'd acted in bed. Whatever else was going on with Bernie, it was about sex.

So Lucky

Meda

We worked a day between Christmas and New Year's, just to keep up with stuff and I went into the office to empty the trash, because half of what Bernie and Celeste did was make trash. Bernie wasn't there; he was at some meeting.

"Is it weird dating Mr. Raleigh?" Celeste said. "I mean, because he's your boss. I'd think it would be a little weird."

"Not really."

"Not that he isn't a nice guy, and he's cute, but I think it would be awkward." She giggled and said, "Are you going to the Hall of Fame dinner with him? I sent in the RSVP card and he said he was taking a guest, so I thought that was probably going to be you."

"I don't know."

"You're so lucky. It's really formal. I bet it's going to be wonderful."

"What do you mean by formal?" The last time I had to dress up for anything formal was when I was the Winter Homecoming Queen.

"You know, black tie, like tuxedos and evening gowns." She took the invitation out of a drawer and showed it to me. It was printed in gold.

"That's nice," I said, knowing she was trying to make me nervous. It was working.

"Are you going to the party at Mr. Tveite's?" When she saw I didn't know, she said real smugly, "He's the Chairman of the Board at Raleigh Industries. Are you going with Bernie to that party?"

"I don't know."

"I bet you are. I bet he asks you. You're so lucky." I really wanted to whack her when she started going on about what a fabulous house the Chairman had, about how she'd gone there for a Christmas party last year. "It was just an employee Christmas party, you know, where they invite everybody, but his house is like a mansion, even more than this house. I mean, this is a really nice house, but Mr. Tveite's house is a lot newer and it's enormous, even bigger than this house. Imagine how bad it would be cleaning that. And it's so elegant, just really beautifully decorated."

She kept saying how amazed she'd been and how fancy it all was, and I nodded like I knew all about it, but it pissed me off that Bernie hadn't been totally honest about what he was getting me in for.

Lady's Choice

To go dancing with Meda, I had quarters for the jukebox, a roll in each of my front pockets. I'd submitted to boots, which I hadn't worn since I was about eight. I'd submitted to a shirt with snaps, but when she handed me the straw Stetson that she insisted would be "great," I tried to take a belated stand against public humiliation.

"I draw the line at that hat," I said.

"No, you don't. And why do you do that to your hair?"

She took the hat back and directed me to the bathroom where she made me sit on the toilet and submit to her erotic hair styling efforts.

Erotic, because the way she tormented my hair was electrically arousing.

Erotic also because when she pronounced me finished, I looked in the mirror and said, "That's nice, you gave me oral sex hair."

"What hair?" She started laughing.

"Oral sex hair. The hair you end up with from some woman grabbing onto it during oral sex." She laughed harder and gave me a look that distinctly accused me of knowing not whereof I spoke.

"It is," I insisted. She subsided into a giggle. When I reached up and tried to smooth my hair down a little, she pushed my hands away. I took the hat and jammed it on my head, wondering if that had been her intent all along—to get me to wear the hat.

The evening was beginning to qualify as a good date against which to measure all others. We had a pitcher of beer and danced and talked. She showed me how to lead on a half-time two-step and we actually got comfortable with it. She wore a pair of boots that added about four inches to her height, a nice surprise that made it easier for us to dance. When we sat down for a break, I asked about the boots, and she obliged me by putting a foot up on my lap. More accurately she slid her foot up the inside of my thigh and brought it to rest in my crotch. I got the strangest feeling she'd given up entirely on having sex with me and only wanted to rattle my nerves.

The boots laced up the front and were form-fitting around her calf. Above the top of the boots, her legs were bare, an invitation that reminded me of being mercilessly pressed against her, feeling her soft, bed-warm legs. I had drunk more beer than was advisable and felt sufficiently loosened by it that I slid my hand up the back of her calf, enjoying the transition from slippery leather to the damp, velvety flesh behind her knee. I slid my hand a little higher, and skimmed her skirt up off her knee, giving me a glimpse of her thighs. Her legs bristled with gooseflesh, and she blushed. Thinking about how easy it would be to end up in some incredibly lonely moment with her, I flicked her skirt back down. When I gave her the next four quarters, she said, "Lady's choice."

After we closed down the bar, we drove out to a truck stop for breakfast. The place was decorated with the traditional wagon wheel chandeliers, with jackalope pictures laminated to the table tops. I didn't see anyone who looked like he'd put in a full day's work driving a truck. Instead, the restaurant was crowded with people of our own ilk, who had stayed out too late and drunk too much.

We'd gotten our food just a few minutes before when I felt Meda shiver next to me. I followed her gaze to where she was burning holes in the plaid shirt of one of a group of non-descript guys being seated at a booth not far from ours. The guy looked back at her and smiled.

Meda's fingertips, like the planchette from a Ouija board, traveled to the scar on her mouth. She didn't say a word. She didn't say, it's the man who cut up my face, who scarred me. She didn't say, it's the man who raped me. She didn't even say his name. It was an omission that spoke volumes to me. What would I say if I ever saw the man with the ether rag again? There's the man who—what? Took me? Kidnapped me? There's the man who—I didn't know. The thought made the hair on the back of my neck jolt up and filled me with almost as much panic as I imagined Meda was feeling.

In a movie, he would be a stereotype, maybe a roughly handsome guy with cold eyes a little too close together and a hard smile. Instead, if I had passed Ray Brueggeman on the street, I never would have noticed him. No outward manifestation of evil was in his face, nothing to show what he was capable of.

"I want to go," Meda said and stood up. I left money on the table and got up to follow her. To leave, we had to walk past where Ray and his friends looked at their menus in between glances at Meda. It might have been better to wait the thing out, except that Meda was miserable.

"Hey, Meda, baby. Lookin' good," Ray called out, and winked at her. She kept walking without looking at him and I followed her, thinking of Robby, of what Robby might have done in the situation. It made me feel pathetic. Robby was the Raleigh brother Meda needed.

"What a cunt," Ray said, louder, emboldened by his friends' laughter. Meda didn't pause and my gut churned to hear him reduce her to the thing he'd done to her. The truth is that every fistfight I ever had, most of them with Robby, ended with me getting the worst of it. I was not prepared to take on five guys. I wasn't afraid. It's not like my nose was ever going to be straight again, but it seemed futile. I think even by the kindest standards I was something of a weakling, but I had only that one chance to do the right thing. Then it occurred to me: I didn't have to take on five guys. Ray Brueggeman was so intent on Meda's retreating back that he hadn't even noticed me.

Half-Cocked

Meda

I've seen guys fight. I've even had guys fight over me. Most guys get some friends together and they go out in the parking lot and they bluff a bunch. Maybe a few punches get thrown, and their friends scuffle a little. They don't go off half-cocked and punch somebody out in a restaurant full of people. That was what Bernie did. And he didn't just hit Ray, he punched him in the face like he was trying to ram his fist down Ray's throat. Then the other guys at the table jumped on Bernie and it turned into this pile of broken glass and guys punching each other. It's hard to get a clear idea of Bernie's strength, because he's skinny, but he's not one of those toothpick tall guys. He's big enough that, except for Ray's friends, nobody else wanted to get involved. Still, there was no way he was winning a fight against four of Ray's asshole friends, and I was glad when a sheriff's deputy came over from the smoking section and broke it up. Before the deputy decided to arrest people, I grabbed Bernie by the arm and got him out of there.

Bernie didn't say anything on the drive back, even when I asked him how he was. Sometimes he was a little spacey, but I hadn't ever seen him like that. Once we got back to his house, I turned the dome light on to get a look at him. He wasn't pretty, but he didn't look very hurt, either. There was a gash on his cheek, his lip was split and his nose was bloody, but it didn't look more broken than it usually did. I shook his shoulder and said, "Are you okay? Come on, Bernie, are you alright?"

"I think so, but my hand hurts," he said, like he'd been talking to me all along.

His left hand looked bad, all puffy and cut up, and he still had it in a fist. When he opened it, I laughed so hard I almost peed my pants. For the whole fight he'd had a roll of quarters curled up in his fist. As soon as I stopped laughing, I hauled off and whacked him on the arm as hard as I could.

"That was so stupid. What was that supposed to prove?" Bernie doing that over some stupid insult pissed me off so much I didn't even know what to say. I'd accepted the fact that there was nothing I could do about Ray. "Why would you ever think that was something you should do?"

"I didn't want you to walk away from him saying things like that. It didn't seem right for him to say that, after what he did."

I knew someone would tell Bernie about Ray, about me, about what happened. It was easy enough to find out everything I wanted about Bernie, because those things went both ways, but I hadn't been looking forward to the moment when it would come up. Then Bernie did the exact opposite of what I thought he would. Split lip and all, he kissed me, long and hard, so that I tasted his blood in my mouth. I forgot to breathe; it was that kind of kiss. I pushed him back a little and looked at him. I didn't have a clue who he was. I'd never met him before. Then he blinked and said, "I'm getting blood all over you. I'm sorry." He wiped the blood off my face with his shirtsleeve and he was Bernie again.

Beauty and the Beast

I stayed in bed most of the next day, nursing something between a hangover and whiplash. It felt like a grenade had gone off in my hand and I vaguely remembered Meda's anger and kissing her. The three things seemed to have a cabalistic connection.

In the evening, she came out to pick me up for the New Year's Eve party at the Chairman's, and was kind enough to try to fix me up. She re-wrapped my hand and put a butterfly bandage across a cut on my cheek, remarking that it was probably from a piece of jewelry.

"His senior class ring. That's what cut me was the stone in his ring," she said matter-of-factly, without any hint of her earlier terror.

Despite an ice pack the night before, the left side of my face was swollen, and the white of my eye was bright red. The split in my lip was black with dried blood, but it hurt too much to clean. Only Meda's handiwork on my cheek gave the impression that I'd made any effort. I was irremediably ugly. Meda on the other hand looked heavenly. Her hair was down on her shoulders, and she wore a hazy lavender sweater set with the necklace I'd given her for Christmas. The pearls were almost as creamy and elegant as the neck she was wearing them around. As we drove, she took some lip-gloss out of her purse and smoothed it on, dreamily working her lips against each other. Admiring that last minute attention to her toilette, I had no worries.

The anxiety didn't surface until we reached the Chairman's neighborhood. Mr. and Mrs. Tveite lived in a gated community in Nichols Hills that was awash in white Christmas lights. When we pulled into the driveway at the Chairman's house, a uniformed valet stepped off the curb and opened Meda's door. She rolled her eyes at me.

Although I had wondered what I should say about my appearance, there was some social contract that precluded anyone from asking. Introducing Meda went smoothly. Mr. and Mrs. Tveite met me in the foyer and I said, "This is Meda Amos. Meda this is Mr. Tveite and his wife."

Meda smiled, and in a sweet, docile voice I didn't recognize, said, "I'm so pleased to meet you. You have a lovely home."

Without a word between us, we conspired to pretend we were other than what we were. I intended to cling to Meda, in an effort to present a unified front for our mutual protection, but the Chairman cut me off from the herd, forcing me to take part in a tour of his home theater with a group of men from the corporate office. The tour came complete with exhaustively boring commentary on the technology involved, and some innuendo about my date.

"That's a beautiful girl," the Chairman said

"Isn't she on your staff?" someone else asked. Several of them had been to the funeral reception, and there was no way they had forgotten Meda.

"Well, a girl like that, I imagine you can get past that," somebody else said.

"Past what?" I said. I didn't want to be a troglodyte, but even more did I not want to have that conversation. After the tour, I regrouped with Meda, who was being monopolized by some upper management type who slithered away when he discovered he was hitting on my date.

The Chief Financial Officer was not in on the social contract, or else he'd had too much to drink, because upon seeing Meda and me, he greeted us by saying, "Hey, Beauty and the Beast. Bern, what did you run into?" He laughed at his own joke. "Does Beauty have a name?"

"I'm Meda Amos," she said in that new, kittenish voice. "And Bernie had a little misunderstanding with someone."

"He understood me perfectly," I said. Meda scowled at me, and then slipped her hand into mine. We held our own against the CFO until the Chairman came back and broke us up. Trailing behind him was Lionel Petrie.

"You're a hard man to track down," Lionel said.

"If we could just borrow your young man, for a moment," the Chairman said to Meda. Short of making a fuss, I couldn't see any way out of it. They took me into custody and walked me across the house to the den, where there was an impromptu marketing meeting happening.

"Look at what they've done with their advertising," the Executive VP of Marketing told me, even though I'd missed the beginning of the conversation. "Consumers love the feeling of purchasing a product from a company that has history. Plus, you're younger and better looking." He hesitated, not wanting to mention my current condition. "You'll sell, Mr. Raleigh. You really will."

"Lionel, you've got to get out to the house, and see Mr. Raleigh's study. That was the original corporate office in 1928," another marketing type said.

"A sense of heritage," Mr. Tveite said. "That's the thing."

After nearly half an hour of it, I excused myself to go to the restroom. In the Chairman's glistening black-tiled crapper, I found I had sweated through my shirt and the lining of my jacket. In the quiet, I realized what was wrong. The galvanizing fear had nothing to do with Meda meeting these people. I was afraid of them. I needed to find Meda and get us out of that place.

Insulting Meda

Meda

Celeste was dead-on about the Chairman's house. The front hallway was the size of Gramma's house, and three stories high. The whole house was full of glass and chrome and black leather and marble. Thank God it wasn't my job to keep it all polished.

Mainly I wished that Bernie had stuck around to protect me, or something. The Chairman's wife kept talking to me, and I tried my best to be what Bernie wanted me to be, but I could see how she was looking to make me feel like crap. She and her daughter wouldn't even let me out of their sight. I got up to go to the bathroom and the daughter, Marcia, said, "I'll go with you." Afterwards she walked me right back to her mother.

"I have to say. You'd really be doing yourself a favor if you had some work done," Mrs. Tveite said.

"M-hm," I said. I was supposed to know what she meant.

"It's not that you're not lovely, but it's all about maintenance and improvement, like road work, my dear." She and her daughter laughed, but I kept my mouth shut. They were a pair of hyenas. "Really, a girl with a face as pretty as yours should have a smile to go with it."

"I never heard it put that way." I did the thing I swore I wasn't going to do. I picked up my drink and finished it.

"You work for Mr. Raleigh, don't you?" Mrs. Tveite said.

"Really? I didn't know you worked at RI. What department?" Marcia said. It was the middle of the winter and she had her toenails painted to match her fingernails, like a French manicure.

"I don't."

"You don't? I swear I heard Daddy say you worked for Mr. Raleigh."

"At his house. I'm his housekeeper." I felt like a liar. Housekeeper was a nice way of saying maid or cleaning woman. I didn't know why I said it. It was Bernie's word. The two of them smiled at me so hard I thought their faces would break. What were they going to say if I said it for them? "I clean his house."

When Bernie put his hand on my shoulder, it was too late. I glared up at him, because he'd left me to fend for myself with those evil, stupid women making their nasty assumptions.

"Oh, Mr. Raleigh," Mrs. Tveite said, practically cooing. "I was just going to give Ms. Amos the name of my daughter's orthodontist. I know you'll like him, dear, and he's wonderful. Marcia had a bit of an overbite, but you'd never know it from looking at her now. Beautiful work." Marcia showed off her teeth like we were at the goddamned county fair, and she wanted a ribbon. Mrs. Tveite liked what she'd said to me so much that she said it to him, too: "A girl with a face as beautiful as Ms. Amos' ought to have a beautiful smile to go with it, don't you think? I can recommend an excellent cosmetic surgeon, too."

I waited to see what Bernie would say, but he was staring at Mrs. Tveite. Second time I'd ever seen him at a loss for words. So I said what I was thinking: "Do you always insult people who come to your parties?"

I didn't think I said it that loud, but maybe it was one of those times when something bad gets said at the exact same time everyone else is taking a drink and the band is coming to the end of a song. Whichever it was, everyone turned to look at me.

"I suppose you know a good sculptor who can put arms back on the Venus de Milo, too," Bernie said. Mrs. Tveite looked up at him and blinked a couple of times.

"I'd like to go now," I said.

Insulting Bernie

The Chairman followed us into the foyer, hemorrhaging apologies, although I don't think he knew what his wife had said. I wasn't entirely sure what all had been said that needed an apology, but

Meda refused to acknowledge him, and it wasn't my place to accept or decline an apology on her behalf. Once our coats were produced, I handed Meda into hers and followed her out into the night. When she looked back at me, she wore a dark, wrathful expression that was fearsome and arousing; a look that both asked and answered the question of why I had gotten involved with her.

"What's that Venus de Milo remark about?" she said as we drove away.

"Even without her arms, she's considered a great work of art."

"I'm not a work of art."

"No, but who is she to be suggesting improvements to you?"

"You like me better with my stupid broken teeth, anyway," she said, disgusted.

"I like you." It was suspiciously like agreement.

"What if I got them fixed? Would you like me less?"

"I don't know what that's supposed to mean."

"I think you like me because you think I'm 'damaged goods.' Like you." To be fair, she seemed shocked she'd said it.

"Meda, that necklace you're wearing. I don't remember exactly what I paid for it, but somewhere close to $10,000. I bought it because I thought you'd like it. If you wanted to get your teeth fixed, I'd pay for that, too. It doesn't matter to me. I like you for what's in you, even when what's in you isn't that nice." I was trying not to be angry.

"Oh my God! This necklace cost that much money?" She put her hand up to clutch at it in horror.

"I would have bought you a new car, except our relationship would be over if you had a better car." I regretted saying it immediately. Another plea for her pity, and I didn't feel pitiful. I felt worthless.

"I'm sorry." She didn't sound it, but she didn't say anything else.

I couldn't tell if she was giving me the silent treatment or if she was just feeling pensive. When we got to Muriel's trailer to pick up Miss Amos and Annadore, Meda declined to give me any signals about her state of mind, so I entered the fray prepared for the worst. Muriel had filled the trailer with flashing multi-colored lights, and every horizontal surface was covered with shabby Christmas knick-knacks. Miss Amos sat on the sofa watching TV, and in the kitchen, Loren and Muriel were talking to Meda's Aunt Rachel.

Muriel made a big fuss over my face until Meda dismissed her with a short, "He got in a fight, Mom," confirming to me that she was accustomed to that behavior from the men in her life. Then Meda poured herself a glass of wine out of the gallon jug sitting open on the bar that separated the kitchen from the living room. To my horror and fascination, she drained it like it was water. Then she refilled it.

"Actually," Loren said, "I heard that you got in a fight with Ray Brueggeman."

"Don't say his name in my house," Muriel snapped.

"I wouldn't call it a fight. He didn't even get a chance to hit me."

"Somebody hit you," Rachel said.

"Well, his friends beat the crap out of me," I admitted modestly.

Muriel hugged me around the waist. "You're a nice guy, Bernie," she muttered into my chest. She was drunk, and Meda was headed there after three glasses of wine. By the time I realized how much they'd all had to drink, it was too late to steer the conversation back from the cliff edge. Saying things better left unsaid was apparently an Amos family tradition. I supposed that was why I hadn't been invited to the Amos Christmas.

Asked how Mrs. Trentam's Christmas had been, Meda said, "Aunt M. didn't have a lot of fun, I think. It was a real blow to Miss Oklahoma not to feel like she was better than everybody else."

"What could have made her feel like that?" Loren gasped. "She is better than the rest of us, isn't she? Isn't she?"

Meda lifted a finger from the rim of her glass and pointed at me: "Meet Mr. Bernham S. Raleigh. He's better than everybody."

"He's taller than everybody, too. How tall are you?"

I shrugged, lied: "Six-six." The truth was so monstrous I wasn't willing to admit to it, even on my driver's license.

"What's the S. for, Bernham S. Raleigh?" Loren said.

"Sevier." I didn't like the interrogatory trend of the conversation.

"Savior?" Loren shrieked. Drunk as a lord and not twenty-one. "Like, as in Jesus?"

"Sevier." I spelled it. "It's a traditional family name. Like Meda."

"It's my mother, you know, who's at fault for Cathy's name," Muriel said from the living room. "You can't imagine what she got me to name my son. We called him David, but his first name was Hezekiah. I can't figure out where she gets this idea that we're Jews. She lights her candles and mumbles her prayers, and makes us do the weird thing for Christmas, but I've never even been in a Jewish church. Come on, how many Jews have Christmas trees?" She gestured to the unlikely article in the corner of her living room.

"Then in fourth grade, Cathy decided she wanted to be called Meda, because of this girl she didn't like who was named Cathy. My mother got me to name her after my great-great grandmother who was a whore. It's her way of saying I don't have any room to talk about us being come down from a whore." Muriel put emphasis on the word and glanced at her mother. "It's true I've had bad luck with men. Meda's father, he worked as a custom cutter. Well, you know, lots of college boys came out in the summers and work the harvest. Meda's father was a college boy."

"So you and Mary Beth made up over Annadore and the Little Miss Pageant?" Rachel asked Meda, as though Muriel had been discussing the weather.

"As long as she doesn't try to pull a stunt like that again, we're made up."

"You just don't appreciate how far that kind of thing can take you. I mean, everybody knows who Jane Jayroe is."

"That's because she has a street named after her. Nobody remembers Susan Powell."

"Who's Susan Powell?" I said.

"See?" Meda was triumphant. "Just like Jane Jayroe, she was Miss Oklahoma and she won Miss America. Only she doesn't have a street named after her."

Rachel shook her head and said, "If Mary Beth hadn't made the mistake of marrying my brother, Ari, she could have made something of herself. She had a college scholarship and everything from the Miss Oklahoma pageant. And Cathy could have done a lot better for herself than Travis if she'd tried a little harder at those pageants. If she'd worked even half as hard at it as Mary Beth did."

"I'm so tired of everyone telling me I ought to be grateful for what Aunt M. was trying to do for me," Meda snapped. "Everybody acts like she was doing it out of the goodness of her heart, but she gets off on that stuff. She likes doing the pageants and the dresses and the whole nine yards. That's why she did it to me, because poor Terry wasn't pretty enough and Aunt M. got tired of bringing home Miss Congeniality awards. That's when she latched on to me. That's why she's trying to do it to Annadore, too. I wish Terry would have another daughter, a pretty one."

The rest of the Amos family barely registered Meda's outburst and Rachel turned to the topic of the Amos family curse.

"As Muriel so politely puts it, the other Meda Amos, our great-great-grandmother, was a prostitute. She was pretty like Meda. Muriel was a knock-out, too, when she was younger. Had tons of boyfriends in high school. Same with Meda, our Meda. Muriel was good-looking, but you want to see beautiful, you should get Mary Beth to show you some of Meda's pageant pictures. She was, she used to be really…wow."

I wasn't brave enough to mention within Meda's hearing that I had seen the pictures, or that I vastly preferred Meda to the girl in those pageants. Instead, I said, "I think she's 'wow' now."

"I mean before." Rachel let the unspoken words hang over us, like unshriven ghosts. "Too beautiful for her own good." She made it sound like Meda's fault.

"Yes, Meda's gorgeous. Lucky for me I'm the smart one," Loren said bitterly. "Since I'm never going to be the pretty one."

"We're in deep shit if you're the smart one," Meda said.

"Fuck you, you fat bitch."

"Girls. I won't kid you, Mr. Raleigh, my sister is a kook. I don't know exactly what happened to her, except the drinking." Rachel glanced at the wine in Meda's hand. "But Meda, our Meda's just too dumb to get out of this town and make something of herself."

My Meda was stonily quiet through most of her aunt's recitation, and even honored me with an arch look at one point, until she remembered she wasn't speaking to me. She stood at the bar, looking into the living room, and sipped her wine with some semblance of calm.

When Rachel stepped out to smoke a cigarette on the porch, Meda said, "Crap, I'm so tired of hearing her 'make something of yourself' speech. She thinks she's done so well because she got married and moved into the city. You know what she made of herself? She's the night manager at a Circle K in Norman. If that's making something of yourself, I'd just as soon clean your house for the rest of my life."

"This town has been against this family from the word go," Muriel said, morose and drunk, standing in the kitchen doorway. "When Cathy was born, I was going to put her father's name on the birth certificate, but the nurses at the hospital wouldn't let me. Said they couldn't since he wasn't there to say it was okay. They didn't believe me, and my letters all came back, so that never got done. Sure, it's easy to look at my life and say, 'She shouldn't have had three kids with three different men.' It's not like I started out with that intention. Who plans for that sort of thing?"

As beautiful and destructive as a glacier, Meda turned toward her mother. "I feel like I'm still in first grade, when you came for open house and humiliated me."

"Oh, God, Cathy. Do we have to—"

"Don't 'Cathy' me. You named me Meda!" Muriel walked back into the living room, ignoring Meda, who turned to me to finish what she'd wanted to say to her mother. "Halfway into the open house, she shows up drunk and starts telling my teacher and all the other parents about being abducted. Just picture, she's six months pregnant with her third bastard—no offense, Loren—and she's standing there smoking, in a grade school classroom, talking about being abducted by aliens."

I longed to flee from the blast radius of Meda's fury, but fearing the consequences of my cowardice more than I feared her anger, I stayed to hear her out.

"What did you think?" Meda shouted, asking the trailer at large, then subsided. "Of course the nurses wouldn't put his name on my birth certificate. What did you think?" She was shouting again: "What was it, again, Mom? What's my father's name?"

Muriel was defiant. "David Cohen. His name was David Cohen."

"Cathy Cohen, doesn't that have a nice ring to it?" Meda asked quietly. Her hand was shaking when she set down her drink. I rested my hands on her shoulders and when she didn't object, I put my arms around her. She leaned into me and we stayed that way for a few minutes, with me trying to carry part of her burden. Her mother coughed several times in the front room, prompting Meda to pull away from me and say, "Let's get out of here."

Breaking Up

Meda

He started to ask me if I wanted to go to his house, but I stopped him. "I just want to go home."

I knew what I was going to have to say when we got there, but I wasn't sure how I was going to get to it.

"She wasn't just a whore," Gramma said from the backseat. "She spoke four languages. She played the piano. She painted. She painted a mezuzah with Judith killing Holofernes."

"What's a mezuzah?"

"You little idiot, it's a place to hold a sacred scripture at the doorway to your house."

"If we have one, why isn't it on the door? Maybe I wouldn't be such an idiot. So who are Judith and Holowhozits?" I said.

She grumbled.

"Holofernes," Bernie said. "If I remember correctly, he was the general of an army that was fighting the Jews. Judith killed him to save the Jews, but she had to seduce him to get close enough to kill him, I think."

"She lay down with the enemy," Gramma said. "And then she cut off his head with his own sword. That was what Meda painted on her mezuzah. Judith beheading Holofernes, only she gave Judith her own face. Your face. When I die it will be yours, and then you'll see she wasn't just a whore."

"Why not show it to me now? God forbid we should know anything about being Jewish. You see? You can't just spring it on us and think we'll know what you're talking about."

"What do you know about it? Nothing. Nothing is what you know."

"What else about her? About Meda Amos?" Bernie said, just when Gramma was finally quiet again.

"Her father was a tailor, brought his family out from New

York. She was sixteen. When her parents died of the influenza, Meda was sixteen and her sister was thirteen and they were all alone in the world. There was no foster system, no caseworkers. No one to come and make sure they had food, not like for you, Meda. They didn't have any money, or any family or anywhere to go. They were all alone in the world. Sixteen years old, she had to lie down with strange men to get food to eat. That was what she had, just how pretty she was."

Bernie didn't ask any other questions. I felt the way you ought to feel on New Year's Eve. I was ready for things to be over. I wished I could take Annadore and walk away from all the things people expected from me.

When we got to the house, Bernie pulled into the yard and turned off the engine, so I said the first thing that came to my mind: "I can't do this anymore. It's not going to work."

He took a deep breath and I knew he was waiting to hear what else I had to say. I hoped there would be less of a scene with Gramma there, because I didn't think I could handle a scene.

"Now you've seen my family. That's them. You know the trailer my mother lives in? It belongs to her boyfriend Ted, who's in prison. That's what kind of people I'm related to. Wouldn't you love to have them get together with your friends and family? Can't you picture my mother at your friend's party? Celeste was right." I hated admitting it, but there was no way Bernie and I were going to have a normal relationship. It wasn't just that we didn't have anything in common. It was a bigger problem than that.

Bernie took another deep breath and said, "One: Mr. Tveite is the Chairman of the Board of Directors at Raleigh Industries. He's not my friend. Two: I can barely picture myself at his party. I didn't enjoy it, except for being with you. They're not my kind of people. Three: What was Celeste right about?" That was the thing he sounded most upset about.

"She was right that I'm going to be uncomfortable and out of place at that stupid Hall of Fame thing. She's right that it's weird for me to be dating you. It freaks everybody out, so no more helping me, or giving me presents. No more furnaces, no more $10,000 necklaces. Just no more. Okay? No more of it." I reached up to unfasten the necklace, hoping I wasn't going to have to ask him to help me. I wasn't proud of what I was doing, but it seemed like the only way to go.

"Do you hate me?" he asked.

"No, of course I don't, Bernie. Don't be stupid." I didn't like hearing Aunt M.'s words coming out of my mouth, but I didn't have any pity for him right then.

"Then please don't be hateful to me." He said it so quietly I knew it wasn't one of his pretend injuries. He wasn't trying for pity. I looked over at him and he was sitting there with his hands in his lap, looking straight ahead.

"I didn't mean it to sound that way. You're so nice to me, but I can't date you. You said I could say stop any time. I guess you'll do whatever you're going to do, but I'm saying stop."

"Okay. I accept that," he said.

"Thank you."

I wished that Gramma wasn't listening to us, because he deserved a better explanation that I could give him with her sitting there.

"I'm sorry if the necklace upset you, but you and Annadore and Miss Amos need the furnace, just as much as Muriel needs surgery. You can't tell me to take that back, and it was a gift given, as much as the rest of it. So, please don't try to give stuff back."

It was pretty small for a scene, so I nodded, trying to agree with some of it, without agreeing to all of it. I got out of the car and started getting Annadore out of the back seat. Bernie got out of the car, too, and opened Gramma's door for her and helped her out. He unbuckled Annadore's car seat and carried it up the steps. I was worried he would come in and make me dump him hard, but he didn't. He leaned toward me and put his hand on my shoulder.

"It's almost midnight," he said and just barely kissed my

mouth. It was a sad kiss.

Dumped & Sued

"Happy New Year," Meda said, but she kept shaking her head at me. "I can't. I like you, but I can't."

She shut the door. I drove back to the house with a head full of complicated diagrams, like sentences from a Henry James novel. It was already shaping up to be a great year. I didn't bother to get up at all Sunday. Celeste woke me up the following morning by knocking on my bedroom door with all her powers of perkiness. Giving into the inevitability of it, I got up and answered the door.

"Good morning, Mr. Raleigh. You know we have a pretty busy day today—are you okay?" She was smiling at me in the weirdest way. Then I remembered why she was looking at me like that and ran my tongue over the split in my lip. It hurt.

"I'm fine, Celeste. I just overslept. I'll be down."

"Okay?"

She didn't move, so I shut the door on her. I looked at myself in the mirror before I showered and saw I didn't look even a little better. I looked worse, and nothing I sang made me feel better. I ran through the first few lines of a dozen songs, but then I was clean, and without a song, there was no sense staying in the shower to sing.

I waded through a bunch of paperwork and sat slack-jawed through a conference call on a subsidiary of RI that I was supposed to talk to shareholders about at the annual meeting. Celeste took meticulous notes and smiled at me relentlessly. Thinking about the foundation instead of Raleigh Industries did improve my mood, so I spent lunch working on a list of people I wanted to invite to serve on the board of the foundation. Mr. Tveite had sent me a list of recommendations, which I mostly dismissed out of hand. Just glancing at the list, I could see his recommendations were all bigwig types like himself, including him. They were all men who served on a dozen charitable boards, and left all the real work to their assistants, or women who were married to the Mr. Tveites of the world, and showed up at meetings dressed in thousand-dollar pantsuits. My mother had been one of those women. For all I knew, she still was.

My list was less glamorous, but it had people on it I thought might actually have some ideas about how to help people. I picked three local doctors, including Dr. Hendershot. To them I added a woman I'd read about in the paper who ran the local food bank, a grade school counselor, a nurse from the county consolidated high school, and a city maintenance worker who had also been in the paper because he'd given half his annual salary to charity. With a sense of randomness, I put on the list the man who had been the librarian when I was a child, although I was unsure if he was still the librarian.

I was getting ready to call the library, when Mrs. Trentam came to the study door to tell Celeste that someone was there to see me. Believing the calendar created reality and not the reverse, Celeste didn't understand how such a thing was possible. There was no appointment on my calendar, therefore no one was there to see me. In the end she cleared my desk and showed in a man who introduced himself as Ethan Darryl, an attorney representing Mr. Raymond Brueggeman.

I asked Celeste to show him back out and to get my attorney on the phone. As with my other lawyers and accountants, I'd inherited Stroud, Stroud and Whitley from my grandfather. The younger Stroud, Alex, was in my study less than an hour later, looking flushed and curious. He was forty-ish, baby-faced, and he gave the impression that he'd actually run over from the city. I told him everything I could think of, from the actual fight, to the real catalyst for the fight. Not just what Ray had said, but what he'd done. Alex listened carefully, asked questions, and there was a spark in his eyes that was slightly frightening.

Celeste showed Mr. Darryl, dollar signs in his eyes, back into the study. The attorneys were introduced and Mr. Darryl produced medical records detailing his client's broken jaw and teeth, and with a flourish, several Polaroid pictures of a swollen and blackened Ray Brueggeman. In one photo, he grimaced, showing the metal scaffolding that held his jaw together. I couldn't stop myself from smiling and Alex admonished me with a look. Mr. Darryl pointed out that I couldn't deny the fight—my hand was evidence—and his client had nine witnesses who would testify I had struck him without provocation. He had merely greeted my date familiarly and I assaulted him.

Alex smiled pleasantly and said, "Is the word 'cunt' considered a familiar greeting where you come from, Mr. Darrow?" It was such a beautifully mean-spirited malapropism that I laughed out loud.

"It's Darryl, not Darrow," the victim said.

Alex smiled again. I sat back to watch the show.

"Of course, I'm sure your client is thinking of my client's bank balance in asking you to file this suit, but consider that the entirety of that balance can be brought to bear against your suit. I assume you're working for a percentage of any settlement? So let me just say, there won't be a settlement. Ever. At this point, you've probably only got a few hours of work in this, so why not cut your losses now? You're not going to see a dime, no matter how much time and energy you put into it." Alex gave the impression of being an older brother, offering advice.

"I beg to differ. The law is clearly on my client's side. The First Amendment provides every citizen, no matter what his financial situation, a right to say what he likes."

"The supposed merits of your case aside, let me tell you what's going to happen if you proceed with this. Unless you drop your suit, my client has instructed me to pursue any and all legal recourse on behalf of Meda Amos against Mr. Brueggeman for his 1988 assault on Miss Amos."

"I—what?" Darryl said, suddenly seeing the conversation gone terribly wrong.

"It's common knowledge that Mr. Brueggeman battered and sexually assaulted Miss Amos in November of 1988. He only avoided criminal prosecution because his uncle is the county sheriff. That won't protect him now." That last piece of news startled me, because my grandfather had always pretty much decided who was elected to what office in the county. Alex was counting on political obligation trumping family connection. I had a sheriff in my back pocket. Defeated, Mr. Darryl began gathering up his reports.

"I'll make you an offer," I said. Both lawyers turned and looked at me. "You can recoup the cost of some of your wasted time. I'll give you $100 for that picture." I indicated the uppermost Polaroid on the stack of pictures he had laid out.

"You're kidding," the estimable Mr. Darryl said.

"Not even remotely." I took out my wallet to demonstrate that I was in earnest.

"My time's worth more than that."

"I doubt it," Alex said.

"Make it $200 and it's a deal."

Darryl waited for me to count four fifty-dollar bills into his hand. When he pushed the photo across the desk to me, Alex shook his head in disbelief.

"I'd report him to the bar if I thought he was a real lawyer," Alex said, after Darryl had escaped with his unethical money. "Ray Brueggeman aside, I think we should make an offer to Pal Shrader to pay for damages at the restaurant."

"That would be good."

"I'll take care of it. You don't want to get a bad reputation," he said.

I kind of thought I did. Alex picked up the picture and looked at it.

"Well, I wouldn't have guessed it about you. One punch?"

It was a small lie, a lie of omission, so I let it ride.

CHAPTER SIX

SUBMITTING

I KNEW I should wait and give Meda some space, but after Alex was gone, I buckled. I didn't get an answer when I called, but I knew she was home, because the HVAC technicians were there installing the new furnace. I knew that because I called the company's dispatcher. I was stalking Meda.

"Your appointment isn't until two. Aren't you going to have lunch?" Celeste said in a proprietary tone, when I voiced my intention of leaving early.

I almost said, "I want a divorce," but knowing she wouldn't get the joke, I said, "I'll get something on the way."

I drove past Meda's house twice before I parked next to the van in her front yard. When she opened the door, she was obviously expecting it to be one of the techs, because she gave me a look of frustration, but let me in. I didn't intend to have a full-blown argument with her, but that was what she wanted. In Meda's narrative, the Hall of Fame dinner was a metonym for our relationship. She didn't have anything to wear. She would be out of place. She wasn't the right kind of people. She would embarrass me.

I countered with the fact that she had been impeccably behaved at the Chairman's party. It was Mrs. Chairman who had embarrassed me. Meda had been lovely and charming and amiable, I recalled. I sat down on the sofa, gearing up for more flattery—is it flattery if it's true?—when one of the furnace techs knocked on the door to tell Meda they were breaking for lunch. When she came back, she stood over me with her hands on her hips, obviously thinking of her next attack.

"You already said you'd go," I said preemptively.

"Can't you take someone else?"

"I'd rather take you."

"Besides, it's weeks away. Maybe you'll be sick of me by then."

"Maybe I already am." I smiled at her, but she wasn't falling for it. "Hey, maybe your mom would go with me."

"Shut up. God, take Celeste. She'd love to go. She said the party was going to be so fabulous and elegant, but what she meant was that I wasn't going to fit in and she was right. That's why that woman was rude to me. She knew I didn't belong there. And this stupid thing, it's a black tie dinner. Did you even tell me that? No. A formal dinner. You've already seen the nicest clothes I own. Have you seen anything you think goes with a tuxedo?"

"Meda, there's a world of fabulous clothes out there waiting for you to buy them." I took out my wallet and tossed it to her. She caught it reflexively, but dropped it on the coffee table as if it had burned her.

"Why don't you take Celeste? She'd like it and I think you'd both have a much better time."

"I'm sure I'd have a great time if I took my little assistant as my date." I was only thinking of my distaste for Celeste, not of what it might sound like to Meda.

"You're right, it'll be a lot better introducing your date as your housekeeper." It stumped me because I rarely thought of her as my employee. If anything, I felt like we were both employed by that larger entity: the estate of my deceased grandfather. It was like working for a museum I also happened to live in. "I noticed how quick you were to introduce me that way at the party."

"Well, you weren't exactly volunteering the information when you were introducing me to people at the bar."

"Because they already knew who you are."

"Fine, I'll introduce you as my housekeeper at the Hall of Fame. Is that what you want?"

"I want you to stop it!" She threw her hands up at me, sounding truly angry.

"Maybe I could just introduce you as my girlfriend?" I asked, trying to return the conversation from the brink of madness.

"I'm not your girlfriend."

"Why not?" I put my arms around her and tried to kiss her, but she pushed me away.

"Annadore." She looked toward the playpen, hardening her mouth. "And I'm not your girlfriend, and you don't even want me to be. Honestly you don't, and I can't. You should go. I want you to leave."

She picked up the basket of laundry she had been folding and went down the hall. I stood at the front door, intending to obey her, but then I had an epiphany. I had wanted to avoid getting seriously involved with Meda, because of all the torments I imagined would result from the relationship. Half of them were already being visited on me.

I went down the hall and found her in her bedroom, putting away laundry. I felt like I was apologizing for something I hadn't done.

"Why aren't you my girlfriend?" I said, feeling unwanted and lonely without being alone. Meda looked at me for a long time, and then at last she submitted. Or I submitted. It was hard to know where to draw the line. She pulled off the shirt she was wearing, reached back to unfasten her bra, and dropped them both on the floor. Pushing her hair out of her face, she looked at me with something akin to a challenge. That's why I wasn't her boyfriend.

Her breasts were a testament to God's love for humanity, like beer, as Benjamin Franklin suggested. They were so pale I could see the blues and greens of vein and artery under the surface. The undersides of her breasts and her belly were shot through with fading streaks of opal, where her flesh had given way to internal pressure. There were mysteries about her that I would never in a lifetime be able to fathom. She looked uneasy and half crossed her arms across her chest.

"Stretch marks. You know, that's what you get from babies," she said.

"I know."

She shrugged and stepped into me, to stop me from looking at her. Putting her arms around me, she strained up on her toes to kiss my neck, pressing God's blessing against me.

Seducing Bernie

Meda

It was like trying to get a priest to seduce me. I had to take off my clothes and offer myself to him to make him do anything. His hands were shaking when he touched me, he was that nervous. Physically, he wasn't like a little boy—not all over anyway—just what I had seen before, that he was so thin and he didn't have much body hair. In the only place that mattered, he wasn't anything like a little boy.

Him being so tall was awkward, but once we were on the bed so I wasn't getting a crick in my neck kissing him, it was nice. A lot of guys, you get this feeling that they're rushing to get somewhere, but even though his lip had to be bothering him, he kissed me like it was the one thing he wanted. That's how he was about everything, and once he got over being nervous, he was comfortable. He had this way of looking into my face to see what I thought about what he was doing, not like he was unsure, but because he liked to.

I never have been happy with my body since I had Annadore. I didn't personally mind being heavier or the stretch marks, but I didn't like wondering what someone else was going to think about it. It was like Bernie didn't even notice. "You are so soft," he said while he was kissing my belly. It was my least favorite part of me, the part I thought was still really fat from Annadore, but when I mentioned it, he just said, "One of us has to have some padding. Two skinny people in bed are dangerous and sad, like lawn chairs having sex."

I laughed and he smiled at me, finally relaxed a little. When we got right down to it, I wasn't sure what he was going to do. I was going to give him a condom out of the box in my nightstand, but he had one in his jacket pocket. He never even asked, he just got it out and put it on very neatly, so I guessed he'd done it before. That was a relief, because that would have made it too weird.

He was so polite about the whole thing, right down to the condom. I never thought about how there might be good or bad manners when it comes to sex. It's the kind of thing that makes you wonder how your own manners are, like when you meet someone with good table manners. Later you try to remember, were you talking with your mouth full? Did you have your elbows on the table? I can't even remember if any guy ever offered to use a condom before, let alone used one without me having to ask.

As much as he liked to talk, he was the quietest guy I ever had sex with. I wasn't even sure how close he was, until he grunted really quietly and then rolled off of me. He didn't have that sleepy, stunned look a lot of guys have after sex, either. Mostly he looked relieved. He shook his wrist to bring his watch around to read it.

"You have somewhere else to be?" I asked. He got red when he saw I'd caught him at it.

"I have a meeting at two. I'm sorry."

"That's okay. It's too cold for this anyway," I said to let him off the hook.

He got up and went into the front room to finish getting dressed, where at least it was a little warmer from the gas stove. When one of the heating guys came in to borrow the bathroom,

Bernie was standing next to the stove buttoning his shirt up and tucking it in.

"How's it going?" Bernie asked.

"It's going good, Mr. Raleigh. We ought to be done this afternoon." The guy actually took off his hat.

Sometimes Bernie paid so much attention to what he said and did that it was scary. Other times he seemed unaware, like right then, getting dressed in the front room, talking to that guy. I felt like his mistress, and he didn't have any idea what it looked like, or he didn't care.

"I'm having dinner tomorrow night at my aunt's house. Would you like to go? You don't have to decide now." Bernie said it like he was worried I would say no.

I said yes, because I didn't know why I always had to put up with my family embarrassing me. Let his family embarrass him for a change.

Sexual Favors

When I went into the bathroom to try to make my hair and tie behave, Miss Amos came in from wherever she'd been while—ouch, while I was having sex with her granddaughter. Where had she been? She stood in the doorway, watching me fix my tie.

"What are you doing here?" She sounded angry, and I had to reconsider my assumption that she liked me.

"I just came to see Meda, Miss Amos."

"I know why you're here. I know all about you."

"I'm not Holofernes," I said, hoping she would remember the conversation. She scowled at me and I saw she remembered, but maybe had a different idea about what it meant. "I'm not the enemy, Miss Amos."

"No? Then what is this? What is this?" I wasn't sure what she was asking, because it didn't seem to be a rhetorical question. "You're turning her into a whore." She raised her hand and I saw she was holding my wallet. Meda had left it on the coffee table.

"Don't say that. She's my girlfriend," I said, trying not to laugh at the idea that I was purchasing Meda's sexual favors.

"Lying down with the enemy." She pressed the wallet into my hand, but her anger seemed to have subsided.

"I brought a present for you." I reached into my jacket pocket for it.

She smiled, her anger forgotten.

I left Meda's house and drove to my meeting, not sure of anything. Before my epiphany, I had been thinking about the man who was the head librarian when I was a kid. For all I knew he still was, but when I was little he was already middle-aged, so it was more likely he was retired or maybe dead. If you didn't make any noise and returned your library books on time, he might never look at you, engaged as he was in studiously stamping your card, or shelving books. Now that I know more about the world, I think the odds are high that he was gay. In a town that small, he could have been as gay as the day was long and it wouldn't have mattered. He would never have had a date or a boyfriend or a lover. He would have gone on leading his quiet life: walking to and from work, living alone, eating his lunch with a book in his hand.

That was the thing that made me happy working at the library, when I hadn't been happy anywhere else: the calm. Meda was a force of wholesale destruction of calm.

Not a Fluke

Meda

It wasn't a one-time fluke, which was what I expected. I figured it would be one time and then it would be over. The next day, when I went to work, I expected Bernie to be embarrassed and trying to avoid me, but he wasn't. Instead, right there in broad daylight, he asked me if I'd like to go to his bedroom, and gave me what I guess was his come-on look.

"Am I still on the clock? Are you paying me to have sex with you now?" I said to yank his chain.

"No, whatever time we spend in bed, you're going to have to make up. Maybe you'll have to stay late or skip lunch."

So I let him lead me down the hall and hoped that Aunt M. wouldn't come looking for me. That second time, he had another condom out of a box in his nightstand drawer. It was funny to think about him putting one in his pocket before coming out to my house, because if you'd asked me, I never would have guessed he was thinking about anything like that. Later when I was changing the sheets on the bed, I checked and saw that it was a new box. Just two condoms missing.

He was still polite, even when he wrapped my hair around his fist, and pulled my head back to kiss my throat. I think he did it to see if I would let him. I knew if I said stop, or gave him a look that said stop, he would. Also, he wasn't finicky, although I was kind of sweaty. He didn't seem to think there was anything dirty about the human body. I had figured he was the sort of person who showered right after sex, but instead he lay back next to me and talked, asked about Annadore and about me.

"What do you want to be when you grow up?"

"I like that you're giving me the benefit of the doubt of not thinking I've already grown up to be what I am," I said. He laughed.

"You never stop having a chance to grow up to be something. I wanted to grow up to be a librarian, but now I'm not sure."

"So, what do you want to be?"

He was quiet for a long time, rubbing my shoulder, looking up at the ceiling. Then he rolled over and put his face into my hair, said he didn't know.

I wanted to tease him a little, so when he was getting ready to go back downstairs and gave me a kiss, I said, "You're going back to your office for the rest of the day with cunt-breath? You don't want to go brush your teeth for five minutes?"

He laughed and said, "No, but thanks for not messing up my hair."

In my secret life I'm a high priestess. I live in a stone temple in an oasis out in the middle of a terrible desert. People come to me for advice and the days are filled with singing, dancing, sacred rituals, and sacrifices. I read this book in grade school about a priestess who was reborn after she died. When she died, the other priestesses went out and found her in her new self and brought her back to the temple to teach her how to be a priestess again. She never had a name. Her name and her soul were eaten up by the gods of the temple.

When I get tired of my real life, of being me, I close my eyes and go to that other life. I wear a heavy black robe and stand on cold stone floors in front of strange altars. All of my life is ritual, a road laid out in front of me, not this jumble of things I never seem to have a chance to plan out. In my secret life I don't end up with a baby I didn't expect and that I don't know what to do with. I don't have a crazy mother and an ex-boyfriend who won't give me a dime for the baby.

That was what I almost told Bernie about what I wanted to be. I didn't think he would make fun of me, but I was afraid if I told anyone, it would stop being my secret life. I wouldn't have another life, because someone else would know about it. I'd just have this one.

Of course, in the book, that priestess didn't get to keep her neat life. A wizard came across the desert and confused everything. Then an earthquake destroyed the temple, and the priestess had to run away. I suppose that's the way life is.

Raleigh Family Patriarch

Aunt Ginny

The first thing I noticed about Meda was that Bernie didn't slump when he was with her. Clearly she was trying to be on her best behavior, too, because she said, “It’s a pleasure to meet you, Mrs. Raleigh.” I didn’t want to make things awkward, so I played along as though we’d never met. Then we stepped out of the foyer into the parlor, and I saw Bernie in the lights.

“Bernie! Your eye and your cheek. All of you. What happened?” I was honestly surprised at how such a good boy managed to find so much trouble.

“It’s nothing,” he said, and tried to turn away from me a little, to keep me from looking at him too closely.

“It is something. Your poor eye looks terrible.” I reached out, wanting to hug him, but then I saw the bandage on his hand. “Shame on you.”

“You’re blaming me for getting beat up?”

I squeezed his hand then, and he winced and looked shocked that his harmless old aunt had hurt him. “Didn’t our Savior say to turn the other cheek? It doesn’t look as though you did that.”

Meda hid a smile behind her hand, but she tried to defend him.

“He meant well, anyway, Mrs. Raleigh.” She shook her head, just the way I think a girl ought to when she loves a boy but is exasperated with him. Seeing that, I let it pass and we went in to dinner.

We had nearly finished our entrees when I looked at Bernie’s plate, and saw how little he’d eaten. “You need to eat more, dear,” I said to him.

“I’m not very hungry.” He hunched over his plate defensively.

“You’re never hungry. You’re anorexic,” Meda said.

It struck me as just the thing I had been concerned about. I simply hadn’t thought of any way to talk about it with him.

“I don’t think men can be anorexic,” he said.

“That’s a myth. Anyway, it’s not going to make you invisible,” Meda said.

“Now you’re accusing me of wanting to be invisible?”

“I think putting on a little weight would be good if you intend to take up boxing," I said. I was ashamed of him for that, but he surprised me by smiling at Meda.

"Actually, the invisibility worked in my favor in the fight. He never saw it coming. Hey, is this some kind of intervention?"

"He doesn't like being so tall. That's why he doesn't want to eat," Meda said.

"I am sitting right here unless I've finally managed to make myself invisible." Bernie was a bit annoyed, but he seemed so much livelier. In the past he would have let us talk across him.

"He even lies about how tall he is. How tall are you? Not six-six. Six-nine?" Meda asked.

Bernie mumbled under his breath what I believe was an extremely offensive word.

"He's closer to seven feet," I said. Bernie scowled. "He was only an average baby, maybe smaller than average. Right at six pounds, I think. Such a little sweetie, too. Born with a full head of hair. Little dimples in his—"

"This is not the part of the evening where we look at naked baby pictures," Bernie said, and seemed pleased when we laughed.

"You see how dictatorial he is now that he's the Raleigh family patriarch." I wondered if he would return to his usual deference. He frowned at us, and ate a few more bites of his dinner. Meda winked at me.

"Are there naked baby pictures of Bernie for me to look at?"

"No, there aren't," he said.

There were, but I chose to cede the battle at that point. I liked Meda a great deal. She had the sort of wickedness that is essential for a truly beautiful girl. No one could stand a girl as nice as Meda was beautiful.

"Now, tell me about your little girl, Annadore," I said. Bernie was so relieved to have the conversation move away from him that he cleaned his plate.

Battle Souvenir

Meda

It was a bad habit to get into, but I went to work early to catch Bernie in bed. I knew he was going to try to talk me into getting in bed with him, so first thing I took the picture out of my apron pocket and handed it to him. With his black eye fading and his lip healing, he smiled when he saw it.

"Did you give this to my grandmother?" That's what she'd told me. He nodded. "Why would you give her something like that? Where in the hell did you get that?"

"His lawyer brought it to me when he came to tell me that Ray was suing me."

"He's suing you?"

"Not anymore. I gave it to your grandmother to make her feel better." He tried to hand it back to me, but I shook my head. I didn't want to see it again. I definitely didn't want it in my house.

"How is that going to make her feel better?" I said.

"Because she feels badly that he didn't suffer any consequences for what he did. I thought she might feel better if she knew that he'd been punished a little."

It annoyed me how he could lie there buck naked and look so nice, so damned sincere. I'd been ready to say something mean about him being a show-off, wanting to look like some kind of hero, but he was serious. He thought it would make Gramma happy to know that Ray got his jaw broken. I bet it did, too, but I didn't want to let him off the hook that easily. I wasn't like Gramma. I couldn't let something like that make me happy, because it's no good getting ideas like that about justice.

"You could sit down. You don't have to keep standing there looking indignant." He patted the edge of the bed. I wasn't going to get anything out of him. He looked down at the picture and smiled a little wider.

"You're proud of yourself, aren't you?" I said.

"I don't know about that."

"I thought you didn't have a mean bone in your body."

"I don't. I have a mean roll of quarters." The way he grinned at me I had to leave. He was so cute I knew I was going to end up in bed if I stayed.

"Are you mad at me?" he called after me.

Some Crappy Eliza Doolittle Scenario

I think Meda was just pretending to be mad about the picture of Ray Brueggeman, but when she came to the study later in the afternoon, she was definitely angry. She came in without knocking and stood at the corner of my desk until I told Celeste to leave. As soon as Celeste was out of the room, Meda said, "Your little bitch assistant needs to learn to keep her mouth shut."

"Whoa," I said, like she was a runaway horse.

"My aunt asked me about that stupid Hall of Fame dinner. I wasn't even going to tell her about it, because I didn't want to get into it with her. Three guesses who told her." I didn't need the three guesses and she didn't give me a chance to make them. "It's bad enough I have to put up with everybody thinking I'm some kind of gold digger without her running her trap to everyone."

"I'm sorry you're upset."

"I'm not upset. I'm royally pissed off is what I am." Meda's voice cracked and she squeezed the bridge of her nose. It dawned on me that she wasn't merely angry.

"I didn't realize it was a secret." I had contributed to the problem. Celeste asked about the Hall of Fame and I answered truthfully.

"It's not just that. I hate people talking about us."

"I doubt there's that much gossip going around about us."

"That's because you don't have to go to the grocery store or the Laundromat, or anywhere except your accountant's office.

That's why you think that," she said. The look she gave me implied I was of sub-par intelligence.

"I'll talk to Celeste and take care of it. Is that okay?" I wasn't about to let it turn into another argument. She nodded and didn't look mad anymore, just troubled. When I took her hand, she let me pull her around the side of the desk and put my arm around her. "I'm sorry I wasn't paying attention. Are you okay?"

"Yes." She kissed me grudgingly, making me feel I'd dodged a bullet. At the door, she breezed past Celeste as though she didn't exist.

I spent almost an hour gearing myself up to make good on my promise to 'talk to' Celeste, before I finally called her over to my desk. She made a little salute and said, "Reporting for duty, sir." She must have seen something in my face, though, because her perkiness collapsed marginally.

I decided to keep it simple, to avoid any misunderstandings brought about by too much talking.

"I want to tell you one thing. I don't want to talk about it. I just want you to do it. Mind your own business."

"I don't understand, Mr. Raleigh."

"Celeste, would you ever talk to anyone, say Mrs. Trentam, about the financial information that we look at in this office?"

"No, sir, never," she gasped.

"Then why would you think it was acceptable for you to tell her about anything else that goes on in this office?"

"I would never—"

"I know that you did. As I said, we're not going to talk about it. Mind your own business. You know exactly what I'm talking about."

"Yes, sir," she said. I felt badly for quashing her perkiness, except that it made such an improvement in her personality. She was almost bearable for the rest of the afternoon.

That was how the Hall of Fame and its attendant preparations became a dirty secret. Or maybe it was the relationship that was the dirty secret, but Meda seemed defeated by the knowledge that she'd agreed to it. The relationship and the event. It's not pretty, but her aura of defeat made me want to spend a lot of money on her. The fact that she let me should have set off some alarms.

I started out wanting to wash away the bad taste of all the fighting and the incident at the Chairman's party by buying her some nice things, but then it started to feel like I was rewarding her for giving in. We went into the city for a day of shopping, so she'd have some appropriate evening attire for the Hall of Fame, but it wasn't some crappy Eliza Doolittle scenario. There was no illusion I was initiating her into a higher class. It was just a day of waiting for her to try on clothes, and watching sales people fawn over her. The experience was far from delightful and I concluded that any future venture should involve Meda and my money, but never again me.

On the drive back, the money I'd spent on her hung over us like a pall. The dress, the shoes, the various undergarments and accessories. Once she had been properly outfitted, there was a hard edge to her, as though she was bitter to find that the gap between everyday Meda and society Meda was a gaping maw that could only be filled with thousands of dollars. She rode limply next to me, her gaze occasionally wandering in an accusatory fashion to the bags and packages in the back seat.

"I'll be glad to see Annadore," she said. "I hope Mom didn't let her eat too much candy."

Or let the aliens abduct her. I hoped Meda's irritation was over, but when we had retrieved Annadore from Muriel's house and driven back to Meda's, she refused to take the dress and its accouterments into her house.

"That dress is too nice to even take inside my house. It cost more than the house did." After I helped her get Annadore out of the car, I tried to insinuate myself into their evening.

"I don't really feel like it, Bernie." She meant something else. "I'm not in the mood. I have my period."

"We don't have to do anything," I said, borrowing a page from her, but she made it clear I better not come in. I took the dress home with me.

Meda was so convinced that the dress was too nice to go in her house that the night of the Hall of Fame, she got ready at my house. I was afraid of her by the time she came downstairs. I'd spent a measly half an hour showering and shaving and getting my tuxedo on, while she had been the better part of three hours in her preparation. She stepped into the parlor in a defensive stance, expecting I-don't-know-what reaction from me. I wanted to make some snide remark like, "You're not wearing that, are you?"

I couldn't get the joke out. Looking at her made my throat hurt.

I would identify what I was feeling as lust, but I always thought of lust as a feeling that starts in your crotch and radiates outward. This started in my chest, scorched my liver, and then traveled like an electric shock to my groin. I thought it must be what people call "falling in love." I had the vertigo of a fall from a great height, and in my stomach, the terrifying thump of impact.

The dress was a shadow-filled, dark red, and looked like it had been made to a mold of her. The plunge from her throat to the center of her cleavage left me humbled and incredulous. I had kissed those breasts. She wore make-up, so that if you didn't know what you were looking for, you'd never notice her scars, but it was her facial expression that left me feeling weak in the knees: serenity, edged by a lingering spark of defiance. She licked her lips, revealing a touch of nervousness and said, "I look okay, then?"

The only things we hadn't bought on our shopping trip, I'd borrowed from Aunt Ginny—a mink and silver fox coat—and from my grandmother's safety deposit box—a diamond necklace and earrings. When Meda opened the case, the light touched the diamonds and refracted off them.

"Shit," she said. "I better not lose these."

"They're insured." I helped her put the necklace on, and then the coat. It carried the ghost of my aunt's perfume and enveloped Meda like a cloud. It was strange to think of my aunt as a younger woman being Meda's size, but I agreed with Oscar Wilde that Aunt Ginny must have simply decided she didn't want to be that tall anymore. The other thing I'd borrowed from my aunt was her chauffeur, Ron Grabling, although I'd decided against her sedate Bentley and gotten my grandmother's silver Rolls out of storage. Meda was still giggling when we headed down the drive.

"Hi, Mr. Grabling," she said.

"Hello, Miss Amos. I always knew you were meant to ride in a Rolls Royce." Of course they knew each other.

"Mr. Grabling used to help us fix our bicycles when we were kids," Meda explained. The ride went quickly with the glass partition down, chatting with Ron. When we arrived, the valets at the convention center stared openly at the Rolls and at Meda. Proof I'd achieved my goal of making Meda feel fitted to her surroundings. She glided up the stairs on my arm, but she never quite managed a real smile. She was nervous.

The event turned out to be a bigger fuss than I'd imagined, as there was easily seating for six hundred if they intended to fill it. There were two other inductees, both of them men of my father's age, to whom we were introduced before the crowds began arriving. One of the other inductees latched on to us in a paternal way, or at least his interest in me was paternal. I recognized him from the billboards for his real estate agency. He introduced us to the people he knew, with only a few variations in the response. Half the people we met didn't spend two seconds on me, their gazes immediately drawn to Meda. The other half didn't look at me at all.

The Chairman and his wife had regained their composure and Meda graciously pretended there had been no embarrassing incident at their party. There were a lot of remarks made about what an impressive businessman my grandfather was, but they were mostly made in an effort to keep a dying conversation going around the supernova effect of Meda's presence. As we made our way to our table, people all over the room wrestled with the dilemma of her presence. Heads turned, doing double takes, risking whiplash. At the table behind us, everyone turned to look, then looked away, erupted into whispers, and turned to look again like a flock of penguins. I wondered how it felt to be Meda, knowing I wouldn't like it. When I took her hand under the table it was ice cold and trembling.

As for my own performance, I had tried to work up an anecdote about my grandfather, but the only ones I could think of didn't cast him as anything but mercenary. He was so conniving and vicious at Monopoly that Robby threw the game away to avoid playing it with him. I ended up with a sixty second remark on how happy I was to accept the award in his honor and how much I regretted that he had not lived to receive it. The reality was that he declined to be "honored" while he was alive.

It was all beginning to wear on Meda. Even at the edge of the spotlight, I felt the pressure of that much attention directed at one location.

"Can we go soon?" she asked in a tiny voice, as soon as it began to look like things were breaking up. In the car she turned away from me and was so silent that I said the first thing that came to mind.

"You were so worried you'd be out of place, but you were wonderful. You're always wonderful." She burst into tears with such a passion that I recoiled from her. "Why are you so upset?"

"Because I feel like a freak show! Like I'm not even a real person. And you just took me there so people would look at me instead of you!"

For nearly ten minutes solid, until I contemplated getting Ron involved, she cried. I tried to touch her, but she slapped my hand away.

"I'm sorry." I didn't know what else to say.

"It was like those awful fucking pageants," she moaned at last. I numbly handed her the handkerchief from my breast pocket, finally understanding, and knowing what an ass I was. At the house, I practically had to carry her and she refused to go any further than the sofa inside the doorway of the front parlor.

Real Person

Meda

Bernie turned on the lights as he left the room, and when he came back, he was taking off his tuxedo jacket. He came and stood over me, but I promised myself I wasn't going to get into it with him. All I wanted was to take off those stupid clothes and go home and be alone, and I knew he was going to make it difficult. I hated him so much right then, because it always had to be so complicated with him. He pulled me up off the couch and yanked his aunt's coat off me, so I knew he had to be furious, because he'd never been rough with me.

That's when I saw the kitchen shears in his hand. He squatted down and took hold of the hem of the dress, cut into it, and then ripped it up to my hip. I put my hands on his shoulders to stop him. He didn't look at me, but he went a little slower when he worked the shears across my belly and up to the neckline of the dress. Then he went snip-snip, across the shoulders of the dress, and the whole thing fell on the floor.

I figured he would see the look on my face and stop, but he started in on the rest of my clothes. He slit the slip like he had the dress, cut the garters off the tops of the stockings and then cut the garter belt right in the middle. He peeled the stockings down my legs until he got to the shoes, and not knowing what else to do, I lifted my feet up one at a time to let him take them. Then he worked his way back up, cut my panties off, and then cut the straps off my bra. He slid the shears into the front of the bra, between my breasts, and I held my breath when he cut, because the shears were cold and I knew they were sharp. I didn't feel exactly afraid of him, but I was afraid something terrible was going to happen. He was like he always was, standing there with his bowtie not even a little crooked, not two hairs on his head out of place.

For the longest time, he looked at me, top to bottom, standing naked. Then he took hold of that big diamond necklace of his grandmother's and pulled on it just enough for me to feel the pressure of it on the back of my neck. I braced myself, thinking he was going to yank it off. I waited for him to open his mouth and say, "You crazy, ungrateful bitch."

Instead, he looked right into my face and said, "You're not a freak show. This is not a pageant, Meda." Then he let go of the necklace and pressed his hand over it, pressed it against me. "This is a gift. For you to keep. I wouldn't give it to you unless you were real."

I couldn't help myself. I started laughing and couldn't stop. I picked up what was left of that insanely expensive dress. Six thousand dollars hacked up with a pair of kitchen shears. I swear that dress cost six thousand dollars. I laughed so hard I had to sit down. Bernie looked like he couldn't decide whether to frown or smile. He looked so alone there was only one thing to do. I opened my arms to him and for once there was nothing polite about it.

Mrs. Bryant's Social Call

Aunt Ginny

I was surprised when Mrs. Bryant came to see me, but thinking she'd come on a social call, I tried to be friendly, and asked after her family and her retirement.

"I just came to tell you one thing, and I'll apologize for it. I know it's not my place, but I thought you should know. My daughter, Mary Beth Trentam, you know she's Mr. Raleigh's housekeeper now. She mentioned to me that Cathy, her niece, and

Mr. Raleigh were seeing each other. Were dating." I nearly laughed, except that Mrs. Bryant looked so serious.

"Cathy, they also call her Meda?"

Mrs. Bryant nodded and drew herself up a little.

"Yes, ma'am. I have nothing against her, but obviously she isn't the right sort of girl for your nephew. She had a child, out of wedlock." So, she was there to caution me against some lower class girl who had designs on Bernie.

"I've met Meda and she seems perfectly delightful. And Bernie, of course, is a good boy. I can't see how you could possibly object to them dating," I said, careful to put the emphasis on the word 'you.' It was a struggle to stay polite. I am not a violent woman, but I felt an urge to pick her up and shake her like a terrier shakes a rat. I supposed she'd sat in the same church with me for the last fifty years, worked for my father-in-law for a good thirty years, and exchanged no more than about ten polite words with me at any given time. There she was tattling on my nephew. She didn't improve my feeling for her with the next thing she said.

"I prayed a long time before I decided to come see you. And Father Reginald and I talked about it, because he's worried, too, about Mr. Raleigh. Meda is a good person, but she's not a Catholic. The Amoses are just a different kind of people from the Raleighs."

The truth about Virginia Waxman Raleigh is this: my parents took a good look around them when we moved to town and realized all the wealth and influence in the area was in the hands of Catholics. They never once looked back to their Methodist roots, but even when I was being confirmed, I knew in my heart that they were not my People. I knew why I was there. I told myself, *This is because it must be*, because I was an obedient daughter, but in my heart I never accepted the things they believe. No one can mediate between you and God. You stand alone before him. The numbers are tallied up in each column and the priest will not be there to hold your hand when the judgment is put upon you.

My parents had certainly intended to move up in the world

socially when they became Catholic, but I don't suppose that even in their wildest dreams they expected to move up quite so far. By the time I met Alan Raleigh, I was already twenty-six. He was twenty when he proposed and although his family was polite to me, I can't help but wonder how happy they were when we married. I was seven years his senior and a records clerk at the county hospital.

"You knew my husband, of course, Mrs. Bryant."

"Oh, yes. I was so sorry—"

"It was my husband's habit to interfere with my nephew's personal life, but it isn't mine," I said, silently apologizing to Alan.

Mrs. Bryant excused herself. I did not show her to the door.

Faking It

Meda

Things were better after the stupid Hall of Fame was over. We had a kind of normal relationship, going on dates, and having sex like regular people. One night, though, we went back to my house after a movie and went to bed. I knew that condoms sometimes make things last longer, but after about half an hour I'd had enough.

"Bernie, if you don't stop, I'm gonna be sore tomorrow. Just let me finish you up," I said, but it was like he was in a trance. He blinked at me a couple of times and looked confused. "Are you okay? Tell me what you need."

He shook his head and wouldn't look at me. I thought about the fact that he was usually very focused on me, that I usually didn't do anything for him, except let him do what he wanted. I should have let it go, except I felt guilty, so I kept trying, and he pushed me away.

"I-I-I just c-can't," he stuttered, which I'd never heard him do before.

"What do you mean, you can't?'

"I can't. It feels really good, but I can't come."

"What's the matter?"

"Nothing's the matter. That's how it is."

"Are you saying you can't come now, or are you saying you can't come, like ever?" He wasn't even going to say anything, but then I saw the look on his face and I knew. "Ever? You don't—well, what in the hell have you been doing with me?"

"I usually just pretend. Nobody expects guys to be very dramatic about it, either, so it's never really been an issue," he said and shrugged.

"You fake it?"

"You've never faked it?"

"Well, okay, I have. But I don't do it all the time, and I haven't done it with you, and don't look so smug. What about when I walked in on you that morning?"

"No, I usually do then. It's just with…"

"With somebody else in the room. Oh, Bernie, you're so messed up. You can't sleep with somebody else in the room. You can't have an orgasm with somebody else in the room. I bet you have shy kidneys, too."

I laughed because it was so crazy, but he turned away from me, and he didn't look embarrassed. He looked crushed. I felt bad for teasing him, so I tried to apologize, but he wouldn't answer me. He got up and stripped off the condom, and then he pulled on his shorts and went out to the bathroom. When he came back, he sat on the edge of the bed, staring off into space. I rubbed his back a little and he let me.

"Have you thought about maybe seeing a psychiatrist or something?" I hoped he wouldn't think I was still teasing him.

"You've got to be kidding me. I spent ten years in therapy. My family spent enough money on therapy, it would have cost less if they'd paid the ransom."

Wad Cutter

"Oh my God!" she said in a piercing register I'd never heard from her. "Oh my God!" She sat up in bed and stared at me as though I'd sprouted a second head. "Are you saying they didn't pay the ransom? They didn't pay? What kind of—what kind of…."

Letting the sheet fall away from her, she rose up on her knees, and put both her hands over her mouth. She looked like she was going to cry, which I wanted desperately to prevent.

"Look, it was a matter of principle for my grandfather not to pay. And paying it was no guarantee I would be returned. It doesn't matter, anyway. It's all in the past, twenty years in the past. I don't even think about it anymore."

"Except that it did something to you," she said. "That's not normal, Bernie."

"I don't think that had anything directly to do with this particular problem."

"Well, that's not the only problem you have."

"I almost forgot. I'm damaged goods. Thanks for reminding me, Mom." I was royally pissed off, to quote her.

"I'm not saying that, but it can't be right for you to have that kind of problem."

I pushed her back down on her impossibly small bed, maybe too roughly. I intended to prove that there wasn't something wrong with me, and she let me, but it was crazy-making. Like having an itch in a place I couldn't scratch. She felt wonderful under me, but there was no end in sight after another futile ten minutes of it. I couldn't. There it was: I couldn't what? Let go? Was it that I couldn't let go? Of what?

"That's starting to hurt," she said and made a mild effort to push me away.

After lying next to her for a while, I apologized and got dressed to go. She didn't say anything, so I let myself out and drove home to a dark house. I didn't see her over the weekend, not clear on what had happened, or if we'd had a fight. She hadn't seemed angry, but I spent the weekend not caring that the water was heating. My mother called on Sunday and we had our usual non-conversation, which prepared me for the plunge I knew was on the horizon. I felt it coming on, like you can feel a head cold coming on. What did my mother want from me that she kept calling?

Getting a bullet to its target is wrapped up in matters of barrel length, powder chemistry, gas compression and rifling. Once the bullet gets there, though, it's all about energy transference. To get maximum stopping power and tissue damage, you have to terminate the bullet's trajectory in the target, and that means calculated deceleration. You want a bullet that decelerates on impact, like a wad cutter.

The Crazy One

Meda

I wasn't ungrateful, but I didn't want the headache of explaining to Mom that Bernie was paying for her surgery. He didn't care anything about people knowing he was doing it. He was embarrassed when I thanked him. So I just told Mom it was taken care of and she didn't have to worry about it. I thought that was enough, because she didn't ask about it. Instead she waited until Loren and Aunt Rachel got there for dinner and then she started asking me all kinds of questions. She'd been living in her own world for so long she didn't even understand the real world. It was useless trying to explain it to her. If I'd told her fairies were going to pay for her operation, she would've understood that more than what Bernie was doing.

"Can he do that?" she said.

"I guess he can, but is he really going to?" Aunt Rachel said.

"He already has." I felt like I was talking in a foreign language, because they wouldn't even try to understand me. Every time I tried to explain it to them, they looked at each other like I was the crazy one.

"I saw the check. I held the check in my hand. It's paid for." I only had the check in my hands for a few hours, and it was made out to the hospital for $500,000. Bernie signed it Bernham S. Raleigh in big, black letters. Very official. I didn't know why I was carrying the check until Bernie introduced me to the hospital director. I was there to distract him, to keep him from making a fuss over Bernie.

"I guess I don't understand how he can pay for my surgery," Mom said.

"They did some sort of deal where Bernie donates money to the hospital to buy some piece of equipment and the doctor does the surgery for free and everybody gets to write it off on their taxes. It's paid for. You just have to finish your antibiotics and get over this bronchitis."

I knew I had to apologize to Bernie. Somebody does something like that for you, you have to apologize when you act like a jerk.

"My question isn't so much how, but why," Aunt Rachel said.

"Because she's sleeping with him," Loren said. "Why else would he be doing this? He bought Gramma a new furnace, for Christ's sake. You saw the necklace he gave her for Christmas. Like he's going to give her that because they're friends." She hadn't even seen the diamonds.

"Is it serious, honey?" Mom said. "It must be for him to give you something like that."

"With as much money as he's got, he can afford to give her something like that whether it's serious or not," Loren said.

"Well, it sounds kind of serious to me."

"She's seriously fucking him. I went by your house a couple nights last week and Gramma said you were at his house. She was pissed off at you. 'Sneaking little whore.' That's what she called you."

"She's probably upset because of what happened with her," Mom said quietly, not wanting Gramma to hear. "All those years she worked for Mr. Gertisson. She won't say it, but he was our father."

"Guess we're lucky Gramma wasn't the Raleigh's housekeeper. That would be gross," Loren said.

I stopped trying then, because that was how they thought of everything.

CHAPTER SEVEN

PROBLEM

I ALMOST STAYED in bed another day, but I admitted to myself that my current state was self-indulgent. It wasn't a real depression. I'd slept off the real depression, or burned it off with the intense burst of self-loathing that followed the conversation with my mother. Whatever the cause, the thing had fled by Monday morning, so I got up and took a shower. When I came out of the bathroom, Meda was sitting on the edge of my bed waiting for me. I liked that she presumed the familiarity, although it might have been the prerogative of any pretty girl.

"What song was that?" she asked.

"It's from *South Pacific.*"

"It's nice." When I came over to the bed, she stood up with her hands in her apron pockets. "I'm sorry about how I acted the other night. If you spent ten years trying to get better, then that's all you can do. I guess you're just you."

"Thanks. That makes me feel better, knowing I'm just me."

"I'm really sorry," she said again.

I leaned back against the headboard, and looked at her for as long as she would let me. She turned a little pink and started to leave.

"It's okay. Can I ask why it bothers you? Why my 'problem'

upsets you so much?" I drew the little quotes in the air and she frowned at me. "I don't have to keep trying until it makes you sore, but I got a little caught up in the rhythm of it the other day."

"That's just it. How do you know when it's over?"

"I'm perfectly content to stop a lot earlier, after your orgasm." I enjoyed seeing the way color blossomed in her cheeks. It made me eager to alleviate her anxiety and almost made me forget what I'd been so upset about.

"It doesn't seem fair for you to not to enjoy it." She looked so serious I had a hard time not laughing at her.

I fought the urge and said, "You know, the means are pleasurable in themselves, without consideration for the end. And I'm not afraid of a little manual labor, so to speak."

She laughed more than the joke warranted, and I saw how nervous she was. I felt badly that I'd made her work so hard, and in the silence after her laughter, I got her out of her clothes and into the bed.

Confidence Lost

Meda

I tried not to think about it when we started kissing, but once his secret was out, he'd lost a lot of his confidence. He knew what I was thinking, because he leaned up on his elbow and said, "You know, it's not always. I do manage it sometimes."

"Like when?" I asked and he looked a little surprised.

"I guess I'm a better actor than I thought. The night of the Hall of Fame."

I waited, but that was all he said.

"So, basically, once. What was different about the Hall of Fame?" As soon as I said it, I remembered exactly how it had been different. He had been different. Not quite the same guy who kissed me after the fight, but someone between Bernie and that guy. He had still been wearing his shirt and his bowtie when it was over.

I didn't know if he came—that's what condoms were for—and I didn't want to know. Afterwards I got dressed to go down and see what Aunt M. was doing. Before I left, he said, "Would you stay with me tonight? We'll figure something out about the sleeping, okay?"

"What about Annadore?"

"Bring her."

"It'll be easier on the weekend. How about if we come Friday night?"

"And Saturday night?" he asked.

"And Saturday night."

"And the night after?"

"Hey, are you trying to get me to move in with you?"

"Okay," he said, so I knew he was crazy. Who says something like that? "You can come and stay as long as you want. You don't have to call it 'moving in' if that seems weird."

On Friday, I packed up a box with some stuff for Annadore and me, clothes and toys and bathroom things, so we'd have what we needed to stay over with him. Gramma glared at me when she saw what I was doing.

"I hope he pays you well," she said. "That was the thing I always had to fight with Gertisson about, the money. Stingy old bastard."

"Bernie isn't a stingy old bastard and he's not paying me to—it's not like that, okay?"

"You say. Not the sense that God gave a goat. You're going to be a whore just like your mother."

"Don't talk like that in front of Annadore." I heard enough of that from Gramma about Mom when I was a little kid. Probably her mother said things like that to her. Someone who beat her kids with a shoe would say something like that.

"You know what he's doing to you," she said. I didn't know and I didn't think she knew either. Whoever Bernie was, he wasn't

Mr. Gertisson.

Bernie's idea of me staying with him did not involve sleeping, but he was interested in having sex. As soon as Annadore was in bed, he practically pounced on me. I tried not to think about what his reasons were. When it got late, though, and we were both tired, he went and slept in the bedroom next door. That's how polite he was: he let me have his bed since I was already in it. I tried to ask him again about sex, about his 'problem,' since that's what he called it. I really didn't understand why he was interested in sex, because I could see then why he wouldn't be.

"My pleasure is vicarious," he said.

"Wait here while I go downstairs and look that up."

"I enjoy it if you enjoy it. And it feels good trying to get there."

He wouldn't say anything else, so I hoped he had a good time with himself in the other room.

Sunday night I knew I ought to go home. I didn't have any intention of staying there with him past the weekend, but I didn't want to have to deal with Gramma. She might have forgotten our fight, but maybe she hadn't.

"Well, just stay," Bernie said.

"Yeah, but then I'd have to take Annadore back anyway, because somebody has to watch her."

It made me feel bad, because it seemed like I was just using Gramma to take care of Annadore. I thought I was doing okay by her usually, but maybe I was a bad granddaughter.

Domesticity

"It's too complicated," Meda said, when I suggested that Annadore could stay at the house during the day.

"No, it won't be complicated." We went into the parlor off the kitchen and I pointed out the Dutch door to her and how it would be easy enough to take anything that wasn't safe out of the room. "Even if you're in another part of the house, I can hear her if she needs anything."

For Monday, that was Annadore's playroom, and she wasn't even alone most of the day. Meda checked on her throughout the day, and I read to her and chatted with her. Even Celeste played with her for a while. Mrs. Trentam was notably not involved.

Monday night, Meda went to dinner with her family and I believe she made up with her grandmother, but at the end of the evening she came back to the house. I liked not just her presence in the house, but the fact that she saw it as a safe place. It felt safer to me.

She was smiling as she carried Annadore upstairs to put her to bed. I read for a little longer, looking forward to going up in a few minutes, thinking of kissing Meda, the shape of her back like a cello. Whenever I caught myself thinking of the next day or the next week or two years down the road, I turned it off. Instead, I thought of Meda, right then, upstairs, getting ready for bed. I traveled back in time, remembering how she looked hugging my aunt. Meda's hair had enveloped them both, while her hands pressed gently on my aunt's back. I thought of some clandestine afternoon in my bedroom, how she had glanced reproachfully over her shoulder at me until I got out of bed to zip her back into her uniform. When the future started to intrude, I set aside my book and went upstairs.

When I went into the bedroom, Meda was sitting on the edge of the bed, unlacing her shoes.

"So, how was your grandmother?" I said.

"Oh, she's okay. She doesn't want to be wrong, I think. She wants to be able to say 'I told you so.' That's why she's so mad at me."

"Maybe she's just concerned about you."

"Does she need to be?"

"Are you asking whether my intentions are honorable?"

"Oh, I'm not asking anything," Meda said.

I wanted to reassure her that I did have honorable intentions, but all the ways I knew of to tell her were dangerous. She was a flight risk.

We'd had the playroom set up for all of two days when Aunt Ginny came to see me. Meda stuck her head into the office and told me she was there, but when I went out to the front parlor, it was empty. Thinking I'd misunderstood Meda, I went toward the kitchen, and heard my aunt's voice. She was in the playroom, getting acquainted with Annadore.

"I came to see you, but Meda said you were busy, so Annadore and I have been playing." Aunt Ginny was smiling and a little disheveled. I waited for the question that would require me to explain the situation, but it didn't come. When Meda came into the room a few minutes later, she looked mortified, probably expecting that question, too.

"I hope you weren't waiting too long, Mrs. Raleigh," she said.

"Oh, dear, I never even went in to see him. I wandered back here and was having such a delightful time I completely forgot why I was here. She's such a sweet girl."

Meda blushed and smiled. We chatted a while longer, and then Mrs. Trentam came down the hall, wondering why we were all gathered there.

"I was just coming to check on her, but I guess I'll get back to work," Meda said.

"Good," Mrs. Trentam said. "I want to get started on those curtains."

"No, come to lunch with us," Aunt Ginny said. Meda looked at me in alarm. I shrugged. For all her sweetness, Aunt Ginny was a force to be reckoned with.

"I really have a lot of work to do," Meda said.

"Oh, bother," Aunt Ginny said.

Mrs. Trentam and Meda looked at me, wanting me to put a stop to the nonsense and get out of the way of the work they needed to do. Aunt Ginny gave me a look that demanded I take charge and bring Meda along for lunch. I don't know what they were thinking. I wasn't in charge of my aunt, and it was clear I had no real say over Meda or Mrs. Trentam. I wasn't even my own boss.

"I'd love to go, Mrs. Raleigh, but we have a busy day. Maybe some other time," Meda said.

Aunt Ginny and Mrs. Trentam both frowned, but Meda carried the day. She and Mrs. Trentam went back to work. Aunt Ginny and I went to lunch.

"I don't see why Meda shouldn't have come with us," Aunt Ginny said, but the question about our living arrangements never materialized.

Child Care

Meda

A couple times I went to check on Annadore, and Bernie was with her, usually reading to her. It was so funny to see him in a suit and tie, with Annadore on his lap.

"Bet you never thought you'd provide your employees with day care," I told him.

"I don't see why not. I like the idea."

"I mean, you personally, providing the day care."

"No, this is a nice break. She's only bitten me a few times, and she never says, 'balance sheet' or 'cats are so funny.'"

He seemed happy and Annadore seemed happy. Aunt M. was not happy.

"Mother's very upset about you moving in with him," she said to me at lunch.

"Well, bully for her." I didn't want to hurt her feelings, but it wasn't her business.

"You have to know what it looks like that you're living here."

"I guess you're going to tell me."

Aunt M. glared at me and took another bite of her sandwich. She was either trying to figure out the nicest way to say something bad or come up with the meanest thing she could say. "You're not the only one who's affected by your relationship with him. Try thinking about Annadore, or even about my family."

"I am thinking about Annadore. I think she's happy," I said.

"Now she is, but what about later? Do you want her to be embarrassed for you, the way you were for your mother?"

I got up and left, because there was no way I could say anything and not wish it back. We didn't talk to each other for the rest of the day, except for what we had to say to get the work done. I was a little ashamed of myself, because when I went to sleep that night, I knew part of the reason I was still sleeping at Bernie's was to be contrary.

Abduction Redux

I came up out of the bed, not sure what had woken me, and went through my mental checklist. All body parts functioning, no intruders, and no obvious immediate danger. Then I heard the steady thumping of someone knocking on the front door. Meda was asleep down the hall in my bedroom. She had a perverse sense of things, forcing me to vacate my bed if I wouldn't sleep in it with her. I pulled on my jeans and took the front stairs two at a time, wondering how long the pounding had been going on before it woke me. The doorbell rang distantly, intended to notify some non-existent servant.

Belatedly, it occurred to me that it was the dead of night and someone was rattling the front door on its hinges. I thought of Ray Brueggeman's friends, but it turned out to be two sheriff's deputies.

"Mr. Raleigh? Sorry to bother you, sir," the older deputy said. "We, uh, we're looking for Meda Amos."

"Why?"

"It's about her mother."

"Is she—what happened?"

"She's been out wandering tonight. Got a touch of frostbite on her toes, but nothing serious."

I felt Meda's presence behind me, an instant before she touched me. She put a fingertip on the scar below my shoulder blade, and the pressure of it passed through me, making the intaglio of scar tissue on my chest tingle. I thought of the temporary pathway a bullet creates as it passes through flesh, displacing shredded tissue and shattered bone, air ballooning around the projectile. Later, the cavity collapses around the wound track. Without thinking, I brought my hand up to those misfiring nerve endings, and covered the scar with my palm, inadvertently drawing attention to it. I turned and Meda stepped around me.

"Is she okay?" she said.

"She is, ma'am, but she's disoriented. She's at County, not in lock-up this time. The infirmary. She wanted you."

The younger deputy was quiet, looking at my hand. I lowered it self-consciously. It was an odd sensation, to feel him pull his gaze away from Meda, back to that scar. We went upstairs to dress and to get Annadore, who was awake and belligerent.

Standing in the front foyer, Meda looked rattled as she tried to calm Annadore. I wanted what I had wanted from the beginning, to make things better for Meda.

"What can I do?" I asked.

"I hate to take Annadore. Would you stay with her while I go?"

The deputies were watching us, and as much as I didn't want to, I agreed. Meda looked relieved as she exchanged Annadore for the car keys. Annadore punched me in the neck and went back to her sleepy tirade.

"I remember that spring. My father went out with a search party," the younger deputy said, when he finally found his voice. He looked at my chest, as though he could still see the scar, through my shirt and sweater, through Annadore where I held her against me.

Meda kissed Annadore, then me, then Annadore again. "Be good for Bernie, Baby Girl. Put her back to bed, okay?"

Annadore was nearly asleep against my shoulder, and I was filled with a primeval terror. She whimpered a little when I pulled off her coat and shoes, but by the time I tucked the covers around her, she was asleep again. Her mouth was open slightly, her breath warm on my hand. Her eyelashes were dense and black, like Meda's, and her eyelids fluttered lightly. She was lovely.

For a moment, she was quite still and I slipped my hand under the covers and pressed it to her chest, feeling the intense heat of her, the rise and fall of her ribcage, until I was able to make out the cadence of her heart pumping blood. I knelt there by the bed, my hand over her small heart, learning the rhythm of her breathing. At that point, I was more afraid of leaving than of staying. It was several hours before I heard Meda come through the kitchen door and creep up the stairs quietly. I wished she would be a little louder, would make enough noise to wake Annadore.

Watchfulness

Meda

When I went into the bedroom, Bernie was watching Annadore sleep. "I used to do that when she was first born. How was she?"

"She's been sleeping since you left."

"And you've been watching her all that time? She'll sleep okay by herself, silly."

"I know." He didn't sound very sure of it.

"Come downstairs. I want something to eat." After hesitating a little bit, he followed me.

"How's your mom? Where is she?"

"They're keeping her overnight, just to observe her. To make sure she's okay."

"What happened?" he said.

Even though I knew he was okay about it, I didn't want to tell him, but he was waiting for me to say something.

"She said they took her tonight."

"They? The aliens? How was she?"

"She was like she always is, confused and scared."

"You've seen her after it before?"

"Sure. Lots of times. She's always scared and I do feel bad for her, because it's real to her. The deputies found her practically all the way to the interstate," I said.

"That's a long way for her to walk."

"At least ten miles. Barefoot in her pajamas. You see how easy it is to start thinking it's too weird to be just craziness. I don't know. I think..."

"That something is happening to her. Even if it isn't aliens abducting her, something is happening," he said. I was glad he understood, because I never had anyone before who was mostly normal and sane to talk to about it.

Domestic Hiatus

Our brief little venture into domesticity was put on hold. Meda decided to stay with her mother until the surgery, perhaps with the idea that Muriel wouldn't get herself abducted if Meda and Annadore were there. Meda denied it.

"It's not so much that, but she's more worried about the surgery than she wants to admit. She needs someone to take care of her." I agreed it would be a kindness for Meda and Annadore to stay with Muriel, but I suspected Mrs. Trentam's odd behavior of late had something to do with it.

"I'll miss you," I said. She laughed, but gave me a kiss that made me feel she didn't despise the sentiment.

It was strange to lie in bed that night, fighting the edge of sleep for the simple reason that I was happy and I didn't want to lose the feeling. Meda wasn't there, but I knew she was coming back. The future actually seemed doable.

Miraculously, the good mood carried through into the next day. Not even Celeste got on my nerves, so I didn't make her take a separate car to go to another meeting with the lawyers who were working to set up the Raleigh Foundation.

"It's surprising that you're taking a personal interest in the foundation," Celeste said in the middle of one of her stream of consciousness monologues on cats. "Karen—she works with Mr. Vogle—has done some other work with foundation incorporation, and she said that you're a lot more involved.

"Usually, Mr. Vogle and his staff do most of the planning. People who leave the resources for a foundation usually have ideas for it, but most of the time people in your situation aren't as involved. But then, Mr. Raleigh didn't make any specific arrangements." There was a pause that I thought was Celeste taking a breath, but it was a bit too long. She was waiting for me to speak.

"I want the foundation to do what I want it to do," I said, which was the sort of thing my grandfather often said. *They'll damn well do it the way I want it done.* "And my grandfather didn't make any arrangements for the foundation, because he would not have approved of it."

"Oh," Celeste said.

It was the first time I'd told anyone the foundation wasn't some idea that stemmed from my grandfather's desires. That was why it was called the Raleigh Foundation, and not the Pen Raleigh Foundation. Once said, the fact could not be contained. At the meeting, I blurted it out to Mr. Vogle, apropos to nothing.

"Oh, I'm sure he wouldn't have disapproved," Mr. Vogle said, with a little smile of pleasant doubt.

"Didn't know Pen, did you?" I was suddenly enjoying the moment.

"No, I never had the pleasure of meeting him."

"He hated charity. Hated people who needed charity. He would have hated the idea of his money being used for charity. If he knew I was planning to spend a bunch of his money to help poor people, he'd be rolling in his grave—if he were in it." I said it all before I realized I was breaking my own rule. Mr. Vogle hadn't asked and he didn't want to know. We spent the rest of the meeting talking about the formation of a board of directors, and my goals for the foundation's giving. Eventually we discussed my personal involvement in the foundation.

"Do you want the primary responsibilities to devolve to the board of directors after everything is set up?" Mr. Vogle asked.

"No," I said, a little shocked at how sure I sounded. "I plan to serve as the Chairman of the Board in perpetuity."

"Mm-hm," he said, making notes on his legal pad. He was an excellent lawyer. His approval and disapproval sounded exactly the same.

When Celeste and I left Mr. Vogle's office, I was still feeling good, until we got close to the house and I saw the markers for my father and brother. I was in such a pleasant mood I couldn't stand to see them, and I remembered the resolution I'd made. In retrospect I should not have done it with Celeste in the car, but the road was deserted, and before I could think better of it, I swerved the Fleetwood across the same centerline my father had crossed to his death. The tires sank into the shoulder as the bumper clipped the markers.

Celeste screamed.

I pulled back into the proper lane with plenty of time to make the turn to the house. I apologized and Celeste hiccupped something like forgiveness. To prove she was recovered, she asked whether I wanted her to see about having the crosses replaced.

"I wouldn't have taken them down if I wanted them up," I said.

Mr. Romance

Meda

Bernie was so happy when I asked him to come to dinner that I didn't have the heart to tell him he wasn't going to get laid. I wanted dinner to just be Mom and us, but Loren invited herself and her stupid boyfriend. He always gave me the creeps because he stared at us like he was from another planet, and he was still trying to learn how to speak our language. I was glad when Bernie came and it cracked me up that he brought flowers for Mom and me.

"Oh, Bernie, you're a sweetheart," Mom said.

"Yeah, he's a regular Mr. Romance," Loren said.

"At least he's not a life-size Mr. Potato-Head." I was pretty sure her boyfriend couldn't understand what we were saying. When Mom finally stopped hugging Bernie, he kissed me, and then went into the living room to say hi to Gramma and Annadore.

Mom nudged Loren and said, "See. He's a nice guy."

"He's like everybody else. He wants a piece of Meda's ass. At least he's willing to pay for it."

When Bernie came back, he leaned over me and whispered, "Who's the mouth-breather staring at your breasts?"

That was about the best part of the evening, because while we were eating dinner Mom started in with Bernie about the aliens, since he was the only one willing to talk to her about it.

"The thing that's always worried me is the girls. I've been abducted so many times, and I worry as my girls get older they'll have the same problem, that it won't just be occasional, but that it will be real regular like it is with me."

Bernie looked at me and raised his eyebrow.

The Not Knowing

"I've never been abducted by aliens," Meda said. "And I'd

appreciate it if you didn't go around telling people I was."

"I know it's hard to accept it," Muriel said.

"Bullshit. Never happened."

Meda didn't lose her temper. She shook her head and calmly buttered Annadore's dinner roll. Loren's nameless boyfriend was still spending about half his energy staring at Meda. Loren for once sat quietly, looking down at her plate.

"What about when you woke up on the school grounds and you came home crying and knocking on the door?" Muriel asked.

"I don't remember it like that."

"What about the time the mail man picked the three of you up—"

"We were running away from home." Meda laughed and turned to me to explain. "I was eight, Davy was six, and Loren was two. I think we would have gotten away if the wheel hadn't fallen off the stroller."

"You know that's not how it happened," Muriel said.

"Oh, you were there? We were running away."

"If that's what you have to tell yourself. I was in denial for a long time, but you shouldn't try to confuse Loren. She deserves to know the truth." Muriel looked at me to plead her case, but whatever Loren deserved, it wasn't that. She was crying.

"Leave her alone. Stop filling her head with your bullshit," Meda said, suddenly angry. She grabbed Loren's arm and pulled her away from the table. While they were gone Muriel didn't say anything, so I decided to have a chat with Loren's boyfriend.

"Maybe nobody ever pointed this out to you, but it's really rude to stare at a woman's breasts, especially when her boyfriend is in the same room. Because if I were a certain kind of guy, I would take you outside and kick your ass. Also, you're not winning any points with Loren, staring at her sister like that. Just some friendly advice."

The guy looked at me blankly, his mouth open.

"I try. I try so hard," Muriel said and started crying, too.

When Meda brought Loren back, she took her mother out of the room. I decided I was willing to cry if it would get me a few minutes alone with Meda.

"She's kidding herself if she thinks it isn't real," Loren said.

It shocked the hell out of me, because whatever else I'd thought about Loren, I'd gotten the impression she was hard-wired for skepticism. I felt the same shock that occurs when a particularly worldly acquaintance turns on you and begins to witness that Jesus Christ is the Holy Resurrected Son of God. I had nothing to answer her convictions. All I had were my good manners, which were ill-suited to do battle against alien abduction theory.

Dinner broke up not long after, and Meda walked me out to the car. We sat there for a while, talking about little stuff.

"Could I ask you a favor?" Meda said.

"Anything under the sun."

She smiled and said, "Mom wants me to stay at the hospital with her the night before her surgery, but I don't really want to ask Gramma or Aunt M. to watch Annadore. Everybody's just being so weird."

"You want me to watch Annadore?" I said in disbelief. I wondered if I had radically misjudged how Meda felt about me.

"I thought maybe if your aunt wouldn't mind keeping her for the night..."

"I'm sure she wouldn't mind at all." I was relieved but a little disappointed. I hadn't misjudged Meda's feelings all that much.

"Thanks. I miss you, too." She gave me a quick kiss before she opened the car door. She skipped back up the trailer steps and gave me a little wave from the doorway before going inside.

Driving home from Muriel's, I let myself think of the future. I thought of Annadore at five, at fifteen. It was terrifying, but not so much that I had to stop myself. I wanted to take care of her, to take care of Meda. Once I let myself think of it, I decided I could be happy in Oklahoma, with Meda. Or I could be happy in Kansas City, if she would agree to go back there with me. I just didn't know how to bring up the subject.

After Muriel was checked in at the hospital, Meda handed Annadore to me. She looked nervous.

"It's okay," I said. Annadore apparently agreed with me, because she didn't fuss very much when I buckled her into her car seat. I glanced back to check on her in the rearview mirror, and it must have seemed strange to her, too, because every time I looked back at her, she was looking at me.

I tried not to take it personally that in less than fifteen minutes, Annadore supplanted me as Aunt Ginny's favorite person. After all, I was thirty and my enthusiasm for dolls wasn't what it had been. I got Aunt Ginny's trunk of china dolls out for them, and they spent hours undressing the dolls and posing them and telling stories with them. They passed me the dolls when the fastenings on the clothing were too difficult for my aunt's arthritic hands or Annadore's not yet dexterous fingers. I put my librarian's hands to work buttoning and buckling, zipping, lacing and hooking. Then I undid it and redid it all a dozen times. It was pleasantly hypnotic, dressing and undressing the dolls, listening to the two of them murmuring to each other.

Later they remembered I was there, and Aunt Ginny sent me into the back bedroom for books. It's one of my few skills: I excel at reading upside down so that my audience can see the pictures.

At bedtime, Aunt Ginny enthroned Annadore in the frilly white bedroom that had belonged to my cousin Joan. It saddened me to see that Aunt Ginny still kept the room that way, waiting for a little girl to come stay. Twenty years was a long time to wait.

The next morning, while Muriel was in recovery, Annadore and I went to pick up Meda from the hospital. She looked tired, and when I asked about Muriel's surgery, she shrugged.

"We won't really know much until the biopsy results come back from the lab. The doctor said things looked pretty bad in there, though. He said there was a lot of infection in the left breast." Meda looked away from me while she spoke, so that I was embarrassed for having asked. She looked down at Annadore then, and gasped with dismay at the china doll she was carrying. "Oh, God, she can't have this. What can your aunt be thinking?" Meda tried to take it away from Annadore, who held on tenaciously, biting Meda's hand. "What if she breaks it?"

"She won't." I showed her the knitted socks on the doll's feet that kept them from chipping each other. Annadore took off the doll's bonnet and smoothed out its glossy black hair.

"It's lou, Mama," she said. She had trouble with 'y' words.

"It'll get broke for sure, then." Meda laughed, and let it go.

On our way to Miss Amos' house, we stopped for groceries, and I got a taste of the gossip Meda had complained about. The people in the store watched us too closely, as if they were storing up information for later. In the check out, the cashier said, "How's your mother doing? I heard she was going to have surgery."

"She's fine. The surgery went fine," Meda said stiffly. The cashier went on asking questions while she rang up the groceries, and Meda kept giving short answers. While I paid, Meda turned away, and I saw how the customer and the cashier in the next lane leaned together to whisper to each other.

In the parking lot, Meda held Annadore tightly and said, "Like she cares how Mom is. What a nosy bitch."

Miss Amos greeted us like there had never been a disagreement, and Annadore immediately introduced the doll to her. I joined Meda in the kitchen with the declared intention of helping her cook lunch, but I helped by putting my chair in her path so that each time she passed me, I could touch her. She swatted my hands away, but while lunch was cooking, she knelt down in front of my chair and unfastened my jeans.

It was the act whose image had plagued me from the beginning, the fantasy that had fueled so many wasted mornings and made me so ashamed of myself. As much as I had imagined the act, I had never imagined Meda's actual participation in it. Some girls did, some girls didn't, and some girls didn't have to. Meda was one of those girls—it wasn't necessary—and she did it anyway. I was going toward panic, feeling the world headed for destruction, when she stopped. Looking pleased with herself, she said, "Hold that thought." Then she zipped me back up and went out to the front room to tell her grandmother that lunch was ready. Sitting across the table from Meda, looking at the mobile tranquility of her face, I forgot to eat my lunch until she prompted me.

That evening, we left Annadore with Aunt Ginny again, and took Miss Amos up to visit Muriel, with the understanding that Loren would visit later and bring Miss Amos home. Meda predicted we'd get a phone call at about ten o'clock, because Loren hadn't come. I wondered at how hard it was to change your reputation, because changing yourself was only half the battle and not even the most difficult half. The hard part was convincing the people who knew you that you'd changed.

Muriel looked depleted from the surgery, and when we arrived, her friend Toni was visiting, talking with her about their abductions.

"It's hard sometimes to go to sleep," Muriel said. "I can't help but think they'll be back again. I never know when they'll come. I once was driving at night and woke up in the ditch an hour later. Lucky I didn't kill somebody or myself. The not knowing was hell on my nerves. Cathy, I know you're angry, so you don't even need to say it."

"It's hard trying to live with that. Cathy, you just have to understand what your mother's been through, and not judge her," Toni said.

"You know what? You don't know anything about me, okay?" Meda said. She went out into the hallway, leaving me alone with the other women.

"She thinks I wasn't a good mother," Muriel said. "The drinking makes her mad and the fact that we were always so poor."

"You drank so much, and nothing anyone could say to you would change that," Miss Amos said.

"But I just couldn't hold it all together with what was going on. It was easier to drink until I passed out. If they came then, I didn't know it."

"I know," Toni said. "It takes about everything you've got to keep from losing your mind. My husband used to come home and wonder why the house wasn't cleaned or dinner cooked and I couldn't get him to understand. I get so mad hearing people act like it's a figment of our imaginations."

Rather than hear the rest of it, I excused myself and went out into the hallway to check on Meda.

Excuses

Meda

Bernie came out of Mom's room and frowned at me.

"What's the matter?" he said.

"It's her excuse, whatever part of it's really something happening to her, the rest of it is an excuse for throwing her life away. I'm not going to let her convince me that it's my excuse, too. When you've heard her story as many times as I have, you start seeing how every time there was something she screwed up, it's because of the aliens."

"Just remember that she's not well. Give her a little break."

"I'm giving her a break. I'm not saying this to her, am I?"

"Fair enough. Let's go down to the cafeteria and you can tell me about it down there."

I wanted to claw his eyes out, but I knew he was right, because it wouldn't be good for her to hear me saying that when she was sick. I felt like a radiator, like as much as I wanted to get it out, I wasn't sure how safe it was to take the lid off. I guess he knew, because once we were sitting down, he said, "Okay."

"When she talks about how they come all of a sudden to take her, how she never knows when it's going to happen, that's her excuse for having no control over her life. That's why she didn't pick me up after my eighth grade dance. I had to walk home, by myself, in the dark, wearing my stupid thrift store party dress. That's why she never could hold down a job. That's why we moved all the time. We even lived with Aunt M. for a while, when the State took David away because there was 'insufficient supervision in the home,' which means he got caught playing pool at a bar when he was nine, and we weren't going to school regularly.

"I remember when we were living in a trailer over on West County Road. It was a total dump and we were always about a week away from being kicked out. The landlord would threaten us and yell and then Steve would come up with a hundred bucks or whatever. Steve, he's Loren's father, he was a mechanic, or that's what he said he was. I never saw him go to work. I think most of the money that kept us off the streets came from Steve selling pot."

"That's nice," Bernie said.

Whenever I thought about what his childhood must have been like, I thought of those stupid Richie Rich comics. I knew it wasn't true, and I had to remind myself there were bad things in his life money didn't protect him from. Money had actually caused most of his problems.

"Sometimes when Gramma came over after work, David and I would be watching TV and eating I-don't-know-what. Sometimes we went to the neighbor's trailer and basically begged her for food. We were six and four and we didn't know any better, but it made Gramma so mad, because Muriel was still in bed. Four o'clock in the afternoon. What kind of example does that set for your kids? I know I'm not a great mother, but at least I try. At least I'm making an effort."

"I think you're a good mother," Bernie said. He looked so calm, and so nice, like he really cared. I wanted to believe him. I wanted to believe he was somebody I could trust, that we could make things work out. I almost told him everything right then.

Miss Motherhood Pageant

Meda looked at me like she wanted to say something. She looked, not just at me, but into me, like she was searching for something. I don't know if she found it. Then she sighed and put a hand up to her forehead.

"Everybody tells you it's such hard work raising a baby, but what they don't tell you is that you're going to lie awake at night wondering if you're doing the right thing or if you're screwing her up, ruining her life, without even realizing it."

"Did your mother ruin your life?" I thought I already knew what her answer would be: half agreement, half demurral.

"As close as she could. Didn't she ever just stop and think how all her crazy alien bullshit was going to look to the rest of the world? How they were going to treat her kids because of it? And why did she let Aunt M. put me in all those pageants? For the longest time I didn't know who I was. I thought I was supposed to be the person in those pageants, but I knew there was something wrong with me, because I wasn't this smiling, cheerful little girl. It was a long time before I looked around and saw that nobody's like that, not even the people who are in pageants. They just play at being those people.

"You know how crazy pageant people are? Aunt M. told me the pageant judges could tell if you were a virgin or not, just by looking at you. She said girls who weren't virgins never won. She told me that when I was twelve. I guess she meant well. She was trying to scare me out of ending up like my mother, but for a long time I believed her. I really thought people would be able to tell if I wasn't a virgin."

"Is that why you stopped doing the pageants?"

She stared at me.

I had made a terrible blunder, worse than usual. She might be angry that I had referred to the fact that she had been raped, because we'd never spoken about it in so many words. Maybe she had not thought of that as losing her virginity. Maybe she hadn't been a virgin when she was raped. Maybe she thought I meant something else. I wanted to apologize, but even that was dangerous. What if I apologized for the wrong thing?

"Have you looked at me lately, Bernie?" She put her finger to the scar on her mouth. "That's why I quit doing pageants."

"I forget sometimes." I was a moron. Meda gave me a frown of curiosity.

"You mean, did I stop doing them because I wasn't a virgin anymore?"

I nodded, expecting to get blasted for it. "Well, I never had to find out whether girls who aren't virgins automatically lose, because it wasn't like Aunt M. tried to put me in another pageant after that."

After a few minutes of quiet, Meda said she was ready to go home. She didn't want to go back up to Muriel's room, so I left her downstairs and went back up to say good-bye. I couldn't shake the things my mother told me were polite.

When I went back into Muriel's room, she and Toni were still on the alien topic.

"I mean, obviously there's something about the fact that they took you right before your surgery," Toni was saying. "The doctor didn't find anything during the operation?"

"Obviously they took out the implants, so the doctors wouldn't find them when they do tests on the tissue they took out," Muriel said, and then smiled at me. "Here's Bernie. You know, he's paying for all this. Isn't he the nicest guy ever? Give me a hug." I did, gingerly, worried that I might hurt her. "I know you're doing it because of Meda, honey, but it means a lot to me that you love her so much you want to help me." Muriel held me a little closer, making my back hurt from being bent over her bed. "She's so tight-lipped like my mother, but you do love her, don't you?"

"Yes," I said, even though I was terrified it would get back to Meda.

"Where is she?"

"She's waiting for me downstairs. It's not that she doesn't want to see you, but you know it's not a good subject for her. We'll come back tomorrow. If Loren doesn't show up, call me and I'll come get Miss Amos."

"She just needs to understand there are things in this world that don't fit into some neat little box, things that can't be explained," Toni said.

I patted Muriel on the leg and escaped.

I was beginning to understand that abductees are working toward a linear, literal interpretation of what has happened to them. Muriel and Toni, and maybe all alien abductees, were wrestling with an experience for which they needed to create a tangible description of events, when they weren't entirely sure of what had happened. I understood. They didn't need the narrative to explain the event to themselves. They knew something had happened. They needed to describe the occurrence to other people in a way that didn't sound completely insane. Clearly it was hard to strike a balance.

After I had been in that closet for a few weeks, Amy became more intensely emotional about the situation. Perhaps she finally saw the impossibility of it ending well. I was scared for her, because the other man yelled, "Quit with all that weepy crap. You better knock it off, you little bitch."

Sometimes he took my head in his hands—I wasn't a small boy, but he could hold my skull in his hands—and squeezed it hard, saying, "I could crush your head. I could crush it that easy."

Once when I spoke back to him, some small defiance to prove I wasn't afraid of him, he closed his hand around my throat and squeezed up under my jaw until the world was not merely dark inside my blindfold, but dark inside my eyes. I was scared for the first time.

Until that moment, I hadn't believed I was going to die. I mean, I understood I was going to die eventually. Until he offered to crush my skull, I hadn't believed I was going to die there and then by the hand of a faceless stranger. Later, after he used the bolt cutters on me, he whispered, "I have your soul. God doesn't see you. God doesn't know you're here." I was nine, maybe ten already. I believed him. I believed him more than I had ever believed the priest when he described the unstinting love of Jesus Christ.

At the end, I remember waking up, feeling the shape of someone next to me, and knowing it was Amy. She slept with the stillness of someone drugged or unconscious, but she was warm and comforting. If Amy was there with me, I thought, everything would be okay. Whatever part Amy had in the thing, she had been kind to me. She had stood between violence and me as much as she could. I was sure it had to end soon if she was with me and I wasn't wrong.

I was used to hearing the two men argue, arguments full of the strangely lulling cadences of anger. The last argument was a catastrophic meltdown, where the only words I heard clearly were, "No," "You," "I," and any given expletive. It was one of those fights that destroy your sense of time when heard through a wall. When you're lying in bed at night, listening to neighbors fight, it's the sort of argument that leaves you wondering if you should call 9-1-1.

Amy's boyfriend shouted, "It's no good. It's never going to be any good. You think you can run this, but you can't. I went and I tried, but it's no good." I remember the voice of the other man was darkly calm, impossible to translate.

What I don't remember is being shot: not the sound of it, the sensation, nothing. I don't know if it was what they call fate or the result of a shaky hand, a hand unsettled by fear or haste. A .357 fires bullets at over fourteen-hundred feet per second, and perhaps I was the beneficiary of the fact that, even in the short distance from a man's hand to two sleeping forms on a closet floor, most people are not particularly accurate with handguns. Despite the killing capacity of the .357, its short barrel means that the slightest movement of the hand can radically shift the target area. At such close range, bullets fired from a handgun also tend to exit targets with most of their kinetic energy intact. All four shots fired into that closet were through and through into the floor.

The neighbors had been willing to ignore the sounds of violent arguments, but could not ignore gunfire. The police came and found Amy's boyfriend dead in the kitchen, shot twice in the chest. In the closet, they found Amy and me. They never found the other man at all. Except for the impossibilities of the evidence, he might have been a bogeyman I imagined.

I sympathized with Muriel and Toni, because I was familiar with the difficulties of creating a narrative for something inexplicable. I spent almost a month in the hospital with the FBI hovering over me, waiting for me to tell them something useful. It wasn't their fault; my grandfather rode them like a borrowed horse. I remember him barking, "Get your goddamned sketch artist in here, so he can give you a description."

I couldn't. I couldn't tell them anything. I couldn't get a word out. Even months later when I could talk about it, it was no use. They wanted me to describe the bogeyman, but I'd never seen him. Or if I saw him, I had never allowed myself to know what he looked like. That was its own difficulty, but it was my soul's suspension, my internal reduction, for which I could never properly craft a narrative.

When the police and the FBI had finished with me, the psychiatrists and therapists took over, but I could only offer them the tangible events of the experience. Meticulous details of carpeting and corkboard and angles of light. The mechanics of being shot. I have studied ballistics as a casual observer, just as I have studied what happened in that little suburban house in Tulsa.

When my mother and father tried to get me to talk about it, I couldn't. How could I tell them I'd had my soul taken out and strung like bait on a hook at the end of fishing line, like some allurement to an angry fish god? That was how I started my life as a seafood metaphor. How to tell the truth and not seem crazy? I didn't talk for the longest time, because I didn't trust myself. I wasn't sure what would come out of my mouth. How could I explain that I had been taken out of myself, and make it make sense?

It may seem odd, locked up as I was, that anything could be subtracted. How can you get the gold out of Fort Knox? You can't. It's not a Sherlock Holmes' mystery that features a primate and a chimney. There's no chimney, no windows, not even a door to this room. How do you get the gold out? You don't.

Here's the trick: remove the value of the gold. The soul. Take away its meaning.

When I came home from the hospital, I remember riding in the car with my Aunt Ginny. She left the deathbed of one of her own children to come to me. It was Thomas, her youngest, her last, and she left him to come to me. She let me rest my head in her lap. I don't remember who else rode with us, but only my aunt seemed real to me as she stroked my forehead. I remember the cool pressure of the gold band on the underside of her finger. I captured her hand, held it in my own, against my chest. I toyed with the ring, slipping it this way and that on her finger, and dazzled my eyes by catching the sunlight in the ruby.

She was so alive to me.

CHAPTER EIGHT

BIG NEWS

"THE HALL OF Fame," I said.

For better or for worse, those were the first words out of my mouth when Meda told me she thought she was pregnant.

"I'll know when I go to the clinic. What do you want to do?" She asked it with an air of defeat, and I realized I was in the middle of a conversation she was already having with herself.

"I think that should be up to you." I hoped it sounded diplomatic. For several minutes she sat staring at the floor, her elbows on her knees.

"I'd just like to make one smart decision in my whole life," she said.

"Okay. Why don't we do the most practical thing then?"

"What's that?" It sounded hostile.

"We'll get married." It wasn't very graceful, but I wanted to say it and cut through whatever assumptions she'd been making. Her response was strictly conversational.

"That's your idea of practical?"

"Well, it solves a lot of things like where you'll live and who'll help with the baby. That's practical." I heard myself at fifteen trying to pull my pathetic weight on the debate team. It wasn't so much that it was the most practical idea I had. It was the only one of several that I didn't find repugnant.

"I'm sorry," I said and immediately regretted it. How do you apologize for something like that? Finally she asked what time it was.

"I made an appointment to have a pregnancy test, so I'd have to tell you this morning. I need to go now."

"Okay. I'm ready."

"People are going to find out anyway, but if you go with me, everyone's going to know by the end of the day," she said.

I went.

On the drive, Meda didn't look sad so much as she looked worried, and I recognized the look as one she'd worn for several weeks. Things had been a little uneven for us since Muriel's surgery. Physically, Muriel was better, but the tensions between her and Meda remained. Those tensions seemed to spill over between us, so there was a lot of silence when we were together. I felt stupid for having been so oblivious. I had wondered if Meda was just tired of me.

We went, not to a doctor's office like I'd imagined, but to a small clinic in a shabby concrete block office, next to a bail bondsman. The nurse gave Meda a little plastic cup and sent her into a bathroom. She came back in a few minutes, and sat next to me, holding a magazine on her lap, but not reading it.

"Meda. It's okay, really," I said.

I hoped it was okay, because I was stunned. I wondered what my mother would think; I couldn't help myself. I put my hand on Meda's knee, to remind myself of where I was, to avoid drifting. The way she looked at me, I knew I had been.

When they called her back, I got up to go with her, but the nurse shooed me back to my seat.

"We always counsel the woman first," she said in an undertone. It clinched my impression that I was the villain.

Bryn Greenwood

Knowing

Meda

"I've known for almost a month," I told the nurse. "I don't know why I took so long waiting to have a test done."

"We see plenty of people who are five or six months before they finally have a pregnancy test," she said. At least there was nothing to be embarrassed about with her. Plenty of people stupider than me had passed through her office, including a younger, stupider me.

"I couldn't let myself think about it."

"That's natural, especially if you don't know how you feel about being pregnant."

By the time Mom had her surgery, I'd known I was pregnant, because I missed my period, and started feeling strange all over. I felt like an idiot. The girls' gym teacher always told us it doesn't matter how careful you usually are, if you aren't always careful. At first, I thought about doing something really bad. I thought, well, I can just take care of it and he won't have to know. I knew that wasn't fair to Bernie, but I thought about it all the same. It made me crazy, thinking about what would happen if I had another baby.

I had a little money and I figured I could take a day off and go into the city. Bernie probably wouldn't even ask why I needed the day off, and if I picked a day that was busy for him, he'd loan me his car. That's what I was thinking, and even looking at Annadore didn't make me think differently, because Annadore was Annadore. She was a done deal, but this was a whole new thing. Then I stopped thinking about how badly it was going to screw up my life, and made myself remember how Bernie said he was glad that I had Annadore instead of an abortion.

I tried to straighten myself up before they brought Bernie back, but I'd been crying so much it was pointless. Bernie sat down in the empty chair, looking like he'd been called into the principal's office.

"As I told Meda, the pregnancy results are positive," the nurse said. It was a big relief to me that she told him, because I don't know if I could have. Bernie nodded and seemed pretty calm. "Have you talked at all about what the two of you want to do? About whether you plan to continue the pregnancy?"

Bernie tensed up, but didn't say anything.

"Yeah," I said. "I think that's what you wanted, too, isn't it?"

"Yes," Bernie said. I think he almost said, "Thank you." He reached over and held my hand. I guess it was supposed to be comforting, but it really wasn't.

Midstream

"We'll refer you to an obstetrician to get started with pre-natal care. I'm guessing we don't need to worry about any information on public services?" the nurse said. She knew exactly who I was. Meda was right. There are no secrets in a town that small.

"No," I said.

The nurse gave us a list of doctors and there wasn't much else to say. We were going to have a baby. I looked at my watch. Less than two hours had passed since Meda walked into the study. It was amazing how such a small window of time could radically alter the world. Actually the window was smaller than two hours. The failed mental process that led me to do what I did on the night of the Hall of Fame had probably only taken a few seconds. The world had seemed wonderfully real that night, the way it almost never did. I'd just forgotten how the real world has consequences.

We had no place of our own to go that wouldn't involve seeing other people. Instead we got something to drink and stopped at the empty city park. From where we were, I could see the little path I used to follow on the way home from school.

"I'm turning out just like my mother," Meda said.

"It's not like we're fifteen, Meda. It's not the end of the

world." She didn't answer, so I tried again: "I'm not Travis." She gave me a look with so many layers I couldn't begin to decode them. I was afraid she would cry again. I racked my brain, trying to think of something to make her feel better. "I like Annadore. I'll like having a baby."

"Really? You like Annadore?" I had all of her attention.

"Yes. It'll be okay."

"I guess it'll have to be. I just hate having to tell everyone."

"We can wait to tell people, until after we're married."

I reached for Meda at the same instant she jerked back from me.

"You're serious about getting married? I thought you just said that because you wanted me to have the baby. Are you crazy?"

There was no safe answer. I was serious, but I actually had a medical diagnosis on the other one.

"That's a big thing to do on the spur of the moment," she said.

"I know you don't want to tell people, but you said it yourself, people are going to know. So could we please tell my aunt today? I don't want her to hear it from someone else."

"Sure you can, if you want, but count me out." Meda was convinced my aunt was going to be mad at her, but eventually she gave in.

"That's what they'll put on my headstone," she said. "*She gave in.*"

I didn't laugh, because I wasn't sure she meant it to be funny.

We drove to my aunt's and went through the painful necessity of making small talk until we were settled into the parlor. I tried to relax, to let all of the familiar furniture and filtered light calm me, but Meda was like a brick wall next to me. I had a small, bitter taste then of what it was like being her, when she'd come into the study to talk to me. I took a deep breath, bit the bullet, and told Aunt Ginny. It turned out that my aunt was quite spry for her age, because she leapt up out of her chair and descended on me, fluttering her purple sweater shawl like bat wings.

"Oh, Bernie, sweetheart, oh, that's just wonderful. Oh, how wonderful. Oh, oh, oh!" She practically screamed it, like she'd just won something on a TV game show. Then she swooped onto Meda. I got one brief glance at her face before she was obscured by the fluttering. She looked paralyzed. After hugging and kissing her about a dozen times, Aunt Ginny let Meda up for a breath.

I repented at leisure my own lackluster response to the news.

"Oh, goodness, you've made me so happy. I'm going to be an aunt again! Oh, and Annadore will have a brother or sister—you don't know which yet, do you? Well, when are you getting married? I'll be an aunt again twice, with Annadore. Soon? You are getting married?"

"Yes," I said.

Meda stared at me with something between outrage and what might have been relief, but didn't say anything. I was relieved. I hadn't expected a standing ovation for something that was essentially carelessness.

A Doozy

Meda

Maybe Bernie thought getting married was the practical thing to do, but it scared me. After I got pregnant with Annadore, I wanted to marry Travis. As stupid as I was, I thought we'd get married and live happily ever after. They say you learn something new every day. That was a doozy.

I never knew what to make of Bernie, because I was expecting some long-winded explanation, but he just leaned over to his aunt and said, "Meda's pregnant. We're going to have a baby." Go figure. He's got a hundred words for any simple thing he wants to say, but this one, he doesn't even use up ten of them.

"I think it's totally crazy for you to be talking about getting married like that," I said when his aunt left the room. "When you got up this morning, before you found out I was pregnant, were you thinking about proposing to me?"

"Well, no, which is why I hope you'll forgive me for doing this without a ring." At first I thought he was joking when he got down on his knees in front of me. "Will you marry me?"

I couldn't help myself—it was like my chair was on fire—I jumped up and tried to get away. He surprised me by catching me around the waist and holding me there.

"Meda, please don't be upset," he said. His aunt came back into the room then and saw him on his knees with his hands on my hips.

"Meda?" He really expected me to give him an answer.

"I can't think with you looking at me like that." I didn't care if his aunt heard it all. I felt like I was getting ready to be railroaded. He wasn't the first guy to ask me to marry him, but he was the first guy who'd ever asked me that I really believed. If I said yes, I was going to end up married.

"Bernie, dear, why don't you let us girls have a little time together," his aunt said.

I didn't want to hurt her feelings, but I didn't want to hear what she had to say. I guessed it wouldn't be good, because what does someone like her have to say to someone like me?

"I need to get Annadore," I told them. "I left her with Loren today and she has to go to work at five."

Convincing Meda

Aunt Ginny

Meda looked so upset; of course she needed some time to think.

"Bernie can do that, can't he?" I asked her.

"I can do that."

"Will that be okay, dear?"

Meda nodded slowly, looking as if she wanted to say no. I gave

Bernie a moment to kiss her before I sent him on his way. When I walked him to the door, he gave me a very hard look for such a sweet boy.

"Be nice to her, Aunt Ginny," he said in that wonderful, deep voice he almost never uses.

"Oh, you. You should talk about being nice to her after what you've done. For shame." He blushed when I said it, so I knew he felt badly. After he was gone, I went out to the kitchen and made some tea, to give Meda a few minutes alone to think. We didn't talk at first, simply sat drinking our tea.

"Now, Meda, dear, I don't know a thing about what it's like to be in your situation. Things were very different when I was getting married. So why don't you tell me why you're so upset?" I was confident that if I gave her a chance she would tell me, and she did.

"I don't think it's a good idea to get married because I'm pregnant. Bernie says he wants to, but he's not even thinking about what it would be like being married to me. He says it's the practical thing to do, but there's nothing practical about marrying someone you barely know."

"Are you worried that he doesn't know you or that you don't know him?" I said.

When her eyes met mine, she seemed less upset.

"Both. Sometimes he scares me," she said rather bravely.

"Meda, there's nothing to be scared of. He's a good, good boy. He would never hurt you."

"I don't mean anything like that. I don't think he'd ever hurt me. I'm scared of him for him. He's so depressed sometimes, and he has problems, emotional problems, I guess. He's so easy to hurt," she said.

"He's not made of glass, dear. You know what happened to him, don't you? I assumed you knew about that."

"I know that he was kidnapped, but I don't know what they did to him. Something really bad, I guess. He told me that he's had a lot of therapy."

"He doesn't need therapy. He just needs someone to love him," I said.

I patted her hand and she smiled such a sad smile I felt sure she did love him. I pulled her closer to me, because she seemed like a little girl, like her daughter with her big dark eyes.

"I don't know. He can't sleep when there's someone else in the room. He won't even sleep with me. I mean sleep, not sex." Meda's face got very red and she said, "I'm sorry, Mrs. Raleigh."

"Dear, I'm not his maiden aunt. I assumed, of course, that this was not an immaculate conception. But I did not know that."

"He says his mother doesn't like to see him, because it reminds her he's not perfect, because he got kidnapped, like it was his fault. And he says it like there's nothing wrong with that." She sniffled. With a little urging she put her head on my shoulder and I stroked her hair until she relaxed. Then I began to tell her about what Bernie had been like as a little boy.

"You won't believe me, but he used to love to sing and dance. He was such a silly little boy, well, not that little."

She settled against me more, like I was her very own auntie, and gave a whisper of a laugh. "He still sings in the shower."

"He used to sing everywhere," I said. "But after that terrible thing, something happened inside of him. A great deal of violence was done to him, things he never spoke about. Do you know, they mailed his finger—they cut off his finger and mailed it to us. The sort of person who could do that to a little boy, well, I suppose could do anything. Bernie was very sick in his mind for a long time, even after he'd healed physically. He wanted to hide. He was afraid that man was going to come and take him again."

"But didn't they catch him, the guy who kidnapped Bernie?" Meda said, very deep in her throat.

"Oh, no. No. They didn't catch the third one, the worst of them. For a long time, Bernie was scared to go outside. His grandfather Pen thought that meant he needed to be hidden somewhere safe, so they sent him to that school for his safety. I think also they didn't want to be reminded that they hadn't protected him. Now that I'm an old woman, I'm not afraid to say my husband's family was very wrong-minded about a great number of things.

"They sent him to one specialist after another, trying to get him 'right' again. That was their notion of a cure for his affliction. Not to help him become himself again, but to get him to their idea of normal. They made him into an observer and now he has to learn to live life again."

Meda nodded, but didn't speak. I hoped I hadn't said too much.

The Grapevine

The grapevine went like this: a woman, who was at the clinic to get her birth control pills, called her sister, who called her ex-roommate, who called Rachel's daughter, Stephanie. Stephanie called Rachel, who called Mrs. Trentam, who called Muriel, who called Loren, who was helping me gather up Annadore's stuff when the phone rang. Loren picked it up and said hello. Then she said, "Are you serious? Where did you hear that?" She stared at me, nodding.

"Hang on, Mom." She put the phone down and said, "Bernie, did you get my sister pregnant?"

"Guilty as charged," I said, trying for witty and apologetic.

"Damn!" She picked up the phone. "He says it's true." I had Annadore's shoes on her by then, so I picked her up and started to leave, but Loren said, "Stop right there, you asshole. You're not going anywhere." While Loren was hanging up with her mother, I thought about making my escape, but she looked upset, and I didn't want to leave on that note.

"I'm sorry. I really am, but it's going to be okay," I said.

"No, it isn't going to be okay! It's not fair!" Loren burst into tears. I put Annadore down and stepped into the kitchen, but Loren backed away from me.

"I'm not going to hurt her. I want to marry her."

"She's not going to marry you. She wouldn't even marry Travis and she was in love with him." Loren looked strangely triumphant in the midst of her tears.

"I got the impression Travis was at fault for that," I said.

"Yeah, that's what she wants you to think. That's what she tells everyone, but I was there. He asked her to marry him and she said no."

"I'm sure she had her reasons."

"Yeah, and I'll bet she has her reasons, too, when she doesn't marry you."

"Okay."

I picked up Annadore and left.

Bernie's Idea of Good News

Meda

Bernie and Annadore looked so sweet together when they got back, that I felt better about it. Mrs. Raleigh took Annadore from him and winked at me. "We'll go have a snack and let you two get reacquainted."

After they'd gone out to the kitchen, Bernie said, "Well, I have some good news. If you were worried about having to tell everybody about being pregnant, that's pretty much unnecessary at this point. Your mother called while I was at Loren's and told her, and there's no telling where she heard it."

He came and sat on the couch next to me, so I scooted over and let him put his arm around me.

"What did you and Aunt Ginny talk about?" he said.

"You."

"Is that good or bad?"

"Mostly good," I said to tease him. I tried to get myself ready for what I knew he was going to say next. He gave me a goofy smile and started to kiss me, and then he changed his mind, I guess.

"You know what I'm going to ask you, don't you?"

"You're so romantic."

"The romantic approach worked so well earlier, when you screamed and tried to run away from me," Bernie said, kind of frustrated.

It made me laugh, and Bernie looked relieved. I let him hug me and kiss me until his aunt came back.

Her People Don't Get Married

"Does this mean you've received a satisfactory answer, Bernie?" my aunt asked from the doorway.

"Actually, I haven't gotten any answer out of her." I let Meda up and she made a flustered effort to smooth her hair and straighten her blouse.

"Meda, dear, I'm sure there are several wise maternal things that ought to be said to you at this moment. I don't know what they might be, but I can't possibly think you ought to let him make love to you on my divan without telling him something," Aunt Ginny said. Meda blushed from pink to red and put her hand over her mouth.

She answered me so quietly I had to make her repeat herself. She took her hand away from her mouth and said, "Yes. Okay." It sufficed for me and Aunt Ginny was ecstatic. She hugged and kissed Meda again with all the enthusiasm of her earlier outburst.

"Of course, I knew you would," Aunt Ginny said triumphantly. "My dears, it's only natural to be a little nervous. Now, I think Annadore ought to know."

Because neither Meda nor I had a clue how it ought to be done, Aunt Ginny explained to Annadore that her mother and I were getting married.

"Now, Bernie will be your daddy," she told Annadore, who

stared at her with amazement, as though Aunt Ginny had just performed a magic trick. Then Annadore looked at me quizzically, so I put her up on my lap and hugged her. I had no idea if she even knew what a daddy was, but it was a nice feeling.

"I want to adopt her, you know, if that's possible," I told Meda on the drive home. I wanted to, and I wanted to make Meda happy.

"Okay," she said.

"I wasn't sure if there would be a problem because of Travis."

"Travis isn't even on her birth certificate." She seemed sad, but then she looked at Annadore and smiled.

When we pulled up at Miss Amos' house, Meda stopped me from getting out, and in a rush of anxiety said, "What do you know about being married?"

"As much as anybody does."

"You've never been married, have you?"

"No," I said, "but I don't think you have to know anything special. Lots of people get married without knowing anything about it."

"Well, my people don't get married."

"Your people?"

"You saw us! Like, two people in my family have ever been married. Not my mother. Not my grandmother. Not her mother. My aunt did and it didn't even last a year. And my uncle, that didn't work out either. We don't get married. We've always been Amoses."

"You don't have to stop being an Amos because we get married. I'm not old-fashioned. You should keep your name if you want," I said.

"I don't mean the name." She didn't say what she meant, because she saw her mother standing in the doorway of the house, looking out at us. "Don't come in. Wait here."

She looked so unhappy I didn't argue. Annadore and I waited for her, and whatever blow up there was must have been brief, because in five minutes she came out with a familiar cardboard box.

At my house, Meda was utterly silent on the topic. She talked about other things, but she refused to talk about getting married or even the baby. If I mentioned those things, she stared into space and said nothing until I brought up something else. She wasn't doing it to be cruel; those subjects were simply too much for her at the moment. After a while I gave up trying to talk. I didn't want to piss her off. We were both relieved when Annadore's bedtime rolled around. It allowed us to go to bed and engage in the one mode of intercourse that no longer seemed all that dangerous.

Before we went to sleep, Meda went downstairs to iron her uniform. It seemed silly to me, so I said, "You're not really going to wear that tomorrow, are you?"

"Yes, I'm really going to wear this tomorrow," she said with a glare.

"You know you don't need to."

"Yeah, well, what else am I going to do with myself?"

I wasn't sure how to answer that, or her annoyance, so I kissed her again, and went next door to sleep.

Another Aunt's Love

Meda

I couldn't think of any way to avoid Aunt M. the next morning, except hiding out in some corner of the house, and I couldn't do that for the rest of my life. Instead I decided to bluff my way through it, so I got dressed, made breakfast for Bernie and Annadore, and then started polishing silver. I needed to do something, just to stay busy. Besides, if Bernie got his way, it was going to be my silver soon enough.

"You're five minutes late," I said to tease Aunt M. when she came in, hoping to throw her off balance.

"At least I'm not two months late."

"If you were, I'd congratulate you and Uncle Donald."

"Is that what you want? For me to congratulate you? Congratulations, then, you stupid little shit."

I'd expected her to be mad, but that kind of language was a bad sign. I got the dust mop and the window cleaner and went out to do the front hall before she could say anything else. I took my time, but Aunt M. started in again as soon as I went back to the kitchen.

"Muriel says he asked you to marry him." When I didn't answer fast enough, she said, "Well, is that true?"

"He did."

"And?"

"Why do you care what I said?"

"You always pretend I'm a witch who never cared anything about you. I've spent your whole life trying to look out for you, because your mother certainly couldn't," she said.

"I said yes, okay?"

She sighed. I was trying not to get aggravated with her, but she stood there, shaking her head.

"I can't win with you, can I? What would you do if I'd said no? You'd just sigh and shake your head. What would make you happy?" I said.

"Maybe if you could think about anything you do, instead of acting like a chicken with your head cut off."

"We were being careful. It was an accident."

"So your whole life, and Annadore's life, and this baby's life, they all get decided by an accident," Aunt M. said.

I shrugged. There was no use arguing. That made her even more upset, and she started yelling at me.

"Sleeping with your boss isn't an accident, Cathy. It's stupid. It's worse than stupid. It's sleazy and it's thoughtless. It makes this whole family look bad and it doesn't make the Raleigh family look great either. And it makes you look like exactly what you are."

She was gearing up to go like I hadn't seen since I was a teenager, when Bernie opened the kitchen door.

"Mrs. Trentam. Please don't talk that way to Meda," he said really calmly. "I can hear you down the hallway." Aunt M. didn't say anything and she looked so shocked I started laughing. Bernie smiled then and came over to give me a kiss. "How are you?"

"I'm fine," I said. "How are you?"

"Excellent. I wanted to ask you when you want to do the ceremony. I thought Saturday, in two weeks?"

"I'm sorry, Mr. Raleigh," Aunt M. said.

"It's okay. Would you like to go home, Mrs. Trentam?"

"Are you firing me?"

Bernie gave me a terrified look that was very funny.

"Not at all," he said. "I thought maybe you needed a day off. I know things are a little tense."

"Yes, sir." Nothing like herself.

"Two weeks seems really soon," I said.

"I thought you preferred sooner to later. Three weeks?"

"Yes, sir," I said, but Aunt M. didn't even notice. After Bernie went back to the office, she snapped out of it, but just barely. "You should go home, Aunt M. You look upset."

"I am upset," she said.

I thought she was going to yell at me again. Instead, she went home.

When I took lunch into the office, Bernie jumped up and took the tray away from me. He put it on the side table and said, "I don't want you carrying that anymore."

"I'm fine."

"Is three weeks enough time?" He looked down at his calendar and I got the biggest kick out of seeing that Celeste didn't know what he was talking about.

"Three weeks is fine. It's just my family, you know, and I don't want to do anything big."

"It's literally just my mother and Aunt Ginny on my side of things, and I doubt my mother will come." He put his pen on the Saturday on his calendar and wrote "wedding." Then I guess he remembered that Celeste was there. "Meda and I are getting married."

"Congratulations," she said in a squeaky voice.

"What am I not thinking of that we need to do? Flowers? Cake? A dress?" Bernie clearly had no idea what most people go through to get married.

"I had a nice dress but it got torn up."

"That wasn't a wedding dress. Anyway, I don't want to be involved in shopping for this dress," he said.

"You're not supposed to be," Celeste said. I bet she knew about all the things Bernie was forgetting.

Zombie

After Meda left, I suppose I stood there with a sappy smile on my face. The phone rang and I reflexively picked it up.

"Bernie Raleigh," I said, and got an earful of Lionel Petrie's enthusiasm.

"Great! I caught you in. You must be a very busy man. I hope you won't mind if I drop in on you. I'm headed out to L.A., and I was hoping that before I left, you and I could sit down and chat. Just the two of us," he said in a rush.

As I was about to come out with a reason we couldn't meet, he said, "Oh, here's the turn. I'm coming up the drive now. I'll be there in just a second."

He hung up, and I sat paralyzed, waiting for him to come get me. Lionel Petrie was like a zombie. His overtures toward me weren't quick or graceful, but fiendishly inexorable. If you've ever watched one of those movies, and wondered how the shambling undead manage to catch the athletic co-eds, know that it's the inexorability. Just when I thought Lionel had given up, there he was. Mrs. Trentam let him into the house, and from down the hallway, I heard him enthusing about the "timeless" styling of the house.

Celeste looked up at me expectantly. I said, "It's Lionel Petrie."

"The director?" she said, her eyes lighting up. She did his entrance justice. When Mrs. Trentam showed him into the office, Celeste gushed her fawning admiration all over him. She so desperately wanted to do something for him that she made a sad face when she saw he'd brought his own expensive bottled water. Not with an eye to rewarding Celeste, but intending to thwart Lionel, I didn't send her out of the room. She sat as close as she could to him, her notebook on her lap, waiting for him to speak.

"Bernham—" he said.

"Bernie."

"Bernie, then, good. I just wanted us to talk about this, because I got the feeling you weren't really on board. You don't seem to want to do this."

"Actually, I'm not going to do it."

He blinked hard, took a drink of his water. "I'm really sorry to hear that. I guess I just hoped that there was still a chance. I thought Reg Tveite had talked to you about it."

"He did, but I never agreed to be in a commercial, as any part of my role with Raleigh Industries. My grandfather and father were never in any commercials, and neither was my uncle. I think I'll stick to that."

"Well, let me just—let me just assure you there's nothing to be worried about. I absolutely respect the dignity of the Raleigh family. This isn't gimmick advertising. No gimmicks, no slick clap-trap. No Fred Astaire dancing with a vacuum cleaner," he said.

At least Fred Astaire had the dignity of being dead. I shook my head, but the zombie kept coming.

"You know, it's not going to be what you might think of as acting. It'll just be you talking to me, with a camera there. You don't need to worry about that. Just a conversation really, and we can piece it all together in the editing booth later." He smiled, took two quick swallows of water. Celeste was magnetized. I watched the zombie think, trying to figure out why I didn't want to do the commercial. I decided to throw him a bone.

"I don't want to do the commercial, and when you're as rich as I am, you don't have to do what you don't want to do." I wished that was true.

"Why is it, exactly, that you're so set against this?"

"Right now, I'm practically a nobody. When I go out in public, no one knows who I am. You start appearing on television, and people recognize you. I don't want that. No offense, Lionel, but I'm done here. I have other things to take care of." As a not so subtle hint, I stood up. When that didn't work, I said, "Celeste, if you'd walk Mr. Petrie out."

Disturbed from her reverie, Celeste looked at me for a few moments, then seemed to remember her job. She promptly began chattering about how exciting it was to meet the Lionel Petrie. The zombie looked defeated, but I suspected it was another ploy. The undead playing dead. Standing up, he offered his hand to me. My own hands were slick with sweat, so I kept them in my pockets. It was half an hour before I was calm enough to think about anything productive, and I felt like my little glow of happiness had been doused with a bucket of water.

Later that night, as I was trying to lure Meda to bed, her silence broke open like a dam.

"So, is it just the baby then? Is that why you think you're ready to get married?"

"It's a lot of things," I said, before I realized I didn't have anything to add to that. "How I feel about you. And about Annadore. I'm very happy with you. I like feeling like we're a family."

"Why are you so sure we should get married?"

"Look, I've never been in a situation like this, so I'm trying to figure it out as I go."

"You never even had a girlfriend say, 'I'm late'? Where even for a little while you thought you'd have to make a decision like this?"

I thought long and hard, but couldn't think of even a moment of worry. "The night of the Hall of Fame was the first time I ever had sex without a condom," I said. "Sex makes it too easy to get attached to someone when they don't feel the same way. I was always afraid of things getting complicated."

Meda stared at me in disbelief. She didn't understand. Whatever her fears were, they were not sexual.

"If you were so worried about it before that you never did it without a condom, how come you're so calm about this? I thought you were just really shy. That's why I practically threw myself at you, because I thought you weren't ever going to do anything," Meda said.

That was not the way I remembered it. I remembered being brought to my knees. "I didn't do anything because I was afraid of you."

"Afraid of me?"

"I knew you weren't someone I could just fool around with, that I was going to fall in love with you. I was hoping sex wasn't the scenic route to Hell."

"You're such a liar." She laughed loudly. I couldn't guess what she was trying to cover up with her amusement.

Massachusetts Wedding

When I was about twenty-five my mother suggested I get married. Five years later, when I called to tell her my news, there was an amazed silence on the other end of the phone. After a few stunned seconds she said, "You mean here in Massachusetts? Did that law pass already?" That struck me as the voice of dementia, because I couldn't fathom what she was talking about. Then she said, "Well, who is it? Where did you meet?"

"Her name is Meda Amos. She's the dark-haired girl who

helped out before the funeral." I felt unaccountably nervous about what she would say.

There was another painful silence until, hostile with confusion, my mother blurted, "But you told me that you were, that you weren't that kind of person, to get married."

Five years before, that had been my answer to her suggestion. I didn't think marriage belonged on a to-do list like learning Spanish or climbing Mt. Everest. I wasn't *that* kind of person. I reviewed our conversation, trying to assemble some sense out of it. Slowly it dawned on me that my mother had inferred I was "not that kind of person" by dint of my sexual orientation. I tried not to be disturbed by the fact that my mother had believed I was gay for so long. The idea must not have seemed particularly surprising to her, for it not to spark even one further word of conversation in the intervening years. I wasn't insulted, but I was sunk at the reminder of the distance between us.

We came to an unspoken agreement to pretend it hadn't happened.

"It's so sudden. I didn't even know you were dating anyone," she said.

"We're just going to have a small wedding, nothing elaborate." I decided at the last minute not to mention the catalyst for our nuptials.

"Well, when? Where?" I'd begun to tell her, before I realized it was all part of her usual pattern.

"Bernie, that's awfully short notice," she demurred, either trying to get me to reschedule my wedding or to excuse herself for not coming. When we finally disconnected, I didn't believe she would come. To be fair, she would have been disappointed if she had.

"Don't you think people ought to love each other before they get married?" Meda said.

I was halfway down the front stairs, and I turned to look at her holding Annadore at the top of the stairs. Not two minutes before, she'd been prepared to go to the courthouse to get our marriage license. I'd expected some last minute hesitation, so bowing to that, I came back up enough steps to bring us eye to eye.

"I do love you," I said.

"No, you don't. You're just saying it because you think you need to for us to get married."

"No wonder you thought I was crazy when I asked you to marry me. I never said it before, because I knew you'd run in the opposite direction."

"Oh, that's bullshit." She put Annadore down. It wasn't going to be a simple conversation.

"Do you think I'd go through with this if I didn't love you? Think about how easy it would be for me to write you a check and say, 'Good luck with the baby. Call me if you need more money.'"

"Doesn't it worry you even a little that maybe I don't love you?" she said.

"My own mother doesn't love me. It would hardly be a shocking development if my wife didn't."

It didn't sound as funny as I'd intended it. I thought Meda might yell at me, but I didn't expect her to slap me, which she did.

"Don't you say that! Don't say that!" She nearly punched me then, so I had to defend myself by catching her hands in mine.

"Not in front of Annadore," I said.

The color went out of Meda's face, and she put her hands up to cover her eyes.

"How could you say that? You could have just asked me. A normal person, a normal person would have just said, 'Well, do you love me?'" It was all she could say. She couldn't even look at me.

After a couple of minutes, I picked up Annadore. I settled her in her room with a variety of toys, and put the baby gate in place. Then I came back to get Meda off the stairs. She'd calmed down some, but there was no way we were going to the courthouse.

What a Normal Person Would Have Said

Meda

"It was a joke," Bernie said.

"Don't try to pretend you were joking, because you weren't."

Right then I saw how his craziness could grow on me, like my mother's. I saw how it would be if I got used to being with someone who didn't care at all about anything, who didn't even care about something like that. He never even complained about my slapping him and there was the mark on his cheek.

"Maybe I wasn't sure I wanted to know the answer," he said.

"Why in the world would you want to marry me if you didn't think I loved you?"

"Well, do you?"

"Yes." It needed to be said. I did love him. I didn't know if I loved him enough.

In spite of all that, he smiled at me and said, "That wasn't so hard, was it?" I didn't deserve for him to be so nice to me, but he walked me back upstairs and sat me down on his bed. He held out his closed hands. "Old or new?"

"New?" I wondered what I was committing to. He opened his hand and offered me a jewelry box.

"It's just a ring. Don't be afraid, Baby Girl Amos," he said.

I picked the one on the left. The rock was so big it almost blinded me.

"I hope this is a joke." I felt like such a bitch. "It's not that I don't like it, but it's huge. Do I get to see the other one or am I stuck with what I picked?" The other one was pretty, and also smaller.

"It was my grandmother's engagement ring. But I didn't want you to think you were just going to get stuck with her old stuff, so I thought I'd give you a choice. If you want a new one, but you don't like the one I picked out, you can have whatever kind of ring you want."

That scared me. I could have as big a diamond as I wanted. I remembered how he'd said he could give me twenty million dollars and never miss it. It was the sort of thing that made it hard to sleep at night.

"Why don't you keep them both for now and you can think about it." He gave me both ring boxes. When he kissed me I was mostly relieved, because I thought if I sidetracked him with sex, we'd never end up at the courthouse.

Pride

"Loren said you wouldn't marry me. That you refused to marry Travis, even though you loved him," I said.

Meda tensed up all along me, her hands clenched into fists against my chest.

"When you're in bed with a girl, it's not polite to talk about her ex-boyfriend."

"Come on, Meda. You always made it seem like Travis was the one who didn't want to get married, but Loren said you were against it. I was wondering if there's something you're not telling me."

"You're the one with all the secrets." I thought that was all she planned to say, but when I started kissing her again, she pushed me away.

"I was willing to marry him the first dozen times he suggested it. But after he changed his mind so many times, I—I had to have a little pride. He kept breaking it off and crawling back and breaking it off. So I did the one thing I could do and the next time, I said no. That's what Loren remembers. She doesn't remember all the times I said yes. She thinks it was my fault, but would you want to marry someone who changed his mind ten times? Oh, hell, it was more like twenty or thirty times. It was so many times I don't remember."

"You don't have to defend yourself to me."

"Yes, I do," Meda said with vehemence.

We got all of fifteen minutes, before we were interrupted by the sound of Annadore crying. Meda got up, resplendently naked, and went to check on Annadore. She came back and stood in the doorway, looking like a nature goddess with her child on her hip.

"What did you mean when you said you doubted your mother would come?" Meda said. "You think your mother won't come to your wedding?"

"She isn't coming. She called me yesterday and said it wasn't possible on such short notice."

"That's fucked up." She glanced at Annadore and blushed.

"Don't take it personally. It's not because of you. It's me."

"That's what makes it so messed up."

"But it's how things are. I can't change my mother and I don't think it's fair to blame me for my relationship with her. I try. I really do," I said, gritting my teeth.

"I wasn't blaming you."

I couldn't get Meda's acquiescence in so many words, but it was in her look.

Unknown

Meda

The clerk in the marriage license office was about Loren's age and she immediately started in asking all kinds of questions: the bride's full name, birthday, birthplace, the bride's mother's name and birthplace, the bride's father's name and birthplace. Bernie answered most of the questions for me, but he cleared his throat when she asked that, so I just said, "Unknown."

The clerk thought about that one for a while. Then she started over: groom's full name, birthday, birthplace, groom's mother's name and birthplace, groom's father's name and birthplace, and that was when I realized I couldn't breathe.

I heard Bernie say, "Meda, are you okay? Why don't you sit down here? Meda?"

"Is she a little nervous? You know sometimes people have panic attacks," the clerk said.

I'd never had a panic attack before, so I didn't know if that's what it was. I couldn't stop thinking about what it would mean to be married, how I'd be tangled up with Bernie and he would be tangled up with me, and how I still didn't know half of what I needed to know about him, and how much I wasn't like his kind of people. I was never going to be like his mother or his aunt, and all the money in the world wasn't going to make me like them. I was always going to be this person who barely graduated high school and got a job at a motel and got pregnant and had a baby with some loser, and had a crazy mother, and was never going to be the kind of wife that would make him happy and fit in with the people he knew, and it would be so easy for him to start hating me. It scared me so much I couldn't feel my hands and feet and then I guess I fainted.

CHAPTER NINE

COLD FEET

I TOLD MYSELF that Meda just had cold feet, but Meda's cold feet would have caused frostbite on a lesser woman. She was completely silent on the drive back from the courthouse. Our copy of the marriage license application lay on the seat between us, but in three days we would have an actual license. We'd left Annadore with Miss Amos for the day, so we had to go back to her house. If it had been up to Meda, I don't think she would have let me into the house when we got there, but she simply didn't know how to get rid of me. I helped her off with her coat and followed her into the kitchen. I knew she was rattled, because she didn't even make tea. She made a mug of hot water and left the tea bag on the counter. What word described my mental state I didn't know. Witnessing the scope of Meda's terror had a sobering effect on me. Until then, I hadn't really considered how little Meda might want to be chained to me for life.

"I don't think I can do this," she said. It wasn't an argument. It wasn't part of any argument we'd had. There was no counterargument for it. "I'm not ready to do this. I can't marry you, not now, maybe not ever. I have to think and I can't do it with you waiting. Can you leave me alone and let me think?"

I went home and tried to work, but everything Celeste said

got on my nerves and I wasn't sure how long I could maintain a façade of politeness. I gave it up after a while and, claiming a headache, went to bed at two o'clock in the afternoon. When the alarm went off the next morning, I hadn't even fallen asleep. I'd lain there for close to eighteen hours, staring up at the ceiling. The world was thoughtlessly white and loud all day, so that twice I snapped at Celeste to be quiet and she looked at me like I was an ogre. I felt like an ogre, shouting, "Would you shut up for ten minutes?" Thankfully, she did.

When I heard Meda's voice in the foyer I thought I was imagining it, but when I got up and looked out the study door, she was standing at the foot of the stairs talking to her aunt. Mrs. Trentam turned away while Meda shook her head at me.

"Please, don't, Bernie," she said.

She came to work the next day and the day after, and although I saw her, heard her, and could have spoken to her, she told me with a look that I was forbidden. It was worse than her actual absence, like living with a ghost. Once I encountered the fading smell of her shampoo in the foyer outside the study, and knew she must have passed there a moment or two before me. The situation was not one of ludicrous absolutes. When FedEx delivered a bundle of documents, Meda brought it into the study and asked where I wanted it. I took it from her and thanked her.

At night, I drove to avoid sleep. I drove by Meda's house a lot, taking comfort from the light slipping out through gaps in the curtains.

Celeste and I did what needed to be done for the creation of the foundation, and waded through the innumerable legal mysteries that had piled up in my grandfather's eighty-odd years. I found excuses to ask Meda about things around the house. Occasionally I butted my head against the wall and asked her about getting married, always with similar results: "I can't talk about that. Please don't ask me that. If you have to have an answer right now it's no." Or some permutation of those responses. If I had to guess, I would say she was so firm in refusing to give an answer because of her experience with Travis. She didn't want to say yes and go back on it. Or she just didn't know. I was out of the business of trying to guess what she was thinking. It was straight to Hell and no scenic route.

The Joys of Motherhood

Aunt Ginny

I offered Bernie a drink, some tea I thought, but he came back from the kitchen with an old bottle of Alan's bourbon and a glass with ice. He'd come from some big, important meeting in the city, about a commercial, he said.

"For Raleigh Industries?"

"Yeah," he said.

"Are you going to be in it?"

"Yeah. If you see my spine lying around somewhere, would you let me know?"

"What does that mean?" I supposed it meant he hadn't stood up for himself.

"I don't want to talk about it."

By my count, Bernie had three large drinks in less than an hour. He was wearing a suit when he arrived, but over the course of the hour, he shed his jacket, his tie and his dress shirt, so that he cut quite a picture of dissolution in his undershirt and suit pants with his drink balanced on his knee. I wanted to bring it to his attention, but I decided to ask first about Meda and his cancelled wedding. He didn't want to talk about that, either.

"Sweetie, what am I supposed to think? A month ago you were getting married, and then last week, you tell me you're not. I think you should tell me something."

"It's complicated."

"It can't be that complicated. I'm rather sharp for an old lady."

I said it to tease him, but he wouldn't even smile.

"I'm not smart enough to figure it out." He poured himself another drink.

"Now, Bernie. Ask yourself if you're doing the best thing to solve this problem. Meda deserves better than you sitting there getting drunk."

He sat up straight and put his glass on the table, so that for a moment I thought we might get somewhere. All I accomplished, however, was to make him cry. The poor dear put his head in his hands and cried, as one rarely sees a grown man cry. It was in surprising contrast to my memory of him only five years before, sitting in that same spot after Alan's funeral. I wouldn't have called him a grown man then. As terrible as I'd been to him, he let me put my arms around him and comfort him.

"I'm sorry. I shouldn't have come here," he said.

"You did exactly the right thing in coming to me. You've had a bit too much to drink and need a rest."

He ended up sleeping on my divan and I fetched a pillow and a quilt to make him comfortable. I was quite surprised at myself. I had always assumed the things I was missing most in motherhood were the happy moments.

Good Luck with the Baby

Meda

All those weeks, I was waiting for some kind of romance novel revelation, where I'd go, "God, I can't live without him," but it wasn't happening. If it didn't happen, was marrying Bernie the wrong thing to do?

Part of me couldn't help wondering what it would be like not having to worry about money anymore, and that made me feel guilty. Marrying him because of the money seemed as bad as getting an abortion without ever telling him I was pregnant. Then there was what the money had done to him. It was like he'd been t-boned. He was driving along, being a librarian, with his own life, and then there was the money. I didn't want that to happen to me. Hell, I didn't have half a clue what I was going to do with my life, but I couldn't see how I was going to get one if I woke up and had a pile of money.

There were a lot of nice things about Bernie, but he was like quicksand. He had all these things going on inside of him, and he was different people sometimes. I felt like I didn't know anything about him, especially after seeing him come home at ten in the morning, looking and smelling hung-over. I guess it was better than him lying in bed all day being depressed. I worried he would do that again. I worried he would do something worse. I kept thinking about what he'd done when he was younger, taking all those pills. I worried, but Bernie kept getting up and doing his work. He kept being too thin and a little near-sighted, and growling at Celeste, and slumping off to meetings in his two different suits, and giving me his sad dog smile. Thinking about all of that, I almost didn't answer the door when I looked out and saw the Cadillac parked on Gramma's front yard. I didn't want to, but I let him in and took him to the kitchen, so we could talk in private.

"I'm not here to harass you, but I wanted to make sure everything was okay," he said.

"Everything's fine." I wanted to keep his visit short.

"Don't."

"Don't what?"

"Don't do whatever you think about doing here in the next ten seconds. Please." He reached into his coat pocket and took out an envelope and put it on the kitchen table in front of me. I guessed what it was before I opened it, but I didn't guess how much it would be. It was about half an inch thick and it was all hundreds.

"I don't need this kind of money."

"Well, you have doctor visits to pay for and you need other things. I mean I don't know what you need, but I want to take care of it."

"Is this the part where you say, 'Good luck with the baby. Call me if you need more money'?" He frowned at me, so I said, "I'm not, I'm not."

"You don't seem to want anything else from me, so good luck with the baby."

"Can I ask why it's cash, a lot of cash?" I saw I wasn't going to be able not to accept it.

"It's easy to tear up a check or never deposit it. You might actually spend the cash on things you need."

"There's something I want to give you, too," I said.

I went into my bedroom and brought back the box with his grandmother's necklace and earrings in it. He shook his head and wouldn't take it.

"That was a gift."

"It was a crazy gift. It must be worth a lot."

"I'd have to ask the insurance company to be sure, but I guess a couple hundred thousand," he said, like it was a couple hundred dollars.

"It can't be safe in my underwear drawer."

I swear he put his hand on the box then, knowing it had been next to my panties. He opened the box and the necklace shot out all these sparks of light around his hands. It was beautiful, but it wasn't anything I wanted to be responsible for. That was what I told him.

"It's yours now." He turned it around and pushed it across the table to me. I just wanted it out of my house, I thought, except that it was so beautiful. I hadn't looked at it in a month and I'd forgotten how incredible it was. "I never met a woman who didn't like jewelry. Almost every girl I've ever dated would have traded her right arm for that."

"You should keep it in case your wife wants it. She can trade her right arm for it." I didn't want to be mean, but wanted him to go away.

"Is that your way of saying you won't ever be my wife?"

"I can't do that conversation. I'm just saying you ought to hold onto it until you know for sure."

"You're right." As soon as he snapped the box shut I was sorry. I couldn't even believe he'd given me something like that. He stood up and said, "My aunt wants to send some birthday presents for Annadore. She asked me to find out what size she wears."

"She's a 3T."

"Can you write that down for me? And her shoes?"

"Sure."

While I was in the front room looking for a pen, he said, "I guess since you're not ready to have that conversation, I'm still not allowed to talk to you."

"You can talk to me, it's that you can't talk to me about that." I wanted to explain better, but I knew it would just be another argument.

That must have been all he wanted to talk about, because he left after I handed him the piece of paper with Annadore's sizes on it.

After Annadore woke up from her nap, I went into the kitchen to fix her a snack. The east wall, the ceiling, and the tops of the cupboards were scattered with little dots of light. Bernie had left the necklace box sitting open on the drain board, and hung the necklace on the latch of the sink window, where the evening sun came in.

"Pretty, pretty," Annadore said, trying to catch the sparkles on the wall.

As bad as he was, Bernie was better about it than my family. Gramma went around muttering about how I was going to end up in a 'bad way.' Then Aunt M. brought Mom and Loren over with her, and they started in on me.

"You know, my mother still thinks of Mr. Raleigh as a teenager, when he was so shy and awkward. She thinks Meda took advantage of him," Aunt M. said.

"Mary Beth, that's not fair," Mom said.

"I'm not saying that's what I think. He's a grown man and he should have kept his pants on, but Mama thinks it's Meda's fault. Before you get mad at me, Meda, you've gotten yourself into plenty of trouble all by yourself, and you know I don't mean what those boys did."

I knew all about what Aunt Bryant had to say about that: *What can you expect when you dress and act like that? A girl can bring that kind of thing on herself.*

"I hope you get your money out of him." Gramma was still stuck on Mr. Gertisson.

"I hope you get enough money for all of us," Loren said. "Crap, I'd marry him. He can't be that bad."

"I thought you didn't like him," I said.

"I don't, but who gives a fuck? You don't have to like someone who has that much money. You think Anna Nicole Smith really liked that old fart she married? Don't be stupid, Meda."

"I'm not being stupid. I'm trying to be decent."

"Well, what are you going to do?" Mom said.

"I'm just going to keep doing what I'm doing."

"I don't know about that," Aunt M. said. "Mr. Raleigh asked me about you working. I told him I didn't think you ought to be doing that kind of work while you're pregnant."

"You should mind your own business," I said. Aunt M. glared at me really hard.

"I suppose it is my business when he asks me about it. I know you did work right up until you had Annadore, but then you didn't have anybody to take care of you, either. Mr. Raleigh told me I should hire extra help, because he doesn't want you working."

"I don't suppose she needs to work, does she?" Mom said.

"No, he's perfectly willing to take care of her. If she had any sense she would have married him as soon as he asked her."

"I guessed that was the last thing you and Aunt Bryant wanted. You didn't want me involved with him."

"That was before. Now, at least there'd be some decency to it.

You said you were trying to be decent. That would be the decent thing to do," Aunt M. said.

"If he wants to marry you, why don't you?" Mom said.

"She's her own kind of fool, Muriel."

"I saw how well it worked out with you and Uncle Ari," I said. They were married for all of two years.

"Oh, good grief. What happened with Ari and me has nothing to do with your situation. I was crazy to marry Ari. You're crazy not to marry Mr. Raleigh."

"Why? Because he's rich?"

I already knew the answer. Aunt M. shrugged. Mom nodded. Loren glared at me. I couldn't trust any of them to tell me what was the right thing to do.

Annadore's birthday party

I hated having to ask Mrs. Trentam about Meda's working conditions, but I was scared to talk to Meda about it. I wanted to tell Meda she didn't need to come to work anymore. I was willing to share everything I owned with her, so it was utterly absurd for her to be "working" for me. Honestly, I was afraid I'd never see her again if I told her that. I was counting on that Midwestern work ethic to keep her in my life. As long as she was still on the payroll, she would keep showing up. Also, I couldn't forget the conversation we'd had when I first asked her out. I'd promised her I wouldn't fire her, and short of doing that, there didn't seem to be any way to keep her from coming to work. Meda did what she wanted, including inviting my aunt to Annadore's birthday party.

Aunt Ginny showed me the invitation, and it gave me a melancholy pleasure to see Meda's handwriting. It was made of perfectly rounded cursive letters, almost like a teenaged girl's, except that she didn't dot her i's with hearts or smiley faces.

"She didn't invite me," I said.

"I believe it's implied that you would be welcome."

I didn't believe Meda was implying any such thing. I hadn't made any more visits to her, nor had I repeated my drunk at Aunt Ginny's house. More troubling, I wasn't exactly sure what I did when I wasn't working under Celeste's watchful eye. Ironically, the thing that had initially made me wretched had turned into the one tangible part of my existence. The money that had seemed like a curse was finally coming to life in the foundation. My original idea had blossomed in a half-dozen different directions.

For the most part, I looked at Meda's family and asked myself, what did they need? From there, I extrapolated what any other group of women needed. Muriel needed health care, so I imagined clinics and insurance subsidies. Loren needed an education, so I started thinking about scholarships. Meda had talked about how Rachel wanted to start a business, so I wrote up ideas for a program to provide small business loans to low-income women. It was funny, but I thought even Pen would have approved of that. It wasn't really charity. It was a capital investment risk.

I didn't know how Meda would have felt about me using her family as a template, but I felt like I was doing something useful. When I was working on the foundation, I was aware of what I was doing. My first major task was to choose a Board of Directors and prepare an agenda for the first meeting of the board, so that was what I put myself into eight hours a day. Sometimes it was the only real thing, and I got caught daydreaming about it when I was supposed to be doing other things.

Aunt Ginny patted me on the leg and said, "At any rate, I won't go to the party, if you don't think I should."

"I think you should go."

"No, I think it might be uncomfortable without you."

She insisted on her point, so that eventually she allowed me to concede that we would go a little before the party and deliver Annadore's gifts, but we wouldn't stay.

Choosing Your Relatives

Meda

If you could choose your relatives, everybody would have an aunt like Mrs. Raleigh. She showed up in a fur coat with a pile of packages, and gave me a little wave when I opened the door. I helped her get the packages inside and started to take her coat, but she shook her head.

"Oh, I'm not staying, dear. I just wanted to drop off some presents." She looked back over her shoulder, so I thought she wasn't going to stay because of Mr. Grabling.

I was about to tell her that Ron was more than welcome to join us, when I looked out the screen door and saw who her driver was. There was Bernie, all six feet and however many lied about inches of him slouched up against his aunt's car.

"Oh, no, sweetie. We just wanted to get a few things for Annadore. We don't want to impose." She was still going to give me a chance to get out of it. Her manners were so good I didn't wonder how Bernie could have grown up to be so polite about sex. I guess when you're raised that way, you're polite about everything. "Give the birthday girl a kiss for me, Meda." She gave me hug and a kiss.

"At least stay and see her," I said.

I hated to see her leave that way, and she let me take her into the kitchen where Annadore was coloring. She was only planning on spending a few minutes, but she got to playing with Annadore, and after a while she took off her coat. I went to straighten up the front room, and when I went back in the kitchen, Mrs. Raleigh looked surprised and picked up her coat.

"I forgot all about Bernie! I'd better go, dear."

"It's okay. I'll ask him to come in." I was pretty sure she'd tricked me.

When I went to the door, he was still leaning up against the car. It wasn't a really cold day, but it was cold enough he shouldn't have been standing outside. When he saw me, he looked at me with love, I guess. It scared me to see how he had his heart in his eyes. He didn't even give me a chance to say anything.

"She said she wasn't going to stay, but I knew she'd want to. When should I come back for her?" He opened the car door and started to get in, so I knew whatever his aunt's trick was, he wasn't playing along with it.

"We should be done by five," I said, wondering whether there was any way I could say something else and not have him misunderstand it. He nodded and closed the door.

Chutes & Ladders

When I came back at five, the party was still going on, so I had to wait a while before Meda came and answered the door.

"Chutes & Ladders," she said when she saw me.

"There's no hurry. I'll wait in the car for her."

"Oh, Bernie, come in and see Annadore."

That convinced me. She wouldn't have mentioned Annadore if she wanted me to say no. In the living room, Annadore, Aunt Ginny, Muriel and Miss Amos were gathered around the game on the coffee table. Annadore gave me a hug and kiss, but couldn't be taken away from her game. The reactions of Muriel and Miss Amos were harder to read. They both said hello, but not much else.

"You want some cake? At least this year she didn't destroy it," Meda said. In the kitchen, she cut me a piece and gestured for me to sit down.

Before either of us could speak, Muriel came into the kitchen and whispered, "I need to talk to you, Bernie." I let her take me out into the hallway, thinking she was going to give me some sort of maternal rebuke. She clutched my arm, looking past me to be sure no one else was coming down the hallway. "We need to talk about what my abductions might mean for your and Meda's baby. You know about hereditary abductions?"

"I'm not really familiar with that, Muriel." I didn't want to have the conversation, but didn't know how to get out of it.

"Nobody wants to admit it, but our government made a deal with the devil. Before we got the bomb, the government made a deal with the Grays. In exchange for some technology we needed, they gave the Grays the okay to experiment on certain families. That's why they're called hereditary abductions, because multiple family members, over several generations, are being used in the experiments.

"My mother's mother had what she always called 'blank spells' where she'd disappear and come back and not know where she'd been. At the time they thought she was sleepwalking or blacking out. Some people think the Grays are—are developing a new race. I don't know about that." Muriel stopped with her nervous clutching once she'd got that all out, and started patting me reassuringly. "I don't want to scare you, Bernie. I just wanted to warn you there's a chance Meda's baby might be part of that genetic group that the Grays are studying,"

Great, my baby might be an alien-bred super-mutant. Just what I needed. I stood there with my mouth hanging open, before I managed to say, "That's okay, Muriel. It's better to know these things, better to be prepared."

"Well, sure, they say knowing is half the battle." Muriel smiled brightly, but there was real fear in her eyes.

When I went back to the kitchen, Loren had come in from somewhere and was sitting at the table with Meda. I sat down and took a bite of my cake.

"You know, most people don't invite their stalkers over for birthday cake," Loren said.

"He's not a stalker," Meda said.

That surprised me. I felt like a stalker.

"You broke up with him and he still comes around and calls you and invites himself over. How is that not stalking you? Now you let him stalk you in your own house."

"It's more convenient that way," I said. "Otherwise, you never know where the stalker will show up."

"Did Mom want to tell you about my alien genes?" Meda asked.

"Mmmm. This is good." I took another bite of cake to avoid answering.

"Don't encourage her."

"I'm not. I'm just trying to be nice."

"Why are you here?" Loren said.

"Because your sister invited me in. I'm like a vampire that way."

"I never liked you."

"I liked you until you started being so mean to me," I said. Meda snickered. "What have you got against me, Loren?"

"You're not treating my sister right. Look at how she's living. And making her clean your house."

"Shut up," Meda murmured.

"Loren, I don't owe you an explanation, but I'll give you one and then you can owe me. I'd marry her today and she doesn't have to work if she doesn't want to. I'll write her a check right now for any sum of money you care to name."

"A million dollars," Loren said. She thought I wouldn't do it.

"That seems awfully modest."

I took out my checkbook and wrote a check to Meda Amos for $20 million, the amount we'd once joked about. I wrote, "I love you" in the memo and tore the check out. It would have required a few phone calls to make that particular check clear the bank, but I was good for it. I showed Loren the check before handing it across the table to Meda. "Now, what have you got against me?"

"You're stupider than I thought you were." Loren stood up and walked out. Meda cracked up laughing.

She was still giggling when she said, "I love to see you get her. '*Well, her boobs are big.*'"

"I miss you," I said. She held the check out to me. "Oh, keep it. Put it in the bank for a rainy day."

When I wouldn't take it, she tore it in half and put the two halves on my cake plate. I guessed there were easily several thousand women in America who would have married me sight-unseen for my money. She wasn't one of them.

"Checks *are* easy to tear up," she observed. She started laughing again. "That's quite a love letter, Bernie."

"Here's another one." I reached for my wallet and she protested at whatever she thought I was going to do. I took out the marriage license I'd been hauling around and handed it to her. She frowned when she saw what it was.

"Don't think just because I'm happy to see you that I want to marry you."

"That would never occur to me," I said, trying not to be glib. She refolded the license to put it in her pocket. I hated to see it go, but she didn't offer to give it back to me.

She surprised me by saying, "Do you want to come over after the party to talk?"

Two Stalkers

Meda

It was late when Bernie came back, so I said, "Why don't you put Annadore to bed?"

"She'd probably rather have you." He frowned like he was thinking about saying something else.

Since he'd asked about adopting her when he first proposed, I didn't want to talk to him about his relationship to Annadore. I said, "Put her to bed. You need to know how to help with the baby."

He picked her up then and took her into her room. For a while I heard him reading her a story, but I got worried when it had been twenty minutes and he hadn't come back. When I went into her room, he was sitting on the floor with his hand on her chest.

"You can leave her now. She's down for the count," I said.

Bernie nodded, but he didn't budge, until I took his hand and made him get up. I'd intended to lead him back to the front room, but between Annadore's room and there, he kissed me and we ended up in my bedroom.

I wasn't going to help him out the way I had the first time, so it took him a long time to get around to anything but kissing until he asked, "Is it okay if we have sex? I wasn't sure if you wanted to."

So instead of just letting it happen, he made me agree to it. I was sort of nervous, but he was like always, gentle and intense, but sad. It was so good to be with him that I didn't even let myself think about what was going on in his head.

Afterwards, he pressed his ear to my belly like he was listening for the baby. I didn't have the heart to tell him it was too early.

"Are you really going to let me help with the baby?" he said.

I'd been worried he was going to ask something else, so I was relieved, but it made me think about all the guys in the world who, if they were as rich as him, would have done whatever they liked. That scared me, because I knew he had enough money to hire enough lawyers to get custody of the baby, and part of me regretted tearing up that check. He might not always be that nice.

"It's your baby, too," I said. "If Travis had been even remotely interested, I would have let him do stuff with Annadore, too."

"Then you'd have two stalkers," he said.

"I don't think so. I wouldn't let him…"

"What? Have sex? Thanks. I'm flattered."

"I meant that you and I—look, I didn't mean for this to happen. I really did ask you back here to talk." It was so stupid to be having sex with him. I wanted to tell him how it was that things were different, that I still liked him, that I did care about him. When we talked, he actually made an effort to understand me. Travis never even tried.

"Okay, so talk," he said.

"I just thought we should talk about what we should do when the baby comes."

"You know what I want to do."

"So, if I won't talk about that, you're just not going to talk about anything practical?"

"I promise I'm not trying to harass you about this, but if you would tell me why you don't want to marry me, I'm willing to work on it. Fuck it, I'll go back to therapy if you want."

"Because I don't know if I'll like being married." It was the easiest answer because it didn't involve things he probably couldn't change. That was where he was after ten years of therapy.

"Your people know how to get divorced, don't they? If you didn't like it, you could always divorce me."

It was like I had a broken toe and, after all that time trying to keep it from getting hurt again, Bernie stepped right on it. Before I could stop myself, it all came out.

"I can't marry you because you—you—you are so messed up. I can't deal with that, with you being so messed up and so depressed. And that you don't care about anything and that awful smiling dog look of yours. You can't even sleep with me and I'm not spending the next fifty years sleeping in a different bedroom. I can't stand the idea of waiting around for you to go off, always worrying that something I say is going to upset you. Wondering if maybe someday you're going to kill yourself. I don't even know the half of what's wrong with you. And besides all of your problems, I'm not ever going to be your mother or your aunt.

"Look at my grandmother and my mother, that's what you're going to wake up married to someday, if you marry me. And I don't want to wake up married to your grandfather. For the record, you sound like him. I worked a couple of summers ago for Aunt Bryant and met him, and when you're in there yelling at Celeste, you sound just like him. And it won't work. I'm tired of having to be the only practical one here. Have some sense."

When I stopped, Bernie got up and put his clothes on. I wanted to take it back, but I couldn't make myself. Just because it was mean didn't stop it from being true.

"I thought you were going to tell me to have some pride," he said.

"But you don't."

"No, I don't. I...never mind, I can't remember what I was going to say anyway. If you need anything while I'm gone, ask Celeste."

"Bernie, are you okay?" I couldn't help thinking about him going home and being alone.

"You don't have to worry about me trying to kill myself again. I guess my aunt told you about that. It was a long time ago, but I understand. You do something like that and nobody ever lets you forget." He didn't seem upset anymore, just done.

Bernie Gets It

After my less-than-stellar performance at the shareholder's meeting, I went to Pennsylvania to tour a rural, low-income clinic that was recommended to me as a model of what I wanted the Raleigh Foundation to do. I deputized Celeste to take care of things for me while I was gone. After Pennsylvania, I had a stop in New York, and as a result I was going to visit my mother, because of the supposed proximity of Boston. It was a mutual bluff gone awry. When Celeste was making travel arrangements, I expected my mother to back down, and she expected me to back down.

The visit to the clinic was fruitful, at least for the lawyers, accountants, and prospective board members I took with me. I spent most of the trip trying to reconcile the two feelings I had about Meda in my head. On the one hand, I loved her. I wanted to marry her, as far as I understood why most people get married. I wanted to be with her, live with her, raise children with her. On the other hand, and this was not a polar opposite of feeling, I was afraid of the power she had over me. When she was done detailing all my failures as a human being, I thought she easily could have snapped me in two. I had dated other girls who liked to exert a little power, but I'd always been fairly sure I was going to walk away from the experience. I didn't have that confidence with Meda. If she decided to break me, she would.

It wasn't anything as paltry as her beauty. It was that I loved her and she was that headstrong. Would she have been so headstrong without the grace of her physical appearance? There was no way to know. Would I have loved her? It depended entirely on how interrelated the two things were. If her strength was formed by her beauty, I loved her because she was beautiful. If her will was something altogether separate, she could have been as ugly as a post and I would have adored her. I reconsidered Tilda's Germanic immovability from that angle.

My mother's immediate solution to my visit was to involve third parties. On that first evening we went to dinner with her Uncle Rafe, who was quite old. His was the other funeral my mother and I would see each other at in the near future. I guess my mother hoped the presence of someone else would make the visit go more smoothly, but she made a miscalculation with Uncle Rafe.

"Well, I'll be damned, Robby, haven't you grown," was the first thing Uncle Rafe said to me. My mother corrected him, but to no avail. For the entire evening, Uncle Rafe called me by my brother's name, and I could see my mother going from bad to worse. At first I corrected him, too, but as the evening progressed, the darkest part of my heart began to enjoy watching my mother struggle with her temper.

"It's Bernie. Bernie. Not Robby," my mother snapped at one point. Uncle Rafe blinked in confusion and apologized. I was barely able to stifle my diabolical laughter.

At the end of the evening, I put Uncle Rafe in a cab. He shook my hand and said, "It was good to see you again, Robby." My mother nearly bit through her bottom lip in fury.

Out to lunch on the second day of my visit, my mother's tag team consisted of her friend Evelyn and Evelyn's daughter, Danielle. Through a failure of communication or utter perversity on the part of my mother, I believe they were match-making. My mother started out by complimenting Danielle's hair and clothes, perhaps draw my attention to them. Then she began quizzing Danielle about her interests and her marital status in some bizarre cross-examination. Clearly she already knew the answers she was eliciting.

"Danielle, didn't you sing in the production of *Othello*? I was sure I remembered that you were cast for it," my mother said, after she'd maneuvered the conversation to the topic of opera.

"Yes, for the chorus. It's a large chorus, so they have auditions for amateurs to fill it," Danielle said. "When they do *Aida* next spring, I'm hoping to get another part in the chorus. It was so much fun." She seemed like a nice girl, but she didn't have the sense to be embarrassed about what our mothers were doing. Helpfully, she said, "Are you interested in opera, Bernie?"

"I really prefer musicals." I was still trying to be polite. "I saw the *Cabaret* revival when I was in New York." Danielle blinked and made some non-committal sound. In a flash I realized how my mother saw me. I burst out laughing and clapped my mother on her shoulder. "I get it now, Mom. I get it!"

"What?" my mother said with an annoyed smile.

"Son of a bitch, I just figured out why you think I'm queer."

That was the last thing she let me contribute to the lunch conversation.

Jewelry

Meda

You'd think I hadn't done anything wrong the way Bernie's aunt acted. I wondered if I would have been as nice to somebody like me. I was expecting her to be a little cold, but when she opened the door, she said, "Meda, dear, it's so good to see you. Come in, come in."

"I wanted to thank you for sending Ron Grabling over to give me a ride yesterday." I hadn't expected that would be Celeste's solution to my having car trouble.

"Oh, I wasn't going anywhere. Anytime you need a ride, you should feel free to call him. I'm so glad you came." She hugged me and pulled me onto the couch next to her.

She was so sweet I didn't really want to do what I'd come there for, but I took the jewelry box out of my purse and put it on her coffee table.

"I tried to give this back to Bernie, but he wouldn't take it."

"If he gave it to you, you shouldn't try to give it back," she said.

"I don't think I should keep it now. He said it was worth several hundred thousand dollars."

Mrs. Raleigh raised her eyebrows at me, so I hoped she understood. She opened the box and nodded.

"I don't want to alarm you, dear, but I believe this is worth a great deal more than that. That's a thirty-carat stone. It's an Indian diamond from what I remember and very nearly flawless." She touched the big diamond in the middle and I thought, so that's what thirty carats looks like. "Pen gave it to his wife for their thirtieth anniversary."

"You ought to try it on," I said. "It would look perfect on you. You always look so elegant."

"I never wear jewelry, except for my engagement ring. I sold it all."

"Why would you sell your jewelry?"

"It was nonsense. My late husband and I were trying to raise ransom money, of all things." She said it like she was telling a funny story, but she looked sad.

"Bernie told me they didn't even pay the ransom. He pretends he doesn't mind."

"Rob, Bernie's father, would have paid the money, I'm sure." She went on playing with the diamond, tilting it under the lights. "It was so little they were asking for, only $250,000. But Pen kept us like children."

"Why didn't he pay it, if it was only that much?"

"Rob was at Pen's mercy. We were all at his mercy to make the decisions that affected our lives, and Pen wouldn't pay. It infuriated him. It wasn't that he minded about the money, but he had such a great fear of being made a fool of. All he could see was that it was the inevitable outcome of paying the ransom. I hate to say it or think it, but if it had been Robby, Pen would have paid. And there's this diamond. It would have paid the ransom several times over."

"That makes me want it even less."

"Oh, Meda, I wish you and Bernie could work things out." She wasn't mad at me, because he hadn't told her anything. "I know I'm not supposed to ask about this. Bernie told me before I went to the party that I wasn't to ask, but he didn't say whether it was his rule or yours. Now if it's yours, I won't say another word, but if it's his little dictatorship, I'd like to ask about the wedding."

"Mrs. Raleigh."

"So it is your rule that I'm not allowed to talk about it?"

"Yes." I figured that would make her mad, but she patted me on the leg.

"Please, don't 'Mrs. Raleigh' me, and we'll talk about Annadore. I want her to think of me as her aunt. I want to be her aunt, exactly as I will be for Bernie's baby."

She looked sad, but she went on being nice to me. I couldn't pick my own relatives, but I could pick Annadore's, so I said yes.

CHAPTER TEN

FUGUE

IF MY MOTHER had kept a gun in her apartment, I would have shot myself within the first twenty-four hours of my visit, and then every hour on the hour thereafter.

"If she doesn't want to marry you, there's no sense in making a heroic effort to convince her," my mother said. "There are plenty of other girls out there who would suit you better. Danielle is very nice. And pretty. And she's more our kind of people."

Children are like computers. They do what you program them to do, and for the first time it occurred to me that I'd been programmed to fail. Lacking a gun, my three day visit turned into a six day fugue that was only broken when Celeste called.

"Lionel Petrie called to talk about scheduling for them to shoot you," she said, but she was only talking about the stupid commercial. "He said they're doing it here at the house?"

"Yes, put it on the calendar."

"When will you be back?" she said. According to Celeste's calendar I was already back. Reality was starting to scare her with its unpredictability. "There are a lot of things that need your signature. Should I overnight them to Boston?"

"No, I'm coming back."

"Oh, and only because you said I should let you know if

anything came up, Meda called yesterday looking for you. I thought she knew you were away."

"I don't know."

"She had car trouble, so I called Ron Grabling for her. I hope that's okay, since you pay his salary."

"Sure, whatever." I deserved to be shot for that. "Look, take this afternoon and go buy her a car."

"Buy her a car? What kind of car?"

"Something practical, reliable. Something nice." I wished I had better guidance to offer her, but what I knew about cars wasn't worth mentioning. Then because she didn't say anything else, I filled in the blanks for her: "You're a signer on the household account. Honestly, it's not that hard to walk into a dealership and buy a car. Tag and title. Put it in her name. Then call the insurance agent."

"Okay," Celeste said in a careful voice. She thought I was off my rocker. "Mr. Cantrell called to say that the mausoleum is completed, so as soon as you'd like, they can schedule the re-interments."

"Whenever is fine."

"I think he thinks that you'll want to be there."

"I don't."

I ended the call, hating myself, mostly for saying things that weren't true. I wasn't indifferent about Meda. I wasn't indifferent about my family being moved from their graves. I didn't know why indifference had to be my default setting. In a sane world, in a world where I wasn't pathetic, in a world where I didn't deserve to be shot, that call would at least have gotten me out of bed, but it took my mother's sinister machinations to get me up two days later.

"Bernie, I called Dr. Rosenwasser this morning to come see you. You remember him? It was a mistake going off your medication. I'm going to have him prescribe something for you. You're not well," she said.

I opened my eyes to see her frowning down at me. Her look of concern, the one that masked her indifference, got me out of bed. I started putting on my clothes.

"What are you doing?" she said.

"I'm leaving."

"Where are you going?"

"To the airport."

"But you don't have a flight booked. You missed your flight."

I knew it was her intention to wear me down, that she was in fact wearing me down. I was so weak I couldn't imagine how I was going to resist her, until I remembered that awful summer before I moved to Atlanta, and how she'd convinced me to check into the clinic. If I hadn't done it myself, she would have done it for me. To me. I wondered if she would send Dr. Rosenwasser's minions to the airport after me.

"There are other flights. I'll get one," I said.

"But you haven't showered in days. You look terrible." Standing there, trying to figure out how to put everything into my suitcase, I felt panicked, but I didn't dare let her see it. Instead, I opened my carryon bag and put in some clean clothes and my shaving kit.

"I'm going to send for my suitcase later, if you can have Mrs. Vasquez pack it up for me," I said.

"What do you mean, you'll send for it?" There was an edge of hysteria to her voice that produced an eerie calm in me. I could see the horizon of the moment and feel the curvature of the earth under me. For the first time, the unspeakable weight of her disappointment steadied me.

"I don't want to mess with it right now." I don't know if she thought about stopping me, but she made a moue of distaste when I hugged her. "I'll talk to you later, Mom."

The doorman got me a cab and held the door for me like there was nothing amiss. I didn't get the same reservation of judgment at the airport, and in an effort not to terrorize my fellow passengers, I took advantage of the three hours before my flight to shave and to brush my teeth. The scar on my cheekbone was a fading apostrophe that nagged me like a clichéd string tied around my finger as a reminder of…something. What was I supposed to remember?

Storm

Meda

The rain turned into sleet in the afternoon and I hoped Loren and her friends wouldn't come because of the weather, but they did. Loren couldn't make up her mind if she hated me or if I was her best friend. I was starting to figure out that was how money worked. Maybe it wasn't what Bernie intended, but he told me to spend the money on whatever I wanted, so I bought a new TV with some of the money he gave me. All of a sudden Loren liked me enough to want to bring her roommate and boyfriend over to watch TV.

Loren's boyfriend said. "Straight six, right? Four liter? What, it'll do 130, 140? Sweet ride."

It was the first thing I'd ever heard him say, and I didn't have any idea what it meant.

"Her boyfriend bought it for her," Loren said.

"I wish I had a boyfriend who'd buy me a BMW," Loren's roommate said. They started talking about what they'd do if they had a rich boyfriend, and it wasn't what I was doing with Bernie.

When somebody knocked at the door halfway through the movie, I thought it was another one of Loren's friends, but it was Bernie. If he was looking for pity, he could have mine, because he looked terrible. His hair was dripping wet, and he looked dead on his feet, with dark circles under his eyes.

"I'm sorry it's so late. I just wanted to see you," he said. That's what he wanted, I guess, because all he did was look at me.

"You want to come in?" I said.

He looked surprised. He'd really come out there just to see me and get sent on his way.

"Hey, Bernie, will you buy me a new car?" Loren said.

"Shut up and watch your movie," I said. Bernie didn't look like he was up to fighting with Loren, so I took him into the bedroom.

The Verb That Created God

"You bought me a BMW," Meda explained, after she shut the bedroom door. I glanced around at her room, looking at all the landmarks of happiness and misery.

"I hope that's okay."

I'd almost forgotten about the car, and I was half afraid it was going to cause an argument. When I looked at her, though, she wore a smiling frown. Concerned and a little embarrassed wasn't a look I recognized on Meda.

"I went with Celeste to pick it out, so it's what I wanted. It's really nice. I never thought I'd have a station wagon. Or a BMW. Thank you."

"I wanted to be sure you had reliable transportation, since I haven't been here much. And I know how you feel about driving the Rolls."

"Where were you?" she said.

"I had to go to New York to sort out a problem with a piece of real estate that's a historical property. Pen was in the middle of a lawsuit, so I went to an arbitration meeting. And I went to Pennsylvania on some foundation business. And Boston to see my mother." I heard myself talking, just to be talking. Meda reached out to me, so I said, "I just wanted to see you, I wasn't thinking of—I need a shower."

"I know how to fix that."

Because there was so much kindness in the offer, and none of her usual bristling, I let her take me into the bathroom and turn on the shower for me. It was an old house, so there was a window over the bathtub. Standing there with hot water vapor clouding around me, I looked out the top half of the window and watched the sleet glazing every surface in the backyard: the dead grass, the sagging clothesline, the shed, the house next door, the line of dilapidated houses beyond it.

I didn't resist Meda when she led me to her bed. I put myself in her hands, knowing she wanted to redraw the lines of me. She insisted on it, knowing my intentions when I touched her, how my hands shaped her flesh.

My scars were the places she didn't attempt to rework with her hands and her mouth. It seemed only natural. When I remade her in my mold, I never attempted her mouth. Her throat, her earlobes, her breasts and the crease beneath her breasts, her belly, the heat sink of her vulva. When I touched them, she ceded them to my design. Her mouth was a thing set in stone, an immutable icon to be adored but unchanged unless by the caressing hands of ten million pilgrims. When I kissed Meda, I knew her mouth came before any creation I commanded. Her mouth was not God, but the verb that created God.

She exhausted me with every technique I knew existed and some that were new to me. I think she intended to assert her power, unnecessary as that was, and if it had been only a matter of wanting to submit, I would have. I would have relished the act of submission if I'd been able, but I felt everything receding from me. All I wanted was to stop that going away, to stop watching the world's destruction from a distance.

Frankenstein

Meda

"Stop, stop, please stop, please stop," Bernie said, fast and hoarse. I did, and felt guilty, because he sounded upset and he was shaking all over. We lay next to each other until he was calm enough to talk.

"You could have said stop sooner and I would have stopped," I said.

"You're right. I'm sorry, I should have said stop sooner." He put his arm around me to show he wasn't mad, but I wanted to defend myself.

"I would have stopped," I said. "That's the worst feeling ever, knowing that saying stop won't mean anything. I wouldn't do that to you."

"I know you wouldn't. And it wasn't that I couldn't stop him from hurting me." The back of my neck prickled when I understood he meant the guy who kidnapped him. Bernie was quiet, and I didn't even know what to say. I turned my head into his shoulder, because I didn't want him to see my face. "I mean, it was that, but it poisoned everything, like you said. It changed the way I see the world."

"And yourself."

"What do you mean?" he said.

"What Ray did to me changed how I saw myself. For the longest time, I felt like a monster. You know, like Frankenstein. Like there was something wrong with me, that I wasn't made like other people. That's what Gramma always told me. *We're not like other people.* And after it happened, that was what she said, too. It's what happens to people like us. She said, 'People eat chickens because that's what chickens are for.'"

"Oh, Meda," he said. He kissed my forehead, and I felt guilty, because I'd wanted to make him feel better, and he was trying to take care of me.

"Do you ever feel that way, like there's something wrong with you because of what happened?" I already knew the answer.

"There is something wrong with me."

"There isn't either," I said.

"There is. You said it. I've just—I've been amputated. Something's been cut off, so that I can't—. Maybe it's silly, but I always thought it was my soul. Like they opened me up and cut out that part of me, and after that I was always separated from myself. I can't get back into myself." He sounded so exhausted and sad. "Do you still feel like you're a monster?"

"No. Not anymore. That was the best part about having Annadore. Not in the beginning when I didn't want to be pregnant. But the labor wasn't as bad as everyone said it would be, and when they gave her to me, the first time I nursed her, I felt better. I didn't feel like a monster, because a monster couldn't do something beautiful like that."

"I like that. I wish I could have a baby." He laughed.

"You're going to."

"Not like that, though," he said. "Are you at least a little happy about this baby?"

"I'm not sorry I'm going to have this baby. I hope—" I was scared to say what I hoped.

"I'm sorry it has to be over between us." He whispered it, almost crying, I think because of how tired he was. For the first time since I'd met him, he looked his age. He looked even older than he was.

"It's not over. It's just complicated. You need to sleep."

"No. I'm awake," he said, the way Annadore sometimes did. He was fading and, after a couple of tries, he let me leave. It was after midnight by the time I got rid of Loren and her crew, so I made a bed for myself on the couch. I woke up at about six, thinking I would make Bernie some breakfast, but he was already gone.

Headache

"Are you okay? Do you need some aspirin?" Celeste asked.

"Did I ask for some aspirin?" I'd gotten in from Boston Sunday evening, and except for the blessed but brief rest I'd gotten in Meda's bed, I hadn't been able to sleep.

"You were rubbing your head like you had a headache."

"You're giving me a headache."

I breathed in, out. I apologized. It wasn't her fault. I had to keep reminding myself of that. The first meeting of the foundation's board of directors was scheduled for the following evening, but at that moment there was a film crew set up in the study, displacing Celeste and me into the dining room.

To spare me from Celeste and vice versa, I went into the study, where Lionel Petrie greeted me effusively. He loved "the opulent, old world atmosphere" of my grandfather's study. He didn't mention if he also loved how the wood paneling made the room like the inside of a coffin, or how the desk brooded like an Easter Island monolith. For the commercial, they'd brought a giant painting of my grandfather, father, and uncle from the corporate office, and hung it on the wall behind the desk, displacing the painting of my grandmother that had hung there my entire life.

The commercial was a toll. It was a price I had to pay. I had survived the shareholder meeting. If I could make it through the commercial, I would make it through the meeting with the foundation's board members. If I made it through that meeting, I would be my own man for a few weeks. There would be nothing looming over me, and then. Then, I didn't know.

"Are you about ready in here?" I said abruptly, and heard the truth of Meda's accusation: my grandfather's voice.

I regretted my impatience once filming began, because everyone was unhappy with how it went. I looked terrible, my voice was hoarse, and I hated the script. It started out, "Sixty years ago in this office, my grandfather had a vision, blah, blah, blah," and it got worse from there. At one point, I was supposed to fold my hands on the desk, right over left. Right over left. Half the time, I did it the wrong way, revealing what no one, least of all me, wanted revealed: that ugly stump of a finger. Subconsciously perhaps, I was indicting my grandfather.

By two o'clock, Lionel looked nervous, and everyone else was cursing the misbegotten marketing brainstorm that had brought us to that point. We agreed to try again the next day.

Reburying the Dead

Aunt Ginny

Meda answered the door in her housemaid disguise and kissed me on the cheek. With a laugh, she said, "Consider yourself warned. He's not in a good mood today." She was already the lady of the house, whether she wanted to admit it or not. I hated myself for being a snob so late in life, but it was clear to me that Meda was who she was all of her own doing. Her family was not charming enough to have produced her. I couldn't help thinking it was imperative for Bernie to marry her, primarily to improve himself, and secondarily to rescue her from her family.

Bernie came out of the study just then, and Meda's warning was quite accurate.

"Celeste, why is everything scheduled for today?" my not-so-sweet nephew snarled when he saw me.

"You said, I'm sorry, sir, you said you didn't care. That I should schedule it whenever. I'm sorry."

Bernie gave the poor girl a look that was dangerously like Pen.

"Now, Bernie. If we're a little late, I suppose that Mr. Cantrell will wait on us. There's plenty of daylight left," I said.

He nodded and apologized to the girl, but the dark look stayed.

At the cemetery Mr. Cantrell awaited us with a crew of workmen. The air felt wonderfully sharp and a little damp. The sort of air that reminded me, even in a cemetery, that things were done with winter and ready to start growing again.

"I wasn't sure if you wanted to say a few words. We have Mr. Raleigh here as well." He gestured in the direction of a hearse parked nearby.

"It was all said at the funeral," Bernie said. I agreed, and once the facing marble from the vaults had been removed, the business of moving coffins began.

"Have you eaten today?" I asked Bernie. He looked ill.

"I don't think I could." He seemed about to say something else, but the workmen came by with the first coffin, and Bernie said, "This is the one from the top right? It's Uncle Alan."

He brushed the dust from the top of Alan's coffin with his bare hands. I was touched that seeing his uncle carried out should affect Bernie so deeply, more so than his father and brother did when their coffins were brought out a few minutes later. Once the moving had been finished, Pen's coffin was carried in, and at Bernie's suggestion, we stepped into the emptied mausoleum.

I didn't want to upset him, but because she had called me, I said, "Your mother was worried about you."

"She was going to Baker Act me."

"Oh, I'm sure she wasn't." I had feared she might, particularly since she'd done so before.

I was reluctant to part with Bernie for the night. Not that I was convinced I could do anything for him, but I was frightened of the black mood on him, maybe even a little afraid of Pen's ghost. I put my arm into his as we walked back to the car. Wanting to make him think about something positive, I said, "Now that I have some money of my own, I want you to tell me what you think I should do with it. To help with the foundation, the work you're doing."

"I think you should hold onto it, and if you like you can leave it to the foundation in your will."

"I hope I can do a bit of good before I'm quite dead." He didn't even smile at my little joke.

Medicine

"I'd like to go to pray, if you wouldn't mind taking me," Aunt Ginny said, as we were leaving the cemetery. I didn't have the energy to resist. When we went into the chapel, I half expected to see a casket flanked by flowers at the front. I looked around like you can't at a funeral, at the holy water font, the banks of candles, and the discreetly martyred saints. It was all in good taste, with none of the garishness that bespeaks real passion. I dutifully went through the motions on Aunt Ginny's behalf, but seeing her fragile neck bowed so earnestly, I was ashamed of my cynicism. For the first time in my adult life, I tried to pray.

It was more like wishing on the candles of a birthday cake, because I remembered only my childhood prayers, the calling down of God's blessings on a list of people. I stumbled in making that list, because most of the people I had been taught to bless were dead. So I prayed for something good for the people I could think of. That was all, just something good for Meda and Annadore, and for Aunt Ginny, and for Muriel and Miss Amos, even for Mrs. Trentam, Mrs. Bryant, Celeste, and Loren. For my mother, too.

My spiritual healing or whatever it was didn't survive the preparations for filming the next day. To get past the taboo about drinking in the morning, I told myself it was like taking medicine. I needed something to calm my nerves, I thought, and then I knocked back a glass of scotch. Once I'd crossed that invisible line, I felt I was capable of a number of things that had been prohibited before. It wasn't a good feeling. When Mrs. Trentam and Meda came into the kitchen, I was relieved. As bad as it was, at least it wasn't a secret then. There were witnesses to the appalling depths to which I had sunk.

"What are you doing?" Meda said.

"I'm getting ready for my close-up, Mr. DeMille." Missed reference. They stared at me. I could see my epitaph so clearly then. Moody, alcoholic billionaire with a bad habit of knocking up his employees. On my headstone, something fit for the 19th century: "He was a bad 'un and we're well shut of him."

"You're drinking, what?" Meda picked up the bottle. "Scotch, at nine in the morning."

"But it's good scotch."

I offered her my glass to refill, and she poured in more than I thought was necessary to make her point. Watching her pour, I marveled at how her face seemed to be lit from within, ruled by its own mystical chiaroscuro. I wanted to ask her if it was a dream that she had said our relationship wasn't over, but I was afraid it was.

"Aunt M., maybe you could go outside for a sec," Meda said. After her aunt was gone, she looked at me and shook her head. She put her hand on my arm, her touch as insubstantial as a snowflake. "You don't look very good."

"You're about the fifth person to tell me that this morning."

Lionel Petrie wasn't any happier about my appearance. I had a tic over my left eye that I hoped the alcohol would cure. Meda's face was so kind I couldn't bear to look at her, and she started to put her arms around my waist. I pushed her away from me and barely made it to the sink before I vomited.

"What's the matter? Please don't say it's because of me."

"It's not you. It's this stupid commercial."

"Don't do it, if you don't want to," she said.

"I have to."

"You have to?"

"I'm trapped. There are all these things I'm responsible for. That's bad enough, and then there's this thing with you. You used to make me happy."

"I'm sorry you've got all these things weighing on you, but I can't be the one who decides if you're happy or not. That's not right." She said it like an apology, but with the confidence that she was right.

The library had made me happy, but it was no use to me there. I couldn't win. If I didn't do the commercial it was one more thing I failed at, one more responsibility I shirked. That wasn't even the worst of it. The camera, the eye of the world, that was the most monstrous part of it.

"I can see why you don't want to marry me," I said. "I really am messed up."

"It's not so much you. It's this whole situation." I didn't press her on that, not wanting her to withdraw the kindness.

Bernie's Close-Up

Meda

One of the guys on the film crew opened the door and said, "Mr. Raleigh? Lionel says we're ready for you." Bernie looked horrible, leaning over the sink. I thought he was going to puke again.

"He'll be ready in a minute." I wasn't so sure, but the guy nodded and left.

"I don't like them filming me. I hate the idea of being on television, of being filmed. It makes my flesh crawl," Bernie said.

I remembered what his aunt had said about him not wanting to be noticed, and then I thought of something that scared me so much, I was glad Bernie wasn't looking at me. To keep from freaking out, I pinched the inside of my arm as hard as I could. Somewhere out there was the guy who hurt Bernie. He was out there, sitting around, watching TV. I put my hands on Bernie's back and hoped he wouldn't feel how much they were shaking. I made my voice as cheerful as I could and said, "When you were little didn't you like to perform? Your aunt said you sang and danced and put on little shows. Think of it that way, like you're performing. I used to pretend I was a queen getting crowned when I went to those pageants. Or sometimes I pretended I was a slave getting sold at market." He gave me a funny look over his shoulder. "You know when you're a kid, weird stuff seems cool. Seems romantic."

"I thought a drink would calm my nerves. What should I do?" I thought he meant about the commercial, but then he said, "Just tell me what you want me to do. Do you want me to stay here to try to work this out? Or should I go back to Kansas City and leave you alone? I'll do whatever you want."

"I think you should do what you want to do," I said, even though I didn't like to give people advice. Since I'd already done it once, I did it again. "Sing something. Sing that Oklahoma song you sing in the shower sometimes."

He started laughing. "I'm not doing a musical number for you in the kitchen."

"Not here, out there. Go out and sing that first and then do the commercial. You'll look stupid right off the bat, so you can get that out of the way, and it's something you're good at."

Giving advice is dangerous. Bernie was drunk enough that he did it. I followed him into the study and on the first take they did, he sang that goofy song about farmers and potatoes and Oklahoma. He sang it like he did in the shower, belting it out like he was on stage. After Bernie finished the song, he bowed. Then he walked out, leaving the director and the camera crew with their mouths hanging open.

Usefulness

I went to the airport with nothing but my briefcase and the clothes on my back, and got on a plane to Kansas City.

I returned to the library with the vow that I would be useful, so on my first day back, I asked Beverly what needed to be done.

"The usual," she said. She wasn't sure what to think of me being back.

"No, I mean what really needs to be done around here that isn't getting done?" She opened her filing cabinet, and pulled out four large manila folders.

"This needs to be put in the database." It was records of missing and replaced items, changes in volume numbers and editions. It took a week of tedious ten-hour days, but I finished it.

"It's not in the budget for overtime," she said when I was done.

"I hope you're not paying me anymore."

She blushed, the first time I had ever seen her so out of sorts.

"I forgot. I just forgot that you're, that you're who you are."

"What else needs to be done?" I said.

"You know we've been wanting to relocate the children's section for years." Beverly suggested it tentatively, not quite daring to hope that I'd take it on. If she had said, *There are these thousand horse stables that haven't been cleaned in ten years*, I would have accepted the task. I wanted to do something that offered tangible proof of the effort involved.

I began drawing diagrams of what would have to be moved to make the relocation possible. It required the piecemeal removal and relocation of two aisles of reference books and another four aisles of adult fiction, plus five computer terminals and the ancient card catalogs, which had taken on a Cheopsean aura of immovability. That was to clear the space for the children's section. The children's section involved moving nine freestanding bookcases and seven sections of half-shelves, as well as all the tables and chairs. The books of course had to be moved in some orderly fashion, temporarily stacked until the shelves were moved and then re-shelved. Somehow simultaneously, the books from the displaced reference section and adult fiction needed to be re-shelved once the shelves had been relocated to the old children's section. Additionally, the displacement would disrupt the order of the adult fiction, putting the T—Z section in front of the A's, requiring that all the books and signs be incrementally shifted to properly order the alphabet again. It had only been talked of for years for a good reason. It was Herculean.

Beverly came out of her office while I was working out my calculations with a tape measure, and I knew she wanted to revoke my commission. She believed I would never finish the job. I decided to view her pessimism as a challenge instead of a prediction.

Spiritual Contract

Meda

Bernie didn't come back after he walked out on the commercial. The film crew wandered around for a few hours, but he never came back. I didn't hear from him that night, and when I went to work the next day he still wasn't there. As much as I didn't want to, I asked Celeste.

"Oh, he flew to Kansas City after his meeting yesterday. Do you need something?" I didn't really, except I wanted to see him. It wasn't a stupid romance novel moment. I just felt sad that he was gone and he hadn't even bothered to tell me. I hoped he was doing what he wanted.

When he called me two weeks later, I had started to think he was moving on with his life. He acted like we'd been in the middle of a conversation.

"I miss you," he said when I answered the phone, no hello or anything. "Do you remember what you said about feeling badly that I'd given you so many gifts and you didn't have anything to give me?"

"Yeah."

"Because I was thinking there's one thing you could give me that I would really like. A gift you could give me."

"You can't ask me that," I said. It made me crazy the way he acted. "Even some obscenely expensive old diamond necklace and a brand new car don't give you the right to ask me for something like that. That's not a gift. That's a—a—I don't care if you believe in it or not, but that's a spiritual contract."

"Well, that wasn't what I was going to ask for, but the invitation is still open, as you like to say."

I wanted to start the phone call over. "I'm sorry. What can I give you, as a gift?"

"Come visit me. I want to see you."

"Why do I have to go there?"

"You don't, but I'm asking you to."

"What about Annadore?"

"I'd like to see her, too. It's not a romantic trip. I promise I won't bother you about that. If you don't want to, just say so." He sounded a little sad, but not that awful sadness he sometimes had. I think his feelings were hurt.

"It's not that. It's just...I've never flown before."

"It's no big deal. I'll send the jet for you."

"Please, don't. I'd rather fly like a normal person."

I felt like a big dummy, but I made him tell me about what you do when you get to the airport, and what you do with your luggage and how you get to your plane and all that stuff. He waited while I went to get a pen and paper, and then he walked me through it. I didn't know how to feel when I hung up. He sounded so normal.

CHAPTER ELEVEN

ASSHOLE

WHEN I MET Meda at the airport, she looked tired, I can only imagine from having to fly with Annadore.

"Take She-Devil, would you?" Meda said.

"Bunny!" Annadore crowed and held out her arms to me. Then in a conversational tone, she said, "Stink, stink, mean Mama."

All around us were people who seemed happy to see each other. I wanted to hug Meda, but it apparently hadn't occurred to her. I felt deflated. As we walked down to the baggage claim, however, she leaned into me a little, and then we stood just touching, waiting for their luggage. Annadore's car seat and a glaringly new suitcase.

"I didn't have a suitcase," she said, when she caught me looking at it. "And I bought new clothes to put in it. Celeste and I both think you're insane for giving me a credit card."

She waited for me to say something, but I decided not to. In the parking lot, Meda looked around, looking for Kansas City perhaps.

"A Toyota," she said, when I unlocked the car door for her.

"A librarian's salary won't buy a Rolls Royce. Or a BMW for that matter."

"With the late fines you charge, I'd think it would," she said with a grin.

She'd had her teeth fixed. Her smile was perfect and uninterrupted.

I'd prepared myself for her annoyance, but she seemed perfectly content to be there until I stirred things up. While we were going into my apartment building my neighbor was coming out and I bowed to the inevitable introduction. "This is Jerry, my neighbor. This is my fiancée Meda and her daughter Annadore."

"I didn't know you were getting married!" He glanced down at Meda's belly, which was larger than I remembered. Of course, it had grown. "When's the happy day?"

"We haven't decided yet," Meda said sharply.

"Well, congratulations."

"Thanks." I felt Meda burning holes in my back as I unlocked the apartment door.

"You promised this wasn't going to be that kind of trip. You promised you weren't going to bother me about getting married."

"It isn't and I'm not and I haven't," I said.

She stepped past me into the apartment and turned to challenge me.

"Then why did you tell him I was your fiancée?"

"You know what I think when I see a guy with a pregnant woman and he introduces her as his girlfriend?"

"That he should have been more careful," she said, either as general commentary or a personal remark on my behavior.

"I think, 'what an asshole.' You're making me feel like an asshole."

"I'm not your girlfriend," she said.

Digging a Hole

Meda

I didn't know why I had to keep upsetting him, but it made him so mad he didn't say anything. He walked out into another room, came back with his hands in his pockets, and then went back the other way. When he came back on his third trip, he stopped in front of Annadore and me.

"I'm going for a walk," he said.

"I thought you were already taking one." Apparently the hole wasn't deep enough for my taste yet.

He looked at Annadore and said, "You want to see some ducks? Some duckies?"

"Duckies!" She knew which side her bread was buttered on. He scooped her up and went to the door.

"Make yourself at home. I dare you."

"I dare you," I said, like Loren.

Once they were gone, I took the suitcase into his bedroom and unpacked some of my stuff onto a chair. I took a shower with his soap and his towels and put on my nightgown. Then I turned the thermostat up and tuned his stereo to a station that was playing country music. I looked in his nightstand drawer and saw his lip gloss, nail clippers, and his book of "erotic paintings." After I flipped through it, I knew why he didn't think I was fat. He was jerking off to some seriously fat girls.

The second bedroom had a desk and a toddler bed. I looked at the stuff on his desk. Pens and pencils, his address book (he had me listed as "Miss Meda Amos"), and his bizarre little lists and notes. "Are abductees working toward a linear narrative interpretation of an event that is essentially non-linear?"

Then, because he'd dared me, I went and looked in his closet, but there were just clothes in there. Then I looked under his bed and pulled out the boxes that were under there. There was a box marked "ROBBY" that had a bunch of old letters and some plastic cases of dead butterflies stuck with pins. The second box was full of photo albums and postcards. I put it up on Bernie's huge bed and made myself comfortable to look through it. That's what I was doing when Bernie came back with Annadore.

"Hungry duckies," Annadore said. "They eat it all up. I don't like big duckies. Big duckies mean."

"They were big, but they're swans. The big ducks are swans," Bernie told her.

"Swans. I hate swans. They try to bited me."

When Bernie walked into the bedroom he was smiling, but he frowned when he saw me and said, "What are you doing?"

"I'm making myself at home. Did you feed the duckies, Baby Girl? Were they hungry?" He lifted Annadore up on the bed, and took off her coat and hat and mittens. She crawled across to hug me, and her cheeks were so cold I was a little angry with Bernie. She seemed happy and he seemed so bothered by me looking through his pictures that I let it go. He lay down across the foot of the bed while Annadore told me about the ducks.

She made her hand into a duck bill to show how the big ducks had tried to bite her. Bernie made his hand into a bigger duckbill and made it quack at her and nibble on her fingers so that she started giggling and hopping around. I couldn't help myself, I started crying. Bernie sat up and held Annadore still and dead serious said, "Meda? Are you okay?"

"It's just hormones," I said.

"Oh." He sounded scared instead of relieved, but he lay back down. After a while Annadore petered out and lay down on his chest with her head tucked under his chin. It was strange to see how small she was compared to him. I kept thinking she was getting so big. When I offered to move her, he said, "She's okay."

"Girlfriend?" I held up a picture of him looking uncomfortable, and some bored-looking woman who reminded me a lot of Celeste.

"Good eye. That's Caroline, my ex-girlfriend." It was cute that he was trying not to get pissed off about it, because he really didn't like it.

"How old are you there?" I showed him a picture of him and his brother in baseball uniforms.

"Little League," he said. "Eight or nine."

"That's Robby, right? I thought he was your older brother."

"I was five feet tall in the second grade. As soon as I had enough teeth to eat solid food I was bigger than Robby." He lifted his head and smoothed down Annadore's hair.

"Were you good at baseball? I didn't know you played any sports."

"I was a good pitcher. Having a long arm helps with that."

"Do you play anymore?"

"No," he said and yawned. "My pitching was no good after I was shot." He'd never talked about it and part of me wanted to pretend it was the first I'd heard of it, and say all shocked, 'You were shot?!' Except he looked so peaceful and sleepy that I didn't want to stir him up. Instead, I leaned over them and gave Annadore a kiss. I gave Bernie a kiss, too, just on the forehead.

"You two have a nice nap," I said.

His eyes snapped open, and looking down into his face I saw how freaked out he was. He sat up fast enough that his head whacked mine, and Annadore started crying.

"Annadore, it's okay, shh." He rocked her until she was quiet again, but he wouldn't look at me. It made me sad that he was afraid of what I was going to say. "I'm sorry."

"It's okay. You know, Bernie, nothing bad is going to happen if you go to sleep. It's safe. I'll sit right here while you sleep and make sure you're safe."

That was what I used to tell Loren when she was afraid to go to sleep because of the aliens. He shook his head and sat there for a long time holding Annadore, looking down at her.

"Do you want me to take her?"

"No, I like holding her."

"You really do like her?" I said to get him out of his funk.

"Yeah, and she's a lot better about letting me love her than you are."

After a while he carried her into the other room to finish her nap. When she woke up, we went out to dinner. Bernie seemed kind of sad and embarrassed. I wondered what he wanted from me, especially when we got back to his apartment. While I put Annadore to bed, he folded out the sofa and made it up. Then he said goodnight to me without so much as a kiss.

Meda's Inheritance

Meda was gone when I woke up. The clock in the kitchen said it was 2:30 A.M. and the bedroom door was standing open. I tried to think rationally, and went to check on Annadore, who was asleep. I felt a crazy kind of panic, and irrationally did a thorough search of the apartment, like Meda was a kitten that could get lost under the bed. I was putting on my shoes, prepared to go out looking for her, when she opened the front door and came in. I let the adrenaline speak.

"Where the hell were you?"

"I went out to get some potato chips." She held up a bag of chips to show me. My head suddenly hurt. "That's how cravings are. I just went down to the gas station on the corner."

"By yourself, in the middle of the night," I said.

Meda's eyes narrowed. Whatever words we said next would be the groundwork for the argument to follow. I wanted to choose wisely, but Meda spoke first.

"I'm an adult, and I don't appreciate being told what to do."

"I didn't tell you what to do. I was just concerned, because I woke up and you were gone and I didn't know where you were. It scared me."

"You thought the aliens abducted me," Meda said.

I felt like a jackass, but a relieved jackass, because the argument dissipated, and she was safe. She sat down on the foot of the sofa bed to take off her coat and boots. Then she opened her bag of chips and ate one. "If you're going to be so fussy about it, I would sleep on the couch."

"You know it's not that I'm fussy, and I'm perfectly happy to sleep out here."

"Fussy."

"You know I can't sleep with you."

"I know. Fussy."

"Is it that important to be able to sleep with someone?" I asked.

"It is. It makes me feel safe, knowing that someone else is there. I think that's why a lot of people have sex, so they'll have someone to sleep with." Meda stood up and went toward the bedroom. She paused in the doorway like a water bird, one foot balanced against her opposite knee. Then she came back and gave me a BBQ potato chip kiss.

Tomato Box

Meda

After we ate breakfast, Bernie got dressed and put on his coat. He leaned over me so that I had to look up at him.

"Do you want me to leave the car? I can walk to the library," he said.

"No, I think we'll just stay in and read."

"I think what you're looking for is in a tomato box in the office closet."

I supposed that was some kind of remark about my snooping through his stuff. Then he kissed my cheek and went around the table to Annadore.

"I love you, sweetie," he said and gave her a loud kiss on the top of her head.

"I love lou, Bunny."

He smiled.

"I love you, Baby Girl," I told her after he was gone.

She smiled her gappy little smile and said, "I love lou, Mama." Things were simpler when you were three.

We spent most of the day painting our fingernails and toenails, reading, and pretending to be different kinds of animals. Since Bernie had put the idea in my head, when Annadore lay down for her nap, I found the tomato box he'd mentioned. It was full of manila file folders of typed reports. It took me a while to figure out they were medical files about Bernie. I thumbed through them and read about one paragraph.

Bernham presents as a courteous and pleasant boy, but struggles when required to attend to something for more than a few minutes, often ignores direct questioning, seems to experience intermittent disassociative states. PTSD. Possible Disassociative Identity Disorder.

I stopped reading there and put the box back in the closet. I didn't know what most of it meant, and I decided I didn't want to know more than I already did. I felt like I'd betrayed him by reading what some shrink had written about him.

Sudden Interest

Meda turned up her nose at me when I got home from work and said, "I didn't know being a librarian involved manual labor."

"I'm moving a lot of books and shelves." Taking the hint, I went into the bathroom to shower. She followed me and watched me take off my shoes, socks and shirt.

"Isn't it hard to move that stuff, you know, with your chest muscle like that?" she said, her gaze settling on the scar.

"Not really, but I have a hard time lifting things over my head. Why the sudden interest?"

"It's not a sudden interest. What do you want for dinner? I could make some spaghetti."

"We can go out or order something in. I didn't bring you here to make you cook for me." I reached out with the intention of closing the bathroom door, but she stayed put. I turned on the shower and finally took off my jeans and shorts.

"What did you bring me here for?"

"To see you. I wanted to see you," I said.

"I thought you brought me here to be your captive love slave," she suggested, which I ignored. "Aren't you going to sing?"

"I'm trying to take a shower. This isn't a concert."

She sat down on the toilet lid and looked at me expectantly.

"I like to hear you sing. Sing that Tom Jones song I like."

Dissociative Identity Disorder

Meda

"Dissociative Identity Disorder," I said while we were eating dinner, because I wanted to ask before I forgot it. Bernie grunted. "Most people don't have their medical files at home. Shouldn't they be in a doctor's office or something?"

"I stole them." That was all he said for a while. Then he looked up and saw me waiting for him to finish. "Graduation day, there was so much going on, I walked into the counselor's office with a tire iron and broke open his filing cabinet."

"How's your spaghetti?"

He gave me a strange look, then looked down at his food and said, "Is this the part where you explain why you can't marry me?"

"Because you don't like my cooking?"

"I didn't say that. It's fine." He took another bite and said, "You read the files, didn't you? Isn't that what you wanted, to know how crazy I am?"

"I didn't want to read all that. And I don't read that fast. I just saw that, Dissociative Identity Disorder."

"Is that crazy enough for you?"

"I don't even know what it means."

"It means I'm not all there. I do things I don't remember later. You know, my elevator doesn't go all the way to the top."

"Like when you get that funny look on your face and your eyes aren't really focusing on anything and I have to touch you to bring you back."

"Really?"

"Yeah, you're a real space cadet sometimes."

"Space cadet?" He looked worried, like he was waiting for me to say something else.

Hair Worth Marrying

After dinner we played Candy Land, which developed some suspiciously mutable rules that helped Annadore win. Once Annadore was in bed, Meda and I played a different game with equally suspect rules. Meda complained that her feet hurt, so I rubbed her feet. Then she said her back hurt, so I massaged that, too, trying not to think about her flesh. She went to the bathroom and came back with a bottle of lotion.

"My skin is so dry. Would you mind putting some lotion on my back?" she said.

I didn't mind, but once she'd unbuttoned her nightgown far enough to slide it off her shoulders, I was beginning to think her requests were not completely innocent. There was no need for false modesty, but having her half naked on the sofa made me nervous. I could see the vague outline of where her bra had cut into her during the day. It squeezed her so tightly, leaving a little roll of skin above and below the band that went around her ribs. I found that excess of her so inviting that I lingered over the places it rested when she was braless.

When I reached the end my tether, I put the lotion on the coffee table and said, "There. Is that better?"

"Much," she murmured and pulled her nightgown back up. After a few moments, she leaned against me, looking at the TV. I'd been watching a show on Civil War era shipwrecks while she got Annadore ready for bed, but it was over and there was a show about lions on.

"Can I put my head in your lap?" Meda said.

She didn't wait for a response before she rested her cheek on my erection and gave a little sigh. Curling her legs up, she snuggled against me and settled her headrest so deliberately I almost begged for mercy. I might have made it, if it hadn't been for that lion show. I was holding my own until those stupid lions started mating. Meda giggled, watching the lion sink his teeth into the back of the lioness' neck, and when I ignored that, she made a purring, growling noise and dug her little claws into my leg, slightly south of the source of my problem.

"That's not fair," I said, and stood up to dump her out of my lap.

"What's not fair?"

"You made me promise that I wouldn't talk about our relationship, but you're, you're—"

"I'm what?" She was kneeling on the sofa looking up at me innocently, the blush rising on her cheeks, her lips slightly parted. She hadn't buttoned her nightgown all the way, providing me with a resolve-weakening view of her breasts.

"You're either trying to seduce me or you're purposefully tormenting me."

"I'm not tormenting you."

"What do you call this? 'Will you rub lotion on my back? Can I rest my head on your lap?' Come on." I was starting to get angry with her.

"I said I'm not tormenting you." She looked annoyed, and I backtracked, retracing what I'd said, remembering how I'd phrased my accusation.

"You're trying to seduce me?"

"Took you long enough to figure that out," she said.

"That's not really fair, either, if I have to follow your rule."

"Does that mean we can't have sex unless we talk about getting married?'

"Am I supposed to do the one without the other?"

"That's what got us in this situation, from what I remember.

Besides, why else did you put Annadore's bed in the other bedroom?" Meda pulled her hair down out of its ponytail and reached for the fly of my jeans. It was an argument I couldn't win, and it left me feeling defeated. I was going to cave in and be that asshole, the one with the pregnant girlfriend.

Despite her protests, I made her leave the light on in the bedroom, and she was so real to me that I was almost there for it all. Afterwards, she pulled the covers up over us and said, "Now that wasn't so bad, was it?"

"I love you," I said quietly, hoping to slip it in under the radar.

"Well, I love you, too." She made it sound like an insult. When I got up to go sleep on the sofa, she exerted her womanly wiles on me to try to get me to stay with her, but eventually I escaped.

The next morning, Meda had one foot up on the toilet seat, rubbing lotion on her leg, while I shaved. She was thinking her innumerable mysterious thoughts, perhaps plotting new ways to torment me. Having finished with her legs, she began to rub her belly with slow steady strokes, using both hands in concentric circles. In the mirror I watched her hands go around and around. I managed to shave without slitting my throat and began the daunting work of making my hair lie down properly.

"That hair, that's the reason," she said.

"It's the reason for what?" I wished I didn't have to ask. I loved her. I desired her. I feared her. I wanted to fuck the will to argue out of her.

"That hair is the reason I can't marry you."

"I know you don't mean it, but for the sake of argument, I'll ask: Are you saying, if I stop combing my hair like this, you'll marry me?" There was no amount of fucking in the world that would stop her, but I was willing to try. Her hands had traveled up from her belly and were separately describing rapturous rings around her breasts.

"No, I'm saying the hair is all about how everything in your life is organized in these boxes with labels, how everything has to fit in a certain place. I'd marry you, if you could stop wanting to comb your hair like that," she said, adding more lotion to herself.

I wanted to explain to her that the organizing, the labeling of everything was necessary to keep my internal chaos at bay. Instead I threw the comb into the trash can and ran both hands through my hair five or six times, in opposite directions. She laughed and turned around to present her back to me. I ignored the bottle of lotion she offered me over her shoulder and put my arms around her.

While moving books that day, I thought about what it would be like to have an actual love slave, because Meda was no one's captive love slave. I might come home and find her reading, or playing with Annadore or cooking dinner and it was all delightfully domestic, but I knew it was mere chance. There were a million other chaotic and stubborn moments that she would also be in.

I came home that very evening to a less blissful domestic scene, with Annadore crying and Meda saying, "Well, I don't like you very much right now, either." When I asked what the problem was, Meda showed me where Annadore had drawn on the wall.

"It's okay. It can be painted over," I said.

"Of course it can be painted over, but that's not the point. She made a little scribble and I told her to quit, but as soon as my back was turned she did that." Meda crossed her arms across her chest and dared me to stand up for Annadore.

"Oh," was all I said, so Annadore was banished to her room until dinner. My punishment was two hours on the phone with Celeste to take care of foundation business, and some lingering issues with my grandfather's estate. It didn't say much for my earlier productivity that I was capable of keeping up with my other life in fewer than ten hours a week. Soon enough, when the board of directors was up to speed and ready to start receiving applications for grants, the foundation would require more of my time, but right then it was a part time job.

When dinner was ready, Annadore was allowed to come back out, and she carried herself with all the elegant, wounded dignity of her mother.

"Scrambled eggs?" she said.

"No," Meda said. "You can have what we're having for dinner."

"Scrambled eggs, Bunny?"

Meda was right about the burdens of parenthood. At three, Annadore already knew enough to play us off each other. Expecting the worse, Meda looked at me.

"No, Annadore. You can eat what we're having." I said it as nicely as I could, and Meda visibly relaxed.

After dinner, after Annadore was in bed, after Meda had presented herself for massaging and moisturizing, after she had been satisfied and I had come as close as I dared, I was feeling a little triumphant.

"I didn't comb my hair all day."

"Yeah," she whispered against my neck, "but you still want to comb your hair like that."

"That's not fair. That kind of test isn't fair."

"You keep complaining that this or that isn't fair. Not everything is fair. I thought you knew that."

"I think that people ought to try to be fair to each other when they're in a relationship together. I feel like you're making a joke."

"It isn't a joke. You and your hair are all about the things that make me afraid to marry you. You've got everything so organized inside of yourself like you're a closet. If there's something that's bothering you, you just put it in a box and put a label on it. Your aunt was right that you're an observer. I think that's why it's so hard for you to have an orgasm. It exposes you and it doesn't fit into your filing system," she said, but it was surprisingly free of judgment.

"How will you know when I stop wanting to comb my hair like that? How will you know?" That was the part of the conversation I felt I could get a handle on.

"I'll know," she said.

The next morning, when I got out of the shower, I spent about a minute looking at my messy hair. Meda's brush lay like a rebuke on the bottom shelf of the medicine cabinet. She'd made herself at home. She'd also broken her own rule, which meant I was free to say whatever I wanted on the topic of marriage.

It was an uphill battle, because Meda had plenty of resources to resist the topic, sex being the foremost among them. Because I didn't stand a chance in any arena where she could strip and get me into bed, I took her and Annadore out of the house on the weekend. We went to the Nelson-Atkins, and destroyed a lot of men's peace of mind. Meda had a new black leather jacket, and a pair of matching knee-high boots, sexy and practical. To go with it, she wore a cute little dress that bared her knees above the boots and revealed quite a bit of cleavage. It can't possibly be right to look at a pregnant woman and think what I was thinking, but it wasn't just me. Everywhere Meda went, men had to reassess their ideas about it.

She was utterly charming and delightful, and herself. She admired Sargent's *Mrs. Cecil Wade,* and stood in awed silence before the enormous Bodhisattva Guanyin that the Nelson has in a latticed enclosure like a temple. She smiled with pleasure at the lovely and diminutive *Amarna Princess* statue, and ooohed over the sparkling light in Frederic Church's *Jerusalem from the Mount of Olives*. She also walked by Willem de Kooning's *Woman IV*, and said, "That's crap. Annadore can do better than that."

In the midst of her charm and delightfulness, I found that we didn't manage to talk about any of the things I wanted to. She made it impossible for me to stay focused. She made me do things I said I'd never do.

I've always been privately appalled by the sexual position people call 'doggy style,' and the fact that she was pregnant made it even more appalling. It was dirty and I did it anyway, because she said to.

"Harder," she said in the middle of it. "Harder, Bernie." I was worried if I did it any harder I was going to crack her skull on the headboard. She'd said it was okay, that I wasn't going to hurt her or the baby, but when she began making the sound, I was afraid I was hurting her. Instead of pulling away from me, she dug her fingers into the sheets, straightened her elbows and pushed back against me. The sound she made obliterated whatever place I'd gone to. It was a wail, low in her throat, that grew louder and was punctuated by every thrust, and I felt like a trap door had swung open under me.

The Dead

Meda

I let him fall asleep partly out of carelessness, but mostly from the pleasure of lying there next to him drifting off, and feeling happy. I wanted him to be able to sleep with me, and I figured there wasn't any way for him to get used to it unless he just did it. His hair was soaked with sweat and his head seemed like it weighed about twenty pounds on my shoulder, but he settled into me a little bit at a time until I thought it would be okay. I don't know what happened when he woke up, because I was asleep, but what woke me up was the sound of him crashing into the dresser. He was down on his hands and knees between the bed and the dresser and I said his name a couple of times, but I don't think he knew I was there.

He put his hands on the edge of the dresser like he was going to get up, but he was shaking so hard the whole dresser rattled. The dresser mirror was broken all over the place and I could see where he'd cut himself on it and was bleeding. I was afraid to touch him, because they say you shouldn't wake a sleepwalker. Since he didn't seem to know I was there, I went to check on Annadore, who had slept through the whole thing. When I came back, Bernie was in the bathroom with the door shut and water running. I swept up all the glass, and when I was done, I knocked on the bathroom door. It scared me that he didn't answer, but when I opened the door, he was standing at the sink, brushing his teeth like nothing had happened. I touched his shoulder, but he looked right through me.

"Are you okay?" I said.

"I'm sorry."

Bernie wasn't even talking to me, but after he finished brushing, he let me lead him back to bed and clean up the cuts on his hands and knees. I had to pick glass out of his shoulder, where he must have hit the mirror. He didn't even flinch when I did it.

"What happened, Bernie? Why did you break the mirror?"

"I what?" He looked at me then, saw me, and seemed to know where he was.

"You broke the dresser mirror."

"I'm sorry. I didn't hurt you, did I? I'm so sorry."

"No," I said, maybe not as nice as I could have been. "I don't want you to apologize. I want you to tell me why you can't sleep with me. That's what upset you, isn't it? That you fell asleep with me?"

Just when I'd started to think he wasn't going to say anything, he said, "The thing I didn't know for the longest time, was that Amy was dead."

"Amy who?"

"She was the girl who worked for us, who helped kidnap me. It wasn't until later, a lot later, that I found out. I knew she was dead, that he shot her, because it was in all the papers. You can read them on microfilm at the county library. I knew she was dead, but what no one told me was that she was already dead when he shot her. He choked her to death, before he put her in the closet with me. The thing that made me think it would be okay, that I would be safe, it wasn't real. Her body was still warm. I didn't know she was dead."

Bernie kept his head down while he was talking and he was so quiet I had to lean my head close to his to hear him. He let me be that close, but when I put my hand on his arm he shuddered. "When I woke up next to you, I knew you were sleeping. I knew it intellectually, but there was that moment between breaths when you were so still."

"Bernie, will you remember this in the morning?"

"I don't know."

"Will you try?" He was so tired, he could barely keep his eyes open. I didn't know what else to do, so I pulled the covers up over him and turned out the light. I fell asleep on the couch finally, and Bernie must have been very early and quiet, because he snuck away to work without waking me or Annadore up.

He left me the car keys and a little note that said, "I'm really sorry. I love you and I hope you can forgive me." I didn't know what to think about that. I wondered if he thought I would leave.

Glorified Volunteer

I was slowly migrating the adult fiction, when Ellen came down one of the aisles. We hadn't been comfortable together since I came back. My change in status upset her view of the world. Only after I stopped what I was doing and stood up to look her in the face did she say, "There's somebody here who says she's your girlfriend."

"Really? She said that?" I thought it was just as likely that Ellen had made an assumption.

"That's how she introduced herself," Ellen said. "Dark hair, very exotic-looking, pregnant?"

"I know, I'm an asshole." I parked the dolly full of books, squeezed past Ellen, and went to the lobby to find Meda and Annadore standing at the front desk.

"You're my girlfriend now?" I asked.

"You were expecting someone else?"

Meda blushed and looked annoyed that I'd brought it up.

"I wanted to be sure I had it right."

Honestly, I was relieved Meda was still speaking to me. Also I didn't mention that some of my ex-girlfriends had come out of the woodwork recently. They were the girls who would have married my money.

I walked Meda and Annadore around the library and showed them what I was doing with the relocation. Once we got to the children's section, though, Annadore wouldn't let us go any further and started pulling books off the shelves that she wanted me to read to her.

"I'm done moving the children's books, but the re-shelving is a nightmare. The reference section and the adult fiction took precedence over this. Later I'll have to come back and put these back in order." Meda smiled indulgently at me, so I knew I was running at the mouth.

"Could I help you do that?" she asked. "It turns out being a love slave is kinda boring. I can alphabetize."

"Sure. I'm nothing but a glorified volunteer here anyway. You might as well be."

"What's that mean?"

"I'm not a librarian anymore or I'm an unpaid one. I guess I'm a professional philanthropist now." It was not what I'd imagined I'd grow up to be.

"Yeah, sometimes I forget that you've got like a billion dollars." Meda could barely squeeze out a smile to support the suggestion that she was kidding.

"I don't know why that upsets you so much."

"He doesn't know why that upsets me so much," she said with an exasperated look.

"Not marrying me isn't going to protect you from that anyway. Guess who gets it all if I get hit by a bus."

"Your foundation."

"The part of it that's being separated into the foundation, yes, but you'll get the rest of it," I said.

She laughed. "You can't do that."

"I already did. If I die, the foundation goes on the way I set it up and the rest of the money goes to you, with trust funds for Annadore and the baby." It took five lawyers, four meetings, three conference calls and two separate nearly bloody battles to write my will. The first battle was over the putative paternity of the baby Meda was expecting. That was the one that ended in me almost punching a middle-aged attorney.

The second battle was more philosophical and less pugilistic.

"I think you'll be sorry if you do this," one of the lawyers said. I figured it wouldn't matter to me once I was dead. Because I was the one paying the bills, I eventually won both of the disagreements without punching anyone.

Winning any disagreement with Meda was a whole different story. Her amusement evaporated as what I'd said finally soaked in. She had a strange look on her face, the same look she'd had at the courthouse. I hoped she wouldn't faint.

"You can't do that, can you? Without my say so?"

"Actually, I can. You don't have to get someone's permission to put them in your will," I said.

"But why would you do that?" Her eyes got marginally wider and darker. She didn't look well. I could have kicked myself.

Whether You Like It or Not

Meda

I had to sit down on one of those little kiddy chairs, because I felt so funny. Maybe it was another panic attack. There was plenty of stuff to panic about.

"Well, primarily, because I want to be sure you're taken care of, and that Annadore and the baby are taken care. Secondarily, because who else would I leave it to? I don't think I'm going to die any time in the near future, but when I do, I'm guessing my mother and Aunt Ginny, neither of whom need the money, will already be dead. Whether you like it or not, whether you're my wife or not, you're my other person in the world."

"There are other people in the world," I said, shocked at how tiny my voice sounded.

"But you're the one who matters to me."

I sat there quietly until the queasy, numb feeling went away, and when I opened my eyes, there was Bernie, sitting on the floor in front of me with Annadore next to him. When you get to the point where you know the worst thing about someone you love, you know the truth about yourself. What I learned about myself from Travis was that I was blind. I only saw what I wanted to see when I was with Travis. Looking at Bernie, I knew I was too hard on him and on me. If he felt that way about me, he deserved for me to try harder. Thinking about all the good things and the scary things about him, I was glad that romance novel moment didn't exist. It was the stupidest thing I ever wished for, like asking to get struck by lightning, when all I needed to do was turn on a light switch. Maybe I wouldn't ever get to sleep with him. Maybe there wasn't any way to undo what those people did to him. Whatever happened to break his heart, it was all he had. He couldn't put that in a box and label it. I opened my purse, took out one of the ring boxes I'd been carrying around and set it on my knee.

"Would you ask again and we can do it right this time?" I said.

Bernie sat there for so long I started to think his pride was kicking in. Then he opened the box and smiled. He looked so happy, but the truth was I didn't choose the ring. It just happened to be the huge rock he'd picked out. He got up on his knees a little awkwardly and then looked down at me, because with me sitting in that little chair, even kneeling he was taller than I was. It got us both giggling and I put my arms around him, so that was how he proposed, with my head on his shoulder.

I said yes, again.

Then some lady with a couple of screaming kids came in and asked if we were having the children's reading circle.

I read to the kids while Bernie went back to moving books.

CHAPTER TWELVE

MEDA'S MOTHER-IN-LAW

Aunt Ginny

BERNIE MISJUDGED HIS mother slightly, as she did come out for the wedding. Perhaps thinking of neutral ground, Bernie decided that he and Meda would pick her up at the airport and go to lunch. I invited myself along, not out of any desire to see the fireworks, but to stand by with a fire pail if I could.

At the airport, Meda carried her belly so beautifully, like a gift. She sat between Bernie and me, holding his hand and wearing an anxious, but queenly smile. Annadore pranced around happily and Bernie looked uneasy. I didn't hold out a great deal of hope that Katherine would make it easy, but the introductions between the two seemed polite enough.

We managed the short trip from the airport to the restaurant without talking of anything more troublesome than her flight and the weather. Things faltered a bit once we were seated for lunch, and I was relieved I had invited myself, because someone needed to keep the conversation going. Absolutely nothing about the situation at hand had been discussed and it seemed inevitable that once we reached the topic, all my efforts would be wasted. It burst through as soon as Meda excused herself to go to the ladies' room.

"You didn't mention that I was going to be a grandmother,"

Katherine said with a touch of smugness I found unbecoming. Bernie blushed. He was sensible to having created an awkward situation.

"I know it's a surprise and I'm sorry, but with one thing and another, I never got around to telling you," he said.

"A pleasant surprise, of course. A wonderful surprise for you, Katherine."

She did not appear to agree with me. At least it was a new irritation for her.

Suffering Contest

Meda

When I came back from the bathroom, before I even sat down, Bernie's mother said, "When are you due?"

"September."

"I see."

She nodded and gave Bernie a disgusted look. He took it pretty well. I was a little mad he hadn't told her before, but I could see why he hadn't, when I was being so stupid. I waited to see what else she would say, but she changed the subject.

"Bernie, did you ever go to the doctor about your pituitary?" She didn't even wait to hear the answer. "I don't know why you're putting it off. You can't honestly tell me you think it's normal that you're still growing at your age?"

"Why does everything about me mean there's a problem? Maybe I'm just tall," Bernie said.

"I'm only concerned for you," Mrs. Raleigh said in a really snotty voice.

"Maybe you could be concerned quietly to yourself."

"Well, perhaps you would have preferred me to be quietly concerned to myself while you were trying to commit suicide." It made me sick to my stomach to hear it out loud the way she said it, for no other reason than to hurt him. Bernie's jaw tightened up, and the tendons in his neck stood out, but he didn't say anything.

"Katherine, I don't see why that's necessary," Aunt Ginny said.

Bernie's mother was quiet for a while and we all pretended to eat our lunch.

"Of course, I suppose it's easy to judge when you've never had to bury a husband and a son and the very same day have your only other child try to kill himself." Mrs. Raleigh couldn't let it go, but I wasn't sure which one of us she was talking to, because I didn't think any of us were judging her.

"I swear to God," Bernie growled, and there was something about hearing that voice and those words coming out of his mouth that made us all sit up and take notice. He said it loud enough that I think everyone in the restaurant sat up and noticed. "We are not having some kind of contest about suffering, because for the record, I think Aunt Ginny has you beat. Only one of your children is dead."

He didn't mean it to hurt her, but his aunt flinched when he said it.

Burden

Aunt Ginny

Meda reached out to touch my hand and after a few moments, our nervous waiter came to clear the table. Once he was gone, Katherine said, "Do you really think this is the best way to start a marriage? You've waited this long, why not wait a little longer? You can't either of you be prepared for this."

"I've waited a little too long," Bernie said. "And I don't think it's the worst way to start a marriage."

"I assume you've already taken care of the prenuptial agreement?" Katherine said.

I regretted that we'd gone out to lunch. It all could have been handled much more nicely at home. Bernie made a visible effort to restrain himself.

"That's none of your business," he said.

"Of course not. I can't imagine why it would be any of my business what you do. I assume you're the father."

"I'm glad we're not wasting our time being polite or anything," Meda said.

I would have forgiven her anything she'd chosen to say at that moment, and I was grateful she'd responded so quickly, because Bernie looked violent.

Katherine leaned toward Meda and said, "Let's not pretend this situation is other than what it is. Obviously you've decided that his money balances out against the fact that he's mentally ill."

"Now that I've met you," Meda said, "I'm amazed he's only as screwed up as he is."

"Perhaps you'll be a bit less quick to judge after he's been your responsibility for thirty years."

"Have I been that much of a burden?" Bernie said, but he wasn't prepared for the answer his mother gave him.

"You can't even begin to imagine."

"Try imagining what it would be like to go through life thinking your mother didn't love you," Meda said.

"Well, that's certainly very melodramatic. Is that what you tell her about me, Bernie?" Katherine said. He didn't answer her.

"Everyone says how much you loved your other son, that you loved Robby more, so I'm not even going to ask you about that," Meda said. "I guess it's not your fault, if that's true. I'm just curious why you treat Bernie like it's his fault he got kidnapped, like it's his fault he has problems. Is it just to keep yourself from feeling guilty?"

Bernie and I were accustomed to Katherine's habit of storming out of the room when she was opposed, but when Katherine stood up and began gathering her things, Meda put her hand on Katherine's arm and stopped her.

Naturally

"Don't touch me. If you're stupid enough to believe everything he tells you, you'll get what you deserve," my mother said. Meda stood up, causing a minor collision between her belly and my mother's narrow hips.

"The only thing he's ever told me about you is that he thinks you don't love him. And that's as true as it gets, because that's what he thinks."

"I don't intend to play this game." My mother's voice was quite loud, much louder than Meda's, and she wouldn't look at me.

"It's not a game. The only reason he thinks you don't care is because you let him think that." Meda was so calm and her voice was so gentle, that if I closed my eyes I could almost forget that she and my mother were having a wrestling match. "If you'd just tell him that you would've paid the ransom, if it had been up to you. I think that would make all the difference in the world to him, if he knew you didn't think it was his fault, that you don't hate him because of it." I would never have the heart to tell Meda it didn't make any difference, but my mother must have known that, because what she said had none of the generosity that Meda intended.

"He's my son. Naturally, if it had been within my power I would have paid the ransom," my mother said coolly, all the fight gone out of her. It wasn't a gift so much as a toll, because Meda let her go after that.

My mother stormed across the dining room, up the stairs, and into the foyer.

Meda sat down and gathered herself before she looked at me. When she finally met my eyes, I think she was embarrassed.

"Do you remember telling me I was a real person? That was the best thing anyone ever said to me. I can't find the people who kidnapped you and punch them out, and I don't know what to say to you that will make you feel real, but you can't go on being kidnapped your whole life, Bernie." Meda took Aunt Ginny's hand and said, "Did you ever tell him about why you don't have any jewelry anymore?"

"No, it never seemed like something to talk about. I should have told you, I suppose, a long time ago." She told me the whole story then, about the weeks of arguing, and waiting, begging Pen to relent, and she and Uncle Alan trying to raise the money on their own. I wanted to stop her, seeing how much it hurt her, and feeling it myself for the first time.

"I was afraid for us, that we loved you so much, and it seemed that Rob and Katherine were resigned to losing you. I don't say that to speak against them. They were hurt, too, but they had Robby to console themselves with. And then when you came back, they took you away from us."

My heart hurt seeing her so frail, fighting tears. I felt paralyzed, like I couldn't do anything for her. I was grateful when Meda put her arm around Aunt Ginny's shoulders.

"Oh, and my engagement ring, we couldn't sell that," Aunt Ginny said, trying to smile. "I still have that, because your uncle was hoodwinked. It's a garnet, not even a real ruby. But then it didn't matter after all, because they'd found you. It all sounds so silly."

"It's not silly," Meda said.

"It's good news for you, Meda." I wanted us all not to cry.

"What is?"

"You ended up with a better mother-in-law than you started the day with."

Aunt Ginny took it the way I intended. She laughed and got up to hug and kiss me in that effusive little old lady way that pleased and embarrassed me.

As we were leaving the restaurant, Aunt Ginny asked the maître d' about my mother. He'd called a cab for her. Like mother like son, she had apparently cut her losses over her luggage. It was still in the trunk of my car.

Certainty vs. Romance

The day of the wedding, the weather was dismal. Meda wore my grandmother's diamonds and a blue silk dress that made her eyes almost grey. We had a retired judge out to the house and were married in the formal parlor with what there was of our families: Aunt Ginny, the Amoses, and the Trentams. I carried a small tape recorder in my suit pocket and, in a last ditch hedge against cold feet, I took Meda, Aunt Ginny, Mrs. Trentam, and the judge into the kitchen before the ceremony. There we signed the license.

"This is a little irregular," the judge said.

"It's legal, though?" I said.

"It may be legal, but it's not particularly romantic," Aunt Ginny complained.

I preferred certainty to romance, and as a show of good faith I signed the license first. Meda held the pen over the license for a few seconds, readjusting it in her fingers a few times. My stomach turned over as she did.

"Once I sign we're actually married?" she said, but before I could answer her, she put the pen on the paper and signed. Aunt Ginny and Mrs. Trentam signed as witnesses, and it was a done deal except for the ceremony. Afterwards, Meda's aunt Rachel seemed especially eager to see the signed license, and teased Meda about how shakily she had written "Raleigh" after her name. That surprised me most, that she had signed the license Meda Raleigh, that she was Meda Raleigh, even if there was a hiccup in the curve of the 'R.'

The next morning, the first day of our honeymoon, of our married life, Meda watched me try to shave through the steam her marathon shower had left on the mirror. It was one of the two most important shaves in my whole life, and I was trying not make a botch job of it. Maybe trying to be helpful, Meda wiped the mirror with her palm, but that made it worse.

I kept thinking she would go out and open the door, clear the mirror, but she hovered right at my elbow. Twice, I bumped her when I went to rinse the razor. A little too casually she said, "Aunt M. said we ought to have real wedding pictures taken after the baby's born."

"Really?"

"So we'd have wedding pictures where I wasn't the size of a VW bug."

"I like Volkswagens."

"Thanks. She says in twenty years nobody will even remember that they aren't the actual wedding pictures." My elbow made grazing contact with her breast again, but she didn't move. "So, what do you think?"

"If you want, we can have fake wedding pictures taken." I preferred not to confuse the issue by referring to them as 'real' wedding pictures. The shave was as good as I could get it under the circumstances. It would have to do. I rinsed my face and toweled off.

"But what do you think?" Meda said.

It was the point in my morning routine when I once would have combed my hair. After a month of not combing it all, which had not been the goal, according to Meda, I had to have a radical haircut to get rid of all the knots in it. I didn't have much hair not to comb. Meda was waiting for me to answer.

"I think…I want to remember all of it," I said.

In my clandestine recording of the wedding, Meda held her breath for a good fifteen seconds before she exhaled, "I do." She must have remembered the signed license at last and got the words out.

"What if it doesn't work? What if this doesn't work out?" Meda said.

That was the real question, not the question about the

pictures.

"It's never too late to change your mind." I immediately wished I could take it back. It wasn't the right answer or even an honest one. I thought of all the things I'd left unfinished under the guise of changing my mind, when that had never been the real reason they were left undone.

"It's too late to change your mind about this baby," Meda said.

"We could sell it on the black market." She pinched my arm, not amused. "No, I know, it's too late to change our minds about that, but it's not too late to change your mind about wanting to be married to me. I just hope you'll give it more than a day."

She lifted two fingers to the fogged over mirror and drew a series of elaborate strokes. An alien language only she knew. Then the steam crept in and filled her calligraphy. She cleared a swath of mirror to be able to see me. When that didn't suit, she turned me away from the mirror and looked up at me.

"There are some things you shouldn't be able to change your mind about," she said firmly.

"Okay. No changing our minds." It had a nicer ring to it than 'til death do us part.

"Are you sure you're ready to do this?"

I could see what she was thinking. The same thing I was. *Him*. Him watching me. Sitting somewhere, free, watching TV. Watching me.

"Why? Because I'm not drunk?"

"Psh. Because. Nothing," Meda said.

"Yeah, I'm ready."

The commercial won't be perfect. It won't quite match Lionel Petrie's vision.

If you watch closely, you'll be able to see where I nicked myself shaving. I'm supposed to look right into the camera, but for most of the commercial, I will look at Meda, who is standing beside the camera, trying to smile encouragingly at me, but mostly chewing her fingernails with her perfect white teeth.

In the last few seconds, I manage to look at the camera, and when I deliver the line, "Raleigh Industries is looking to the future," I will actually mean it. When I fold my hands on the desk, I will do it with purpose. I will shift my left hand from the chair arm and fold it over my right hand.

To show two things.

Not just the stump of my amputated finger, but my wedding ring, too. If *he* is watching, let him see that. What he did to me isn't the most important thing in my life anymore.

It isn't anything at all to me now.

CPSIA information can be obtained
at www.ICGtesting.com
Printed in the USA
FFOW02n2139290418
46376838-48074FF